MISSING

A Christine Lane Mystery #2

Dianne Scott

Danforth Press

To the members of my writing group: Ania, Elsie, Elizabeth, Leanne and Roz as well as Lucie and Susana.

Thank you for your years of support, encouragement and thoughtful feedback.

Chapter 1

September 1968

"Lane!" Get over here!" Sergeant Bard swung his arm out the driver's window of his patrol car, motioning Policewoman Christine Lane over.

"What have I done now?" Christine asked her partner. They were just exiting the ferry that had piloted them to Toronto Island for their afternoon shift.

"Better you than me," PC Geoffrey Fillingham said as he slipped on his sunglasses.

Holding her breath against the ferry fumes, she hustled into a jog and headed for the utility patrol car parked forty feet away. PC Morano opened the passenger door and retrieved a blue bike with white tassels from the back of the car. When she arrived, he dropped the bike in front of her, the tire slamming down on her black Oxfords.

Ignoring the pain in her toes and Morano, she grabbed the bike's handlebars. Leaning her six-foot height down to the open driver's window, she queried, "Sergeant?"

"I need you to take a call," Sergeant Bard said.

"Yes, sir." Usually at shift change the outgoing officers gave a brief oral report on the day's incidents to the incoming staff, then hurried onto the waiting ferry back to the city. The new shift then drove the patrol car back to the Center Island Police station a five-minute ride away.

"What's the nature of the call, Sergeant?" she asked.

He slid his sunglasses down his nose and regarded her with clear blue eyes under bushy gray eyebrows. "Women problems," he said, sotto voice.

Women problems could be anything from complaints about tourists trodding in residents' gardens to rape or child abuse. Christine was familiar with the latter calls. For the past four years, she had worked in the Toronto Police's Women's Bureau, where most of the force's female officers were stationed. She had also worked with Vice and the Youth Bureau, whose cases involved women, children and the elderly.

"Women problems?" she repeated. "Can you clarify, sir?"

Shoving his sunglasses back up his nose, he barked, "Why don't you ride that abomination of a bike over and find out! Sixteen Fifth Street."

She raised her eyebrows but said nothing, stepping away from the car window. Looking over her shoulder, she watched her partner approach, his head tilted to catch the late summer sun.

"You go," Fillingham said when he reached her. He must have heard the sergeant's bellowed instructions. "I'll see you back at the station."

Fine, she thought. Let her partner finish report with Sergeant Bard, a boss who vacillated between blustery anger, humor and the occasional profundity.

Christine tucked her uniform skirt underneath her hips, hopped on the bike and began pedaling, mindful of rubbing chain oil on her new nylons. She had ruined a pair yesterday. Nylons weren't cheap—especially in Extra Tall. She didn't have the pin money to be buying a new pair every shift.

Her sergeant was right about one thing: her bike's flower-entwined baskets, icy blue color and handlebar streamers were ridiculous. It was a gift from her favorite Islander, Mrs. Polotov, and Christine loved every overly decorated inch. And although most officers preferred patrolling the Island by car, Christine and her partner liked the freedom and activity of biking the Island's pathways.

Rolling past the Centreville Amusement Park, she was struck by its quietness; a singular employee in overalls watered a tub of geraniums. Now that summer was over, Centreville was only open on weekends. Although it was Monday, she could still smell the cotton candy, as if the scent had soaked into the wood panels of the merry-go-round and the rickety tracks of the roller coaster.

Her bike's white plastic streamers tickled her calves as she veered left at the forked pathway. The ferry bellowed a last warning for passengers to embark. She pedaled toward Ward's Island and its community of a hundred cottages, her shoulders warming under the sun. Wildflowers edged the concrete path, blurred into smudges of muted gold and royal purple as she pedaled by. A few sumac leaves were tipped red. Fall was just around the corner.

Was a child lost? she wondered. Surely, that was not a "women problem"—and Sergeant Bard would have included Fillingham in the search. Likely it was a man peering in a resident's window or pestering bikini-clad women on the local beach.

She pressed on the pedals with more force. Being assigned to the female complaint calls bothered her—as if they were the only tasks she could handle. Had Sergeant Bard forgotten that she and Fillingham had arrested a murderer last month?

But if the complaint involved abuse or rape, it was better that she respond rather than an officer like Morano. Christine imagined the coarse officer crossing his arms as he listened to the woman's teary story and his subsequent questions: *What were you wearing? Were you flirting? Why were you alone? Don't you have a husband?*

Attacks weren't common on Toronto Island. A few visitors or boaters drank too much, resulting in the occasional fisticuffs, but it was more common to interrupt two lovers on a secluded beach than to receive a call about a man on the prowl.

She approached a wooden bridge that joined the main island to the Algonquin Island community of cottages. Trudging over the arced structure was a line of young boys with school knapsacks slung over their shoulders. A flurry of waves. No doubt they would dump their satchels for tackle and fishing rods. The lagoon was a favorite fishing spot for children and adults alike.

Merging onto Willow Street, she glided by a line of cottages, tiger lilies leaning into the pathway, before reaching the field where Island families challenged each other to weekly baseball games. Her eyes searched for the number 16 from the row of houses fronting onto the field.

Geez. Who was on top of the house by the baseball diamond?

Three naked men angled themselves on the roof, basking their glistening tanned backs and bare bottoms in the sun.

Christine quickly scanned the area for civilians. No one was around, thank goodness, but families walking through the narrow cottage streets, picnicking in the field or heading to Ward's Island Beach would see them.

Her bike bumped across the grassy field. As she neared, she spied the number 16 in tarnished brass under a porch light.

So this was the women problem: three naked men. Her boss's idea of a joke. Make the female officer blush and fumble through a public nudity complaint. Ha ha.

Since she'd started working on Toronto Island four months ago, the Center Island Police Station had received a handful of calls about the "hippies" leasing houses on Ward's and Algonquin Island. Complaints ranged from marijuana use and lax house maintenance to loud beach parties.

Most Islanders were liberal and open-minded. They recognized that young people gravitated to the Island's cheap rental housing, and Islanders welcomed all types of residents.

But as far as Christine was concerned, sun-tanning naked in a public space went too far. If the men wanted a uniform tan, they could head to Hanlan's Point Beach on the other end of the island, where adult nudity was accepted.

Dismounting, she lowered her bike onto a tangled skein of ivy greening the front lawn. Her heel crunched a milkweed plant as she backed up to view the men baking in the sun.

She cupped her hands to her mouth. "Hello! Policewoman Lane. Toronto Police."

A rustle of shifting bodies. A red-bearded man turned, propped himself on one elbow and raised his other arm to block out the sun as he regarded her. For a second, his muscled torso reminded her of Hawk, her secret lover, and she felt a warmth spread across her chest.

"Sir," she said, returning her thoughts to the current situation. "We've received a complaint. I need the three of you to get dressed."

Red Beard's voice was low and friendly. "A policewoman. I've heard about you. You're the one that found Ginny's killer."

The other two men, a blond, bearded man sporting a navy bandana on his head and a clean-shaven one, propped themselves into sitting positions to look at her.

"Hello," Blondie said.

"Sir, you need to put your clothes on."

Red Beard pushed himself to standing, one bare foot pressed against the roof slant, his nude front as nutmeg-tanned as his back. He had a copper necklace hanging around his neck, which looked like a Celtic symbol.

He caught her staring at him. She felt a blush prickle up her neck.

"Why don't you come up?" Red Beard asked.

"We'll make room," Blondie said, patting the towel he sat on. All three laughed.

Christine gritted her molars. Her sergeant and Morano were likely choking with laughter as their ferry docked at the mainland terminal.

"You, sir." She pointed at Red Beard. "What's your name?" She pulled her memo book from her leather police purse.

"Climb up and I'll whisper it in your ear," he said.

They were like children, even though they were her age. "I'm losing my patience," she said.

Blondie said, "Come and get us," in a sing-song voice. He rolled back onto his stomach, the round globe of his bottom several shades lighter than his back.

She let out an impatient sigh. Shoving her memo book back in her purse, she spotted an aluminum ladder leaning against the house beside a spindly fir tree. As Christine ascended, clasping the hot metal sides, the ladder swayed under her weight. She was as heavy and as tall as the men.

Her head reached the roof line, level with the eavestrough that was storing beer bottles, cigarettes, matches and a jug of orange juice. Stepping onto the inclined roof, she pressed one foot against the slope for balance, her skirt drawing tight. What she would give for lightweight summer pants. And to be rid of these itchy nylons.

"Gentlemen," she said to the naked men lying prone below her.

No one responded.

She announced, "Let me list the charges I will be laying before parading you through Ward's Island in handcuffs."

Blondie and Clean-Shaven looked over their shoulders. Red Beard rolled onto his back.

Thumb in the air, she said, "Charge one is indecent exposure." Her index finger joined her thumb. "Because this rooftop is in view of passing children, the next charge is indecent exposure to a minor—a crime that puts off employers, I can tell you." She recalled that several hippies on Ward's Island were working on a municipal lake water project. She nudged a beer bottle with her toe and held a third finger up. "I'll add public drinking to the list, which comes with a hefty fine. My friends at *The Star* will be happy to publish your name and photo alongside these charges in tomorrow's paper." She was making up that last part, but bluffing was part of policing.

All three scrambled to a sitting position.

"We didn't do anything in front of kids," Red Beard said.

"Your names?"

"Karl Olsen," said Red Beard.

Blondie said, "Mike Hampton."

Clean-Shaven: "Joe Hill."

"Thank you," she said. "I understand you want to enjoy the warm weather, but this rooftop is not the place for nude sunbathing. Get dressed." She sounded like a schoolmarm.

The men bent to gather towels, cigarette packages and bottles.

As Christine waited, eyes averted from their nakedness, she scanned the neighborhood. Up here, she had a panoramic view of the houses. Toronto Island was basically a spine with fifteen connected islands, with Ward's Island anchoring the east, Center Island in the middle and Hanlan's Point in the west. The two residential communities, Ward's and Algonquin's, populated the eastern section of the Island.

As Christine gazed down, the residents' rooftops were partially obscured by the leafy boughs of maples and aspens. Her eye caught a flash of blue and white by the sumac bushes down the road. Was that the white cab of the patrol car? Leaning down, she discerned two dark-clothed bodies in the front seats—Fillingham and Sergeant Bard? They were spying on her! Waiting to see what the naïve police-woman did with three naked, noncompliant men.

She shook her head. Now she knew what they were up to. Police officers were notorious pranksters. At the Women's Bureau, they teased each other all the time, making Louise Fairbanks think she forgot her shift and Fanny Albrook frantically clean her untidy desk when told the chief was coming for an inspection.

Island officers were jokesters, too. They had dressed a mannequin in an old police uniform, labeled it *PC Pilkington* and sat it a station desk, poking fun at Pilkington, who chose permanent desk duty. Christine, the only female officer on the Island, had found pink washing gloves, a toilet scrub brush and an apron in her locker when she first arrived at the station...as if she were the station's new house-keeper. Ha ha.

Karl paused beside her, following her gaze down the street. "What's going on?"

She said, "My fellow officers are hiding behind a bush, watching my response to this call."

Karl smiled, white teeth showing in his red, lush beard. "Why don't we give them a show?"

"A show?"

Karl turned to Joe. "Can you find a mattress, a big one?"

"Sure, there's one in the shed," Joe responded. Quite a few Island sheds functioned as sleeping quarters, since the houses were small and the city had few rentals.

"What do you have in mind?" she asked Karl.

He held up a finger to show he would answer in a minute.

"Joe and Mike," Karl instructed, "head down the ladder, like you're cooperating. Then pull the mattress around to the south wall of the house."

"Mr. Olsen?" She was getting impatient.

He stood up, arms wide. "Throw me off the roof!"

"What?"

"Kids jump off the roof all the time. Houses are what, eight feet high? Single level. You bring a mattress around or a trampoline, and it's circus time!"

She thought for a second.

"I won't get hurt," he added. "We do it all the time. And you'll be showing them," his head tilted toward the patrol car, "how you handle these pesky calls." He leaned over the edge to watch the two men place a mattress below and gave them a thumbs-up.

Karl turned back to Christine and rotated his hand. "Start it up."

"Start up what?"

"Your spiel about me getting off the roof. What laws I'm breaking. Blah, blah, blah."

A smile tugged at her mouth.

Karl's eyes widened in encouragement.

"Mr. Olsen," she said, "follow your friends down the ladder and get dressed."

"Louder," he whispered.

She took a deep breath and bellowed as they faced each other, "Mr. Olsen! I've asked you twice to get down off the roof."

"I don't have to follow your rules," he yelled back.

"All citizens need to abide by laws," she said. "Public nudity is an offense under the Criminal Code, Section 174, paragraph 1b." For the next minute, she outlined the details of the charges, her voice ringing clear across the roof shingles.

His thumb pointed at his bare chest, touching his medallion. "This is my house, my property!"

He was cute under all that facial hair, eyes a flash of royal blue under blond eyebrows.

"Sir," she said, letting impatience sharpen her tone, "it's not a request. It's an order."

He motioned her forward.

She took a step nearer. "You need to come down. Now!"

Karl waved his hands in front of him while shaking his head. "No way, fascist pig! I'm not coming. Screw you and your laws and the lawmakers! And get the hell off my roof!"

"*You* get off the roof!" she yelled.

Karl turned away from her, his mahogany nakedness silhouetted against the neighbor's maple tree.

She shoved him hard in the middle of his back, his skin hot underneath her palms.

He screamed and fell off the roof, legs and arms flailing against the backdrop of trees and sky.

Christine scrambled over to the roof edge, fingers gripping the eavestrough.

Karl lay splayed on his stomach on the mattress, then rolled onto his back to grin up at her. She smiled, exhaling with relief. That had been fun. Scary, but fun. She certainly hoped that her fellow officers had seen the performance.

Back on the ground, Christine addressed Karl. "Party's over. Clothes on!"

"Tempted to join me?" Karl said, patting the mattress.

He did look appealing in his Scandinavian way. "In jail?" she responded, smiling.

He made a face.

Joe extracted a pair of shorts from the pile of clothes on a lawn chair and threw it at Karl, who pulled them on.

Christine said, "Do you want a ride to Hanlan's Point Beach?" Otherwise known as "The Naked Beach," Hanlan's Point attracted European tourists who liked to sunbathe nude, "queers," as Morano called them, and naturists. And, often, hippies.

"Sure," said Karl.

"Wait here." She retrieved her bike from the front lawn.

Three minutes later, she was back. "Hop on!" she commanded, pointing at the flat wooden wagon attached to the bicycle she had borrowed from a neighbor. "Keep your shorts on and grab your towels."

After some good-natured shoving, the three men got onto the wagon, Karl kneeling in the middle while Joe and Mike sat on opposite sides, their legs hanging over the wagon's edge, toes almost touching the ground.

Struggling at first with the weight of the men, Christine pedaled hard until she found her rhythm. As she biked along the narrow streets of Ward's Island, the young men hooted, waving to a couple walking hand-in-hand, Mrs. Clancy pulling weeds in her garden and a diapered toddler out for a walk with her mother.

Christine headed toward Fourth Street, where she'd spotted the police car. Approaching the Jeep, her handlebar fringes flapping in the breeze, she jauntily rang her bike-bell. *Triiiing!*

Sergeant Bard and Fillingham sat in the front seat; Morano's head appeared between them as he leaned forward from the back seat. The three policemen stared at her wagon full of men, Sergeant Bard's eyes wide, Fillingham's eyebrows raised and Morano's lip curled in disgust.

Looking back over her shoulder, she caught Karl's eye. With a wink, he pulled down his worn cotton shorts and mooned her fellow officers.

She snapped her head to the front, pretending she hadn't seen it. *Joke's on you, officers,* she thought. She laughed and rang her bell again. *Triiiing! Triiiing! Triiiing! Joke's on you!*

Chapter 2

When she dropped the men at Hanlan's Point Beach, they promised to keep their trunks on until she had wheeled her bike around. Her laughter bubbled up as she rode back to Ward's Island to return the borrowed wagon, remembering Sergeant Bard's shock, Morano's derision and her partner's questioning look. She smiled all the way back to the Center Island Police Station. Karl Olsen had been right. It had been a good prank.

Leaving her bike in the front yard, she headed into the bungalow that had been converted into a police station. It was one of the few houses spared from the bulldozer's blade when the local government evicted Center Island residents a decade ago and replaced their houses with a public park.

The doorbell chimed as Christine entered the waiting room furnished with red leather benches for visitor seating. A long wooden counter spanned the width of the building, separating the office from the waiting area. Behind the counter were two large desks, a radio recharging station, filing cabinets and shelves filled with binders of protocols, criminal codes and municipal regulations.

Fillingham poked his head out from the small kitchenette at the back of the house. "Coffee's on."

"Great." She lifted the hinged counter and walked through the office to the back kitchen, where she stowed her dinner in the fridge. After pouring herself a coffee, she sat at the square Formica table across from her partner.

"Everything okay?" he asked, wide-eyed.

They must have seen her push Karl Olsen off the roof. Or at least heard his scream. "I don't think we'll get a complaint about this group again." Her chair screeched against the wooden floor as she went to the cupboard for the sugar dish and to hide her grin. Turning back to her partner, she said, "When we finish our coffees, we're heading over to the Nature School." The facility was a day school for Island children, as well as an overnight science program for mainland students in grades five and six.

"We are? Why?"

"My stepbrother, Wayne, is attending the outdoor program this week. His teacher asked me if we could speak to the children about water safety." Christine's siblings were fifteen years younger than her, children of Phyllis's disastrous second marriage to the long-gone Eddie Williams.

"From the woman who sinks in water?" he teased.

Fillingham had given her swimming lessons all summer. "I'm improving," she protested. Her dog paddle had developed into a thrashing front crawl. "You can talk about boating safety, since that's up your alley." He sailed for the Royal Canadian Yacht Club located on the Island.

After retrieving their bikes—her floral-covered one and his light-weight silver racer—they rolled along the Island of the Avenues, a pathway that bisected Center Island. The petals of late-blooming geraniums fluttered as the fountains beside the walkway sprayed the air with fine mist. It was hard to believe that ten years ago, before the city-sanctioned demolitions, this road had been crowded with businesses, hotels, restaurants and homes. She had visited the busy strip once as a little girl with her mom; she remembered holding a dripping soft ice-cream cone while listening to the boom of bowling balls from the alley next door. It seemed sad that the hustle and bustle of thriving businesses had been replaced by static flower tubs and fountains, however beautiful.

When they reached Manitou Beach and the lapping waves of Lake Ontario, they angled their handlebars onto the path toward the Nature School at Hanlan's Point. The officers' bike tires crunched on the gravel pathway that veered inland, away from the squawking seagulls and crashing waves. She was glad that the Island prohibited vehicles other than police, hydro and forestry, since it made the Island feel like a sanctuary—a serene getaway from the city's frantic pace and congestion.

A childish, angry voice erupted from behind a scrub of bushes near the school. "Give me a token, you stupid Polack!"

Christine veered down the path beside the one-story schoolhouse.

A fair-haired boy crouched on the patchy grass, blood smeared under his nose and staining the neckline of his white t-shirt. A paper headband circled his head, imprinted with the word *FOX* beside the image of a red-tailed fox. He was glaring up at a stocky boy who stood over him with a raised fist; another boy stood off to the side, watching.

"Roy?" she said, recognizing the boy with the balled fist and *RAC-COON* headband. He was in her brother's class at Lakeview Public School.

Roy's head swerved to look at her, his arm dropping to his side. "Christine?"

"It's PW Lane. I'm on the job. This is PC Fillingham. What's going on here?"

The fair-haired boy scrambled to his feet, then wiped his nose with his forearm, smearing blood across one cheek. From behind the school, children squealed and laughed, their voices advancing and receding.

Roy looked at Fillingham and back at Christine. "Just a game."

Turning to the other boy, she acknowledged, "Patrick." The boy was also in Miss Phillips's Grade 5 class. He looked at her through his shaggy auburn bangs, eyes wide.

"What game?" Christine asked Patrick.

"Predator and Prey," Patrick answered quietly.

A whistle blew three times.

"I think the game's over," she said. She met Fillingham's glance and tipped her head to show he should take Roy and Patrick.

Turning to the blond boy, she asked, "What's your name?"

"He doesn't speak English!" Roy called over his shoulder as he walked away with Fillingham.

"I speak English!" the blond boy retorted in accented English. He yelled a string of words in his native tongue—Polish or Ukrainian, Christine hazarded—directing the diatribe at Roy's back.

Fillingham raised his eyebrows at the blond boy's tirade, then shuffled Roy in front of him. "Let's go find your teacher," he said. Her partner and the two boys disappeared around the corner of the school.

Christine wasn't surprised to find Roy in an altercation with another student. The few times he had come over to their apartment, he had bossed Wayne around, always choosing the games, always managing to win. He was known to be rough, aggressively tackling other students during recess football games. Nevertheless, he was the first one to be picked when choosing teams during gym. He was strong, charismatic and the school's star baseball pitcher, all of which impressed her brother to no end.

"What's your name?" she said again to the bloodied boy.

"Jakub." He paused. "In English, Jacob."

"Jacob, how did you get hurt?" She pointed to his face.

He shrugged. "Just game."

"What was Roy saying about tokens?"

"In game, predator get token if eat prey, but I not prey!" He pointed to his headband. "I predator, too. He cannot eat me. So I no give him token."

"Is that why your nose is bleeding? He tried to take your tokens?"

He looked away. "Accident."

"Are you sure? Because it's not all right for a person to hit you or to take what's yours."

His head swiveled to look at her, his eyes a cold blue marble under pale eyelashes. "In Poland, army took our house."

Christine thought of the news coming out of Eastern Europe, how Czechoslovakia had moved toward democracy before the invasion by Russia. How families like Jacob's had fled to Canada. The boy was a tough customer. Maybe he would do okay against Roy.

Christine and Jacob joined the rest of the students in the school's meeting room, a cavernous space with pine board walls and a sooty fireplace. Students sprawled on beanbags and large pillows. Christine made sure that Jacob sat away from Roy as the students settled in to listen.

A lean, shaggy-haired teacher came over to shake their hands, introducing himself as Tim Hawley. He had been leading a discussion about the game the students had been playing.

Tim turned back to the students. "How many of you prey and predator animals were able to keep the tokens I gave you and survive the season?"

A third of the students raised their hands.

"For the students who were prey," he continued, "the squirrels, birds, mice and groundhogs, what was the secret to survival?"

He called on a pony-tailed girl. "Scrounging in the bushes to find food tokens," she said.

A boy added, "Hiding when the predators came around."

A girl in a brown corduroy dress said, "Camouflaging ourselves with leaves and bark."

"All good ideas," Tim said, nodding at each response. "Exactly what animals do on the Island to survive." He scanned the group of fifty students. "How about the predators? Did you eat enough food to survive the winter?"

"Do predators eat other predators?"

Christine turned at the familiar voice—Roy.

"Yes, they do," Tim answered. "Animals are often both predator and prey."

"So why couldn't we get tokens for eating another predator?" Roy asked.

"Good question," Tim said. "We wanted to keep the game simple because we only had one hour to play. And because we have special guests today." He smiled at Christine and Fillingham, who were standing off to the side. "Toronto Island police have kindly agreed to provide safety tips for your stay on the Island." He looked at Miss Phillips, standing beside Fillingham. "I think a Lakeview student has a connection to Policewoman Lane."

Wayne's thin shoulders hunched as students turned to look at him; he looked simultaneously proud and embarrassed under his brown bangs.

Fillingham nudged Christine in the back, and she walked over to stand beside Tim. "Some of you recognize me because my brother and sister attend Lakeview. I'm PW Lane, and that's my partner, PC Fillingham." She gestured toward Fillingham. "You might have seen officers patrolling the Island in a blue and white utility car or on our bikes or spotted us on foot at the amusement park. Or passed by our Center Island station."

"Have you arrested anyone?" a boy asked.

"Not today," Fillingham said, smiling at the children as he joined her up front. "Most Islanders and visitors are law-abiding. They're here to swim, picnic or go on rides."

"A common call into the station is for a lost child," Christine said. "What can you do if you get lost on the Island?"

Hands shot up. "Tell a police officer."

"Talk to a grown-up."

Another child added, "Go to the police station."

"All good ideas," Christine responded. "Try to find an adult you know first. If you can't, find someone in a uniform who works on the Island: the canoe rental staff, a ferry worker or Centreville employee."

"Did you ever shoot somebody?" a small boy asked, directing his question to Fillingham.

Fillingham smiled, shaking his head. "No."

"Why not?" the boy asked.

Fillingham looked at Christine, eyebrows raised.

"For one," Christine said, "I don't carry a gun. Only policemen do. Although I've been trained to shoot. Second, police officers hardly ever draw their weapon. We want to help keep the peace. Most of the time, we talk to people and help them solve problems."

"Don't you catch bad guys?" a youthful voice asked.

"Yes, we do," said Fillingham.

"Did you ever see a dead body?" a boy asked.

Gosh, these kids are macabre, Christine thought.

Fillingham nodded.

"How about a drowned body?" a girl's voice said.

Fillingham answered, "That's the jurisdiction of the Harbor Police. Their station is down the road from the ferry terminal. They're a separate police force that rescues boaters and tickets drivers for boating violations. They also recover drowned bodies."

"Ooh," groaned several students.

"Didn't your sister tackle a murderer, and then his boat exploded?" a boy near Wayne asked him.

"That's not quite—" Christine began.

"Yes, she did!" Fillingham interrupted, gesturing to Christine. "She rescued him from a burning boat, and then she arrested him."

"Where were you?" a little girl said.

Fillingham pointed his thumb at his chest. "I'm just her sidekick."

Christine made a skeptical face.

"Were you wearing a life jacket?" another boy asked.

These kids were barracudas.

Tim stepped up beside the officers. "That's a good point. Water safety is paramount on the Island. When you go canoeing with Derek, our paddling instructor, everyone needs to wear a life jacket. What else do we keep in mind when we are in a boat?"

Tim continued the discussion about water safety, with some help from Fillingham, and then dismissed the students to wash up for dinner. As the children made their way to the door, Jacob passed Christine, his eyes glued to the floor.

The two officers headed down the hallway to the main doors, accompanied by Tim.

"Didn't realize we had Wonder Woman in our midst," Tim said.

"Hardly," she said.

"Maybe you can lasso me with your rope of truth," Tim suggested.

Fillingham smirked, pulled his sunglasses on and pushed open the door to the outside.

Was Tim flirting with her? "No lasso," Christine said. "Just a billy and standard-issue handcuffs." She patted her purse.

"That'll do," he said.

Christine felt herself redden. She was so bad at this type of banter. She mumbled a goodbye and followed her partner to their bikes.

As they rode parallel, Fillingham made kissing sounds with his mouth.

"What?" she asked.

"He likes you."

Hanging out with Fillingham sometimes felt she was in high school again. "Oh, for goodness' sake. As if Wayne's teacher wasn't batting her eyelashes at you the whole time."

"That's because I'm charming."

"Charm's worn off!" She pushed hard on the pedals, heading back to the Island Police station, Fillingham in hot pursuit.

Chapter 3

Back at the station, Christine checked the red and gold leather police log: five incidents recorded with today's date, all of them closed out. Her head swiveled to a faded list above Fillingham's desk. She and her partner could work on the duties relegated to the slow time when officers weren't patrolling or responding to calls. Both preferred to keep busy, whether it was tidying an office drawer or challenging the other to a bike race. It made time go faster. Plus, she was compulsively industrious, and Fillingham couldn't sit still.

Today, she wanted something mindless and physical to do. She needed to keep busy and press down the fluttering butterflies of excitement regarding the note left in her bike pannier. She was to meet Hawk Johnson at his house on Second Street after work.

They didn't usually do this—meet at his house. His roommates must be away. For the last two months, they had met up on an Island beach or park bench, almost always after dark. Once, they sat on a blanket and watched the planes land and take off from the Island Airport, plane lights blinking neon colors in the sooty sky, until eleven o'clock when the airport shut down for the night.

To keep occupied on her shift today, she would organize the station's attic and sort through the old incident reports. If she could get rid of a box or two, there would be more room for the bench press and free weights piled in the corner. Fillingham had brought them in last month to help him keep fit over the winter when he wasn't competitive sailing. No doubt he would challenge her to a weight-lifting competition, unaware that bench presses and squats had been components of her high school wrestling team training, so he would not have the upper hand.

As Christine climbed the narrow back stairs to the attic, broken office chairs, tangled radio equipment and towers of boxes came into view. Dust-filled light shone through the singular window. Shoved against one sloped wall was a cot used by officers during night shift in the cooler months. The room got suffocatingly hot in the summer.

As she removed the cardboard lid off a file box, the floor waxer buzzed on from below. The smell of beeswax wafted up. Fillingham was polishing the pine floors of the waiting room, a job Sergeant Bard assigned weekly. Sitting on a stool in the circular light of a brass lamp, she sorted the papers into three piles: garbage, shred and keep. As she scanned the contents of file folders and manila envelopes, her mind turned again to Hawk Johnson, and she smiled.

Last time they met, they had gone swimming. She had worn her bathing suit—a new bikini—under her uniform and met him after her afternoon shift. They had frolicked in the water, at first deliciously cold, their skin goose-bumped, until they warmed up enough to dive in. Then he had picked her up, hauled her onto his shoulders despite her shrieks, told her to stiffen her body into a plank and pressed her into the air above his head. She couldn't believe he could lift her. On the count of three, he had thrown her, her arms and legs thrashing as she hit the deeper water.

As Christine placed an outdated first-aid manual on the garbage pile, she thought about Hawk's skin against hers, the weight of his solid, powerful body. Her birth control pills were hidden in a shoebox in her closet at home, samples purloined by her policewoman friend Julie from a west-end medical clinic. For a second, Christine thought about getting caught with Hawk, the repercussions, the outcry, but she pushed the worry away.

As the afternoon progressed, shadows lengthened across the attic's wooden floor, the light coming in from the square window muted. At the Nature School, Wayne would be heading outside for a sing-along and marshmallow roast by the fire. From her quick sighting of her brother today, she could tell he was having a good time. He was an outdoor boy, keen for a game of hide-and-seek, ball hockey or pickup baseball. But a city boy. Learning more about nature and local wildlife would be good for him, as it had been for her.

That poor kid Jacob wasn't having a good time, though. She hoped Roy and Patrick had stopped bothering him.

At nine o'clock, she had successfully sorted one box and headed downstairs for their end-of-shift-duties. After updating the log, she gathered the mail for tomorrow's pickup and placed it on the counter for the courier. As she wiped the kitchen table, her body tingled with anticipation. She was meeting Hawk in less than three hours. Work couldn't finish fast enough.

As they often did, she and Fillingham split up for the last patrol of the Island—her to Ward's Island and Fillingham to Algonquin—both searching for visitors to shepherd onto the last ferry to the mainland, which left at eleven. One couple was still wandering Ward's Island Beach, sandals in hand, so Christine directed them toward the dock. The rest of the streets were deserted.

Back at the station, she placed her radio into the charger and then spent three minutes cleaning her teeth, brushing her hair and styling it back into a chignon.

"Sixteen!" Fillingham yelled from outside the bathroom door. Sixteen was the number on her police badge and her partner's nickname for her. "Let's head out."

On the ferry home, she encouraged Fillingham to talk about his upcoming sailing regatta so she only had to nod, her mind on the six-foot-two man she would see within the hour. With a casual, "See you tomorrow," she headed toward the streetcar stop while he hopped into his white MGB sports car parked in the lot. She had so often refused his offer for a ride home that he didn't ask anymore. Once he had roared away, she called a water taxi from a pay phone to pilot her back to the Island.

Back on Ward's Island, she hurried by the sports field, praying she wouldn't meet a resident out for a late-night dog walk or a smoke. At least she was still in uniform, so she could say she was on shift. Her relationship with Hawk—and what she did with him under his grandmother's star blanket—was private. A secret squirreled away in a hidden chamber of her heart.

A cooling breeze swayed the tree branches, tinkling house chimes, dampening the sound of the crickets from the nearby field. Moths fluttered around porch lights, but most house interiors were dark: families in bed, resting for work or school. As she approached Hawk's house, the long front windows burned gold. He was waiting for her.

The door opened immediately after her light rap. She stepped into the wedge of open door, and he shut it firmly behind her.

"Hi," she said, the pulse in her throat thrumming.

"Hi." His grin pushed his cheeks high, deepening his eyes.

"Anyone here?" She leaned in to view the small living room: lumpy couch, wooden chairs and hulking television. He was so close, she could smell him, that musky man smell that was unique to him, a hint of sweetgrass from his braided hair.

"Harry and Malcolm have gone back home," he said, referring to his two roommates. "I made tea." He motioned to the small kitchen.

"They're finished at Centreville?" she asked as they sat down at the battered wooden table marked with mug rings and water stains.

He poured each of them a cup of tea from the ceramic pot between them. "Just a handful of people left." Hawk's job as a mechanic would soon end because the amusement park was closing for the season. He slid the milk jug and sugar jar toward her.

"How was your day?" he asked. "Catch any bad guys?"

"I sorted a box of papers and kicked lovebirds off the beach."

"Serious police work," he said, his tone teasing. "Did you ride over on your bike?"

She shook her head.

"Next time, bike over. Your back tire looked flat last time I saw it. I'll check if you have a slow leak."

"You're nice," she said. He remembered how she took her tea. Last week, he had brought her roasted chestnuts warm from his backyard firepit.

He smiled. "So are you. And you keep the Island safe from lovebirds."

"Heroic, I know."

She sipped her tea. "How do you know so much about repairing things?" He fixed the leaking taps, broken appliances and faulty lights of quite a few neighbors, including Mrs. Polotov.

He shrugged. "My uncle repaired boat engines, stoves, cars. I learned from him. I was also a carnie for a year, setting up and taking down rides all over the country." He reached over to touch her hand. "What do you want to do tonight?"

"I don't have my swimsuit, otherwise we could find a beach for a dip." Glancing down, she said, "I'm always in uniform when we meet."

"Sometimes you're out of uniform." His smile dimpled his cheek.

Christine forced herself to maintain eye contact and not look away. God, this man made her feel great.

He slid into the chair kitty corner to her and reached for her police hat; his fingers felt around for the pins that secured it in place and gently pulled them out of her hair. After setting the pins on the table, he hung her hat on the back of an empty chair. Turning to her, he gave her the once-over, his glance traveling from her brown hair in its low bun to her white blouse, uniform jacket and dark skirt.

"I like you in uniform," he said. "You look so serious. Like a meter maid handing out parking tickets."

"Very funny." She stood up, and Hawk followed suit. Reaching for him, she tugged at the leather vest he wore over his black T-shirt and dropped it on the chair.

"We done talking?" he asked.

Looking into his beautiful chocolate eyes, she said, "For now."

He led her into a small bedroom that had just enough room for a double bed, a highboy bureau and a corner chair. She let him take off her uniform, clenching her hands in anticipation as he slowly undid her blouse, his knuckles grazing her skin. He layered her jacket, blouse and skirt over the back of the chair.

He laughed when she roughly pulled his T-shirt off, then pulled him toward her, her nails digging into his arms. Inhaling his smell, she hugged him close, trying to press herself against every inch of him.

He unclasped her bra, and she let it slide off her shoulders. Shuffling over to the bed until she felt its edge at her knees, she pulled him down on top of her. They kissed deeply, her arms wrapped around him. She'd been thinking about this moment all day, the exquisite feel of his heavy body, its weight on top of her like an anchor, his long hair tickling her shoulders.

Pushing him off to the side, she hurriedly pulled off her nylons and underwear, hearing him slide off his jeans. She pulled herself on top of him, trying to match him from his shoulders to his feet, one hand touching his face as she looked into his eyes.

"*Gi zah gin*," he said. "You are beautiful."

After, she lay in bed on her side, her top leg slung over his as he slept on his back with his hair spread over his pillow. It was the middle of the night; she wondered if she dared stay longer. What she would give to wake up next to him, then head to the kitchen to find mugs for their morning tea—like they were a couple, a typical married pair.

Propped up on her elbow, she stared at his profile back-lit from the streetlight filtering through the cotton curtains: his slightly curved forehead, straight nose, plump lips that had kissed her body and the square chin that had nudged her as he had moved over her.

His hand reached over and touched her hip, his eyes still shut. "You awake?"

"Uh-huh."

"Let's have lunch tomorrow."

Did that mean he wanted her to stay over? Or meet him again for a separate date? "Okay," she said hesitantly.

Opening his eyes, he turned to her. "You're off until three, right?"

She nodded.

"Let's go to Chapel House."

She stiffened. Chapel House! The restaurant staffed by Islanders and frequented by her sergeant. They might as well broadcast their relationship in the *Ward's Island Weekly*.

"Hector can cook us his special," Hawk said. "Small-mouth bass." He turned on his side to face her, adjusting the sheet around his hips. "It's good. Not as good as the fish we caught at Trout Pond."

"You mean the fish *you* caught," she said. Their first date, a secret, had been night fishing at the pond by the school. "Why don't we do that again—go fishing."

His fingers traced a line down her arm. "I mean it, Christine. Stay here. I don't have to work tomorrow. We could sleep in, hang out. Then go to lunch."

"I–I didn't bring any clothes to wear," she stuttered.

His hand moved up to her shoulder, his palm warming her, and he pulled her in closer. "You keep a change of clothes at the station."

She pushed away from him so she could see his face better. "I couldn't get them. What if an officer asks me what I'm doing?"

He exhaled. "Tell them you are going to lunch with me at Chapel House."

"I...I don't want anyone to know my business," she said, forcing her tone to be light.

Rolling onto his back, he shifted away from her and propped his arms behind his head. "You don't want anyone to know about us."

Silence, except for the sound of squawking cormorants through the screened window.

After a minute, she said, "I'm an Island police officer. You're a resident and a Centreville employee."

He gave an exasperated snort. "That's not it."

A few seconds ticked by.

"Okay." She paused. "You're an Indian and I'm white."

"Bingo." He turned to her. "It's not against the law, now. We're not doing anything wrong."

"I know, but that doesn't make it accepted." She thought of the cross burned on the front yard of a Jewish family in Oakville last year.

His brown eyes looked at her. "Don't let them take this away from us."

"Them?"

"The people you are afraid of. Police officers. Islanders. White people."

"I'm not strong like you." He had told her about his childhood, hiding from the RCMP at his uncle's hunting cabin so they wouldn't round him up for the residential schools for Indigenous children, escaping the brutality his mother and cousins had endured in the church-run schools.

"You *are* strong," he responded. "At work. With your family."

Her hand touched his neck, then slid down his shoulder to his smooth forearm, moving on to cover his hand, squeezing it.

He squeezed back, and they lay in bed, looking at each other.

"Where are we going?" he asked.

"What do you mean?"

"Us. Where is this going?" His finger pointed to her and back to himself.

Fear climbed her throat. "I'm not sure what you're asking."

"Tomorrow. Next week. Next year. Are we still hiding like frightened rabbits?"

She remained silent.

Hawk pushed himself into a sitting position. "I want to be together."

"So do I," she said.

"Let's do it!" he said, his tone excited. He tipped her chin so she met his glance. "Let's be together. Inside this house. And out."

"It's not that simple." She thought about the responses of her fellow officers. Fillingham would shake his head in derision. Marino would call her "Squaw" and ask her if she put out to all riff-raff. It would make it difficult to work at Island station—at any station.

"Christine," Hawk said. "In two weeks, I finish at Centreville. I'm going back to Whitefish to see my *nimaamaa* and to hunt elk with my uncle. I will stay there for the winter unless you tell me to come back because we are together. For everyone to see."

"You don't understand. People will say things about us. Hateful things." Her voice quavered.

"I understand," he said, his hand reaching to touch her forearm. "I've been called those things all my life."

"They will say things at work." She swallowed against the welling tears.

"I know," he said, his gaze sympathetic.

He didn't know policing. It was very conservative and traditional. A male institution, where everyone followed protocol. And if your behavior was deemed out of line, you were bullied and harassed until you quit.

"I can find a handyman job in town over the winter," he said.

She sat up on her knees to face him, pulling the quilt up to cover her breasts. "Can't we continue like we are now? Just us?"

He shook his head, his long hair spreading over his shoulders. "I don't want to hide anymore. I am not ashamed." He clasped her hand. "Don't be ashamed either."

He didn't understand. She didn't want her workplace ruined. Policing was the one thing she was good at. She couldn't see herself doing anything else. And it paid well—she earned the same as the male officers. And every two weeks, she handed her wages to a loan shark to repay her mother's gambling debt. "I can't risk my job. My income. My family depends on me."

"You have your mom."

She crossed her arms, and his hand slipped away from hers. "The last time Mom was in charge, our grocery money bought beer and she pawned our toaster."

"You said that was long ago. That since she's been working at Police Records, she was better," he said.

Christine blinked away tears. "I can't do this."

Their eyes locked for a long minute. His eyes were warm and pleading, then, slowly, they got colder. He turned and swung his legs over the edge of the bed, his back to her, and pulled on his pants. Leaning down, he retrieved his T-shirt from the floor and pulled it on over his head with a brisk motion. He left the bedroom.

Christine quickly dressed, dread filling her. *No. No. No.* This wasn't happening.

Hawk stood near the front door, her police hat in his hand.

She took it from him. "It doesn't have to end this way."

"Be with me. For everyone to see." His brown eyes begged her.

She held his glance for a few seconds, then looked down, silent.

"You have no courage in your heart." Hawk walked back into the bedroom and closed the door.

Christine woke up to the shrill peals of the kitchen phone. It stopped before she could get out of bed. Her mom must have left for work and Donna must be at school.

Last night, Christine had stumbled out of Hawk's house and taken a water taxi back to the mainland. When she got home, her mom was in bed and Donna was bundled in her comforter like a crescent roll fast asleep. Wayne, of course, was bunking at the Island school. In the bathroom, Christine turned on the shower to cover the sound of her weeping. Hawk was done with her. With their relationship.

Pajamas on, she had pondered Hawk's naïve attitude. What did he think would happen if they walked hand-in-hand around the Island—a native man and a white woman? Islanders would be tolerant—they were a liberal-minded community of musicians, hippies, politicians, artists and office workers. But the rest of the Torontonians, including her mother and her fellow officers, would not be accepting.

Fillingham had disliked Hawk from the moment they interviewed him for their last investigation. Hawk had responded to Fillingham with the same animosity. No policeman would think it acceptable for an Indigenous man to be messing with a white policewoman. Everyone knew about the constable from 41 Division with the broken collarbone. His injury was a warning to all Black officers to stay away from white policewomen.

She couldn't allow her workplace to be contaminated—it was hard enough to be one of sixty female officers on a force of four thousand. Her police job was her ticket—her family's ticket—to better things. A better apartment. The payment of debts. Baseball training for Wayne. An education for Donna.

The phone rang again. She squinted at the alarm clock: 9:15. It could be work calling. Or her siblings' school. Grunting, she pushed herself out of bed and propelled herself to the kitchen.

"Hello." Her voice was hoarse from last night's crying.

"Sixteen. What took you so long to pick up?"

"Fillingham?" she croaked. "What's wrong?"

"A kid is missing from the Nature School."

"Wayne?" She squeezed the receiver tightly.

"No, it's not him."

Thank goodness, she thought, her other hand over her heart. Wayne was a good kid, but he could be impulsive and silly. And he didn't always follow the rules. "Who is it?"

"A ten-year-old boy. Jacob...Jacob Nowak. He wasn't present for roll call this morning at seven. Last seen at 10:00 p.m. last night. They've been searching for him for the past two hours."

"Jacob is the name of the blond boy we saw yesterday with the bloody nose," she said.

"It could be him."

"Have they have notified the radio and television stations?"

"No publicity yet, in case he's homesick and arrives on his parents' doorstep. But Sarge wants a complete sweep of the Island. Can you be ready in ten minutes?"

"Sure," she said and hurried down the hall to get dressed.

Children, especially tourist families, went missing on the Island occasionally. Odds were Jacob would be found wandering one of the Island's parks while she and her partner were ferrying to Hanlan's Point. But work would be a good distraction today. It would take her mind off Hawk. And it would be good to find the boy and have a happy ending to something.

Chapter 4

After dressing in her uniform, Christine splashed cold water on her face, trying to soothe her puffy eyes. She hurriedly styled her chignon, trying to erase the memory of Hawk's warm fingers against her neck as he unpinned her hat. At the front door, she quickly brushed the gravel dust from her Oxfords.

Her soles tapped down the interior stairs of her low-rise apartment to the exit. She didn't want Fillingham to see their threadbare couch or wobbly kitchen table. It was bad enough he would roar up to her place in his white convertible, like a Hollywood celebrity, completely out of place in her neighborhood of working families, new immigrants and rooming houses.

Thank goodness her mother wasn't home. Phyllis would gaze out the living room window for a sighting of Fillingham, declaring him "such a lovely man, so charming." And of course, rolling in old Toronto money. Richie Rich was his nickname around the police station, named after the wealthy blond boy from the comic series. Clearly, Fillingham did not need his job, but it was his stepping stone to being a Harbor Police officer—his childhood dream.

With a low snarl, Fillingham's white MGB convertible appeared with its top down, as if he were starring in a James Bond film. His short blond hair was ruffled in the wind, blue patrol shirt rolled up to the elbows showing tanned forearms.

Christine dropped into the low seat, the small car rocking with her weight.

"You look terrible," he said. "You okay?"

"Donna was sick, so I stayed up with her." She hated lying to him, even a white lie, but she could never tell Fillingham the truth. He had warned her about Hawk, about dating native men. He had been right.

"Where was your mom?" he asked.

"Oh, for goodness' sakes. Drive!" Her foot stomped the floor.

"Grum–py!" he said, without rancor as he shifted gears and then did a quick U-turn to head toward the ferry docks.

By the time they boarded the Hanlan's Point ferry, Christine was calm. In uniform, she felt composed and competent. As she brushed a piece of lint off her skirt, she reminded herself of the force's new motto: *To Serve and Protect*. She was on duty now. Her goal was to find a lost boy whose teacher, schoolmates and family were undoubtedly worried.

The gardener from the Island school picked them up in a golf cart, and the trio headed south toward the school. They'd likely find the boy in the next hour or two. A lost child was a frequent call-in to the Center Island station from the amusement park staff. Police would find the child calmly licking a lollipop as he watched riders get soaked from the Log Flume ride, unaware of the search underway.

When Christine and Fillingham arrived at the Nature School, they were directed to an empty classroom, which Sergeant Bard had commandeered as home base for the search. The far wall had a door that led outside to a courtyard. Above the columns of stacked chairs and desks hung frames of pressed flowers and photos of the Island's natural landscape. A chalkboard was spread across the width of the front wall.

In the middle of the room, Sergeant Bard pointed to a creased map laid flat on a large teacher's desk, his sizeable belly pressed against the wooden edge. Three officers looked on: Morano and Reynolds and PC Fairweather from 52 Division, who filled in when they were short.

Sergeant Bard looked up. "Your bikes are in the back of the patrol car. You two check Centreville for the boy."

She felt a flutter of wild anticipation that she might see Hawk at work; with a stab, she remembered he wasn't working today. He wouldn't want to see her now, anyway.

"Is there a photograph of the boy, sir?" she asked.

He pointed to a pile of mimeographed paper on the chalkboard ledge. Christine went over and picked up the black-and-white picture of a fair-haired boy with wide-set eyes, straight nose and high cheekbones.

She tilted the photo toward Fillingham. "It's Jacob—the boy we saw yesterday. The one with the bloody nose."

"What's this?" Sergeant Bard asked.

"We were at the school yesterday," Christine said.

"And?" Sergeant Bard said.

Fillingham said, "Kids were playing a game outside. This Jacob was with two other boys. He looked like he had been punched in the face."

"Somebody hit him?" the sergeant asked.

"He wouldn't say," Christine answered, "but it was probably Roy O'Neil. He's in the same class as my brother."

"Your brother's here? On the Island?" Sergeant Bard asked.

She nodded. "He goes to Lakeview. Two classes from his school are here this week."

"Grab your radios from the car," Sergeant Bard ordered. "Lane, I might call you in later to speak with the students, since you know them."

"Any info on the missing boy?" Fillingham asked.

Morano said, "His family came from Poland six months ago. He doesn't speak great English."

"Did he get lost exploring the Island?" Fillingham said.

Sergeant Bard said, "He took his suitcase with him."

"He's a runaway?" Fillingham said.

"The teacher said his bed smelled like urine," Sergeant Bard added.

Fillingham frowned. "The kid peed himself? At ten years old?"

"Maybe he's embarrassed that he wet the bed," Christine said. "So he took off."

Sergeant Bard nodded. "We're checking the ferry docks to see if staff spotted him last night or this morning. Morano's been talking to the water taxis."

"We'll head out to Centreville," Fillingham said.

"A patrol unit is with the family in Parkdale in case the boy arrives home," Sergeant Bard said. "We notified transit drivers to look out for a blond ten-year-old boy with a tan suitcase."

Christine and Fillingham pedaled eastward, swiveling their heads to scan their surroundings for Jacob. They took turns calling his name, gliding with heads tilted to hear over the crash of the waves against the breakwall.

Dismounting at the entrance sign to Centreville, Fillingham said, "I'll head to the office to get the maintenance staff to open the locked areas."

Christine nodded toward the Bumble Bee ride. "I'll start here. Jacob may have been hiding in a ride seat overnight, waiting for the ferries to start up." Hiking up her skirt, she stepped over the wooden fence surrounding the attraction and peered into each car.

It took two hours to check the grounds of the closed amusement center. With the help of park staff, they searched the rides, storage sheds, farm, locked vendors' carts and the gift store. Employees were asked to keep an eye out for the fair-haired boy with a suitcase. The officers left copies of Jacob's photo in the office.

The partners regrouped on a park bench under a willow tree. Christine said, "Jacob could easily evade us by hiding in the places we already checked."

"He could be hiding underneath a picnic table anywhere on the Island," he added. "He's got eighty-eight acres to choose from. That said, should we check Olympic Island?"

She shrugged. "We could check behind the clump of bushes at the far end. Otherwise, it's open space."

Her radio crackled on her hip: "52-25. Sergeant Bard. Requesting report from PC Fillingham."

Fillingham picked up his radio. "Dispatch, this is PC Fillingham. No sighting of Jacob Nowak at Centreville. Over."

"Dispatch, Sergeant Bard. Requesting PC Fillingham and PW Lane search the Island Airport. Over."

Fillingham turned to Christine. "Think the kid is going to commandeer a plane and fly back to Poland?"

Frowning at her partner's levity, she reached for her radio. "Dispatch, 52-25. PW Lane. Copy that request. Heading to the Island Airport. Over."

As they retrieved their bicycles propped against a tree, he said, "If we don't find him on the Island, odds are he's back in his neighborhood."

She mounted her bike. "Poor guy. He gets punched in the face. Then he wets his bed. That's a lot of shame to bear. Especially for a new kid trying to fit in."

Fillingham hopped on his bike with a practiced spring. "No one saw him leave the Island. If he snuck on a ferry unnoticed, why hasn't he shown up at home?" He glanced down at his watch. "It's two o'clock. He's been gone for at least seven hours. Do you think he got lost on his way back to Parkdale?"

"I don't know if Jacob would remember which streetcar to take back home. Kids don't always pay attention to that. Or if he would have the five-cent fare on him," she said.

"Maybe he's too embarrassed to go home," Fillingham concluded. "Maybe the dad beats him every time he wets the bed. Or maybe he's fed up with life in Canada and wants to be back in Poland."

"Jacob told me his home was taken over by the military. I don't think Poland is a peaceful place for him to return to."

They cycled west along Lakeshore Road, past the Center Island Pier, heading back toward the school. "He could be anywhere in Toronto," Fillingham said.

As they rode, they scanned the surrounding fields and bushes for the boy, the lake breeze keeping them cool as the sun climbed higher. Their tires whirred quietly on the concrete path as they passed the occasional tourist or family pedaling rented quadricycles. Passing the school, she spotted several police officers in the inner courtyard. Sergeant Bard must have called in more staff from 52 Division.

"If it were my brother that was missing," Christine said as they continued westward toward the Hanlan's Point dock, "I would be furious to start, because Wayne had probably done something foolish and was hiding to avoid the punishment. But after a couple hours," she shook her head, "I would be worried. He's too impulsive and doesn't always think things through."

"Lane, I'm sure you've responded to lots of missing children calls as a policewoman. Ninety-nine percent of the time, we find the kid a short distance away—at a friend's house or a neighbor's or playing ball hockey three streets over."

"True..." she said, trailing off. The cases she remembered were not the happy-ending ones: a four-year-old who had hidden in the pantry cupboard because her dad had knocked out her mother's front teeth; the toddler who wandered onto Jarvis Street as his mom lay unconscious from a heroin hit. The homes the children returned to were often as distressing as the missing child call.

She shivered—she was being morbid. "This is the route Jacob would have taken from the school to the closest ferry dock if his intention was to get off the Island."

As they turned north, the strip of land on the west side of the path widened. The mowed grass was dotted with clusters of wooden tables and metal-grill barbeques. Fillingham said, "I'll search the picnic area."

"I'll check by the water," she said. "I'll meet you at the snack bar in fifteen."

While Fillingham crisscrossed the park, Christine biked slowly along the path, dismounting several times to check the bushes and trees lining the inner lagoon.

At the snack bar, they checked the open washrooms. The business was closed for the off-season, a solid metal curtain locked to the counter.

He rattled the lock, which held. "Well, he didn't stay here."

"We should head to the airport. Sergeant Bard is waiting for our report," she said.

As they biked toward the ferry dock, she asked, "How do we enter the airport from the Island? It's fenced off all the way around." She hadn't been inside the small airport before. It was only accessible by a ferry that piloted people across a channel from the mainland to the northwestern tip of the Island.

He veered left at a fork in the road. "I have my ways. Follow me."

The asphalt pathway ended at a gate in the airport fence with two screens chained together by a large steel lock. After dismounting, Fillingham pushed against the screens, creating a gap in the fence. He looked over his shoulder at Christine. "We can make it through."

Her eyebrows furrowed. "I don't think so."

"Watch!" He pushed the front tire of his bike through the gap, then angled the handlebars sideways. With a forceful shove, the bike sailed through.

He turned and unclipped the front basket from her bike and tossed it over the fence.

"Hey," she objected.

He nudged her off her bike, unlatched the panniers from her rear wheel and tossed them over the fence. Holding on to her bike handles, he wiggled it through the gap in the fence.

Christine regarded the two bikes lying on airport property on the other side of the fence.

"Lean on the gate," Fillingham instructed. Kneeling, he pushed on the bottom rails while she pressed on the chain link above him; he angled forward until his head and neck were through the gap, followed by his torso, the metal fence clutching him at the waist. He wiggled, pressing the chain link with his elbows, panting with the effort.

"If you get stuck, I'm leaving you here," she grunted.

With a last heave, he scraped through to the other side. Standing, he tugged down on his uniform jacket, straightening it, scanning for tears in the material.

He gestured to the opening. "You're up, Lane."

"No other way to get in?" she asked.

"We could ask security to unlock the gate, but that would take too long. I think Bard wants to hear from us sooner rather than later."

"I won't fit." Her hips, chest or shoulders could get stuck. And she wasn't a hundred percent certain that Fillingham wouldn't leave her pinioned here as a lark.

"Sure you will," he said. "I'll help you."

An image of him pressing on her hips like a farm boy trying to coax an ox into moving flashed through her mind. "No."

He sighed. "Fine. You'll have to climb it."

Sizing up the ten-foot fence, she wondered if she could make it over without laddering another set of nylons.

"Move away from the fence," she said, gesturing with her hand. "I don't want to land on you."

"That would be my untimely end."

"You're hilarious."

Climbing the fence wasn't too bad; her upper-body strength helped pull her up. The difficulty was at the top. When she attempted to swing her leg over in her narrow skirt, she teeter-tottered dangerously.

"Lie on top of the fence," Fillingham advised. "Hug it with your arms and legs, then let both legs hang down the other side."

Her fingers clawed around the metal fence loops. The grass below was blurring into a smear of green.

Fillingham said, "Let your legs drop—"

In one motion, her legs were over, and she began sliding down the other side of the fence. She pushed herself away so the wire wouldn't catch on her uniform and fell onto her back at her partner's feet.

"Ow!" he said. "You're on my toe."

"How about getting your foot out of my back," she gasped.

He obliged. While she caught her breath, he hooked the paniers and basket back on her bike.

They pedaled across a swath of grass toward the asphalt runways that ran the length of the airport grounds. "How do we reach the terminal without getting hit by a plane?" she asked.

"Take the crossroad." He pointed to a narrow lane that bisected the two long runways. "And duck!"

He took off on his bike, and she followed, her head rotating to check for planes. The air traffic controllers must be wondering who the heck was bicycling on their airstrip.

Arriving at the main terminal was a relief. The two-story white clapboard building featured a smaller third story with large windows that gave air traffic controllers a 360-degree view of the horizon. To the right of the building yawned the open mouth of a hangar housing planes in various stages of function. Parked on either side of the terminal were a dozen small passenger and cargo planes.

Inside the terminal, Christine and Fillingham met the airport manager. Sergeant Bard had called earlier, so the airport staff had already conducted a cursory search for Jacob. The groundsman accompanied the two officers around the property as they checked the hangar, storage cupboards, offices, tool sheds and parked planes.

"He's not here," Fillingham concluded as they returned to the main building an hour and a half later.

"I need to wash up." She showed him her palms, grimy from pawing through the contents of closets and bins. Undoubtedly, she had dirt smudges on her face.

He nodded, then pulled his radio from his belt to report to Dispatch.

Framed photographs hung in the narrow corridor to the washrooms, depicting the airport's history: an aerial view of the amusement park that previously occupied airport land; a Hanlan's Point house floating on a barge to Algonquin Island for resettling; and big band leader Jimmy Dorsey exiting the first commercial flight at the airport in 1939.

Near the washroom entrance was a series of wartime photographs. Christine's mom had told her that Norwegian pilots had trained at the Island Airport during the Second World War.

A pilot posed with his aircraft with a wide smile.

Dad?

It was a photograph of her father before he died in the war—identical to the one framed on their living room shelf at home—except this one was taken from farther away. He was smiling, one arm touching the plane's metal belly as he stood under the wing, his shirt sleeves rolled to the elbows, short hair gelled in a side part. His wrists looked thick and strong, his shoulders wide, neck bullish. Christine got her height and musculature from his side of the family.

She hadn't known that her pilot father had flown out of the Island Airport—she'd have to ask her mom about that.

Christine read the caption below the photograph: *Lieutenant Hans Jansen. Norwegian Air Force.*

What? Her dad was Captain Thomas Lane of the Canadian Air Force.

"Sixteen!"

Christine turned.

Fillingham was waiting at the end of the hall. "Sarge wants you back at the school to interview students."

Without responding, she continued along the hallway into the bathroom and headed for the sink. The cold water blasted her hands, numbing them as her brain scrambled to make sense of the photo. Why did it say her father was in the Norwegian Air Force? He was Canadian. He had been overseas during the war and died in France in 1944 just after Christine was born.

A tap at the door. "Lane?" Fillingham said.

"What?" she barked.

"We have to go."

"Give me a second," she called through the door.

Finding a missing ten-year-old boy was the priority, she reminded herself. That was all she should be thinking about right now. Not this mix-up with her dad. Or Hawk Johnson. Her singular focus was Jacob Nowak.

Chapter 5

"Lane!" Sergeant Bard said. "Do you know all the Lakeview students on the trip?" He stood in the search room beside a somber Tim Hawley. Children's voices chattered down the hall as indoor classes continued with staff.

"I know most of the students in my brother's class," she answered. "I'm less familiar with Miss Patterson's class."

Sergeant Bard said, "No one has seen Jacob at the ferry docks or water taxi stands." He stabbed the map with his thick finger. "We have ten officers combing the Island."

"It's past three thirty," Fillingham said. "Jacob would be home by now, if that's where he was heading."

Sergeant Bard said, "He hasn't been back. The family rents the main floor of a house near Queen and Dufferin. The Youth Bureau has been canvassing the neighborhood in case he is bunking with a friend or hiding in a backyard."

"Does the family speak English?" she asked.

"A little," Sergeant Bard responded. "They came over last March from Poland. Brass assigned a Polish-speaking officer to the neighborhood search because the block is full of them."

"Have they called the Harbor Police?" Fillingham asked.

Their boss nodded. "They've checked the beaches and the lagoons but haven't called in the scuba divers. The boy could have drowned; that's always a possibility on the Island. But he took his suitcase, which points to a planned escape." He addressed Christine. "We've interviewed his classmates, and no one seems to know where Jacob was headed. I want you to dig around. See if you can get some fresh details from the students. His bunkmates are Roy O'Neil, Patrick Williamson and your brother, Wayne. Start with them."

"Okay."

"The boys know you," Sergeant Bard said. "It'll be easier to gain their trust. Put your womanly talents to work. If we don't locate Jacob by dinner, they're sending the kids home."

"I'll take you to the group." Tim indicated the hallway with his inclined head. He touched her elbow to turn her in the right direction. She stepped away, letting his arm drop.

Student art brightened the hallway: a watercolor of the Gibraltar Point lighthouse, an acrylic painting of a male cardinal with his mate, sunset on Lake Ontario.

In the large community meeting room, Miss Phillips leaned against the wood paneling, watching students work in groups. The children were matching footprints and fur to the correct animal photo. Her ashen face matched the beige hue of her ponytail, her pale eyebrows invisible above her brown eyes. Christine felt sorry for her. A student goes missing on an excursion—every teacher's nightmare.

"I'd like to speak with Miss Phillips first before I talk to the boys," Christine told Tim.

Tim approached the teacher. "PW Lane wants to ask you a few questions in the staffroom. I can hang out here."

Miss Phillips shook her head. "I won't let my students out of my sight."

"We can talk here." Christine went over and leaned back against the wall beside Miss Phillips. After Tim left, Christine asked softly, "What do you think happened?"

"Tim said Jacob's bed was wet."

"So he left because of the embarrassment?"

Miss Phillips grimaced. "Kids can be cruel."

"Any other reason for his departure?"

"I don't know," Miss Phillips said. "I...I don't know Jacob that well. The school term just started. I've only had the class for two weeks."

"Did he seem homesick?"

"I don't think so." Her tone was hesitant. "He fell yesterday, when the students were playing a game outside, but he was joining in the activities—making a pine-cone craft, going on a scavenger hunt. And he was keen to play in the baseball game scheduled for Thursday."

"Does he have friends?" Christine asked.

"He is friendly with his classmates, but I don't think he has a particular friend. I've seen him with another Polish boy at recess—Peter—I'm not sure of his last name. He's one year younger, so he's not on this trip. The police checked in with Peter today. He hasn't seen Jacob."

"Is Jacob friends with his bunkmates?"

"I'm not sure if they are good friends. I thought it was nice that they included Jacob when I let students choose roommates."

Wayne had been excited about being chosen to bunk with Roy, and all four boys were on the baseball team.

"Can I talk to Patrick now?" Christine asked, spotting the boy sitting cross-legged on the rug.

Christine directed Patrick into an empty classroom, where they sat at adjacent desks. Christine's body overwhelmed the small student chair, which she angled toward the boy.

He stared down at his desk, his shaggy auburn hair brushing the collar of his plaid shirt.

"Hey, Patrick. I'm here to talk about Jacob."

"I already talked to the police. And the teachers."

"I know. Thank you. It's a drag to retell your story. But let's try it again in case something jogs your memory."

His shoulders slumped as he looked down again at his desktop, hands clasped.

"When did you last see Jacob?" she asked.

Without looking up, he said, "Last night."

"What time was that?"

"Ten."

"At lights out?" she asked.

He nodded.

"What happened after that?" she asked.

"We went to sleep."

"Right away?"

He nodded.

"Did Jacob fall asleep?"

"I guess so."

"When did you notice Jacob was missing?"

He was fiddling with his fingers, picking at the cuticle around his nail bed. "When Tim came in to get us up and he wasn't there."

"Did you see him leave the room during the night?"

He shook his head.

"Even to the washroom?" She leaned on her desk, trying to meet Patrick's eyes. His fair skin looked so pale that his freckles were like tiny burgundy splotches covering his face.

Again, he shook his head.

"Is Jacob a friend?" she asked.

He shrugged.

"Why did you pick him to bunk with you?"

"I don't know."

"So, who are your friends, Patrick?" She smiled, trying for a more casual tone. Patrick was upset, clearly, which was not surprising in the situation where a classmate was missing. But he was shutting down—giving her nothing.

He looked up for a second, a flash of blue eyes fringed with darker lashes. "Roy."

Christine acknowledged his response with a nod. It was clear from the scenario the previous day with Jacob that Patrick was Roy's friend—or at least his sidekick. "Were you having a good time on the Island?"

He nodded.

"It seems like a lot of fun," she said. "Paddling. Hiking. Marshmallows by the fire." She paused. "Was Jacob having a good time, too?"

"I guess so." His hand moved atop of the desk, his thumbnail tracing a crack in the tabletop.

"Was he homesick?"

"I don't know."

"Did he say anything to you about leaving the school or the Island?"

He shook his head.

"Did he talk about going home or to a friend's house?"

Head shake.

"You have no idea where he is?" she asked.

"No."

"Did you notice that Jacob's sheets were wet?" she asked. The boys must know that Jacob wet the bed.

Patrick nodded, his mouth pinching in disgust.

"Do you know when that happened?" she asked.

He shook his head.

"Was Jacob having a good time yesterday when he got punched in the face?"

He looked up quickly, as if surprised, then back down. "That was an accident. We were just playing around."

"Why do you think Jacob left?" she asked.

"I don't know."

"If you know anything about Jacob's whereabouts from something he said or something you noticed, it is important to tell us. He could be lost on the Island or somewhere in the city. He might need help. Maybe something you remember can help us find him."

She waited a full minute. Patrick kept his head down, shoulders rounded, staring at his thumbnail wiggling in the desk crack.

With a sigh, she stood up, pushing the chair away with her legs. "Thanks for speaking with me, Patrick. I know it's an upsetting situation. If you remember anything that might help, even if it doesn't seem important, let me or another officer know."

Patrick silently left the room, averting his eyes as he passed her.

Fillingham arrived in the doorway. "How'd that go?"

"Nothing helpful."

He nodded. "Sarge wants me to talk to your brother."

"Okay." Did her sergeant not trust her to interview her sibling?

Her partner must have read her mind. "Sergeant Bard thinks Wayne might be more honest if a policeman speaks to him, not his sister."

"Fine. I'll talk to Roy."

The conversation with Roy was like Patrick's interview: shrugs, "I don't know" or "No." For the first part of the interview, Roy leaned back in his chair, the soles of his shoes pressed against the desk table legs, balancing himself.

Christine had seen this before: the sneering child unintimidated by police. Most male officers would have shoved the chair down, had

Roy address them with a "Yes, sir" or "No, sir," physically rattling the child. But that just shut the child down or made them lie. Christine had found that when a child was unafraid, things slipped out: boastful rants, hidden facts and alliances.

"Roy, did you get up during the night?" Christine asked from the adjacent desk.

"No."

"Anyone leave the room during that time?"

"I don't know."

"Did you hear anything in the hallway?"

His brown hair brushed against the shoulders of his jean jacket as he shook his head. He was stockier than Patrick and taller by three inches.

"How about outside?" she asked.

He gave her an exasperated look. "I was asleep. I didn't hear anything."

"Tell me about Jacob," she said.

"What about him?"

"How did he end up in your room?"

"They wouldn't let me bunk with Samantha Buchanan." He smirked. He was ten but had a teenager's insolence. And he certainly didn't seem to care that he was speaking with a police officer.

She kept her expression neutral. "Where do you think Jacob is?"

"Who knows?" His tone implied, *Who cares?*

Time for a change in tactic. She pushed the back of his chair, and the front legs thudded to the floor. He grabbed the front of the desk for balance, looking over at her in surprise.

She leaned forward. "A boy is missing. A boy that bunked with you. I'll ask you again. Where do you think Jacob is?"

"I don't know," he said, his tone slightly chastened. "He peed his bed, like a baby. Maybe he went home to his mom."

"Is there anywhere else he might go?" she asked.

"Probably some Polack family."

"Which family?" she asked.

He shrugged. "Don't they all stick together?"

"Did he say he was meeting someone?"

His top lip curled. "He talked about some cousin of his, about how great he was. That he would show us."

"Show you what?" she asked.

"I don't know. Are we done?"

"We're missing something," Christine told Fillingham as she carried the heavy spotlight into the police station's backyard. It had been four days since Jacob Nowak was last seen. Lakeview students had returned home on the ferry on Tuesday night. Christine had relayed Roy's information about Jacob's cousin. The teenager hadn't heard from Jacob; he had joined the officers searching the Parkdale neighborhood, acting as a translator between the police and some of the Polish residents and business owners.

Christine, as well as a swelling group of police officers, Island residents and volunteers, had daily searched the Island for Jacob's whereabouts. Walking in lines an arm's-length apart, they combed through the rough terrain beside the filtration plant and examined every storage box, feed container and equipment closet in Centreville and Far Enough Farm.

Christine and Fillingham had spent the first three hours of their current shift scouring the Island for signs of the boy, checking in several abandoned houses, old sheds and backyards. The Island was quiet, the air cool and damp with the approaching fall. Back at the station, they had a bite of dinner as the sun set and now were heading outside for a wrestling session.

It surprised her that Fillingham wanted to continue wrestling with her. When they were first partnered in the summer, he had cajoled her into giving him lessons after he saw her flip an over-zealous admirer. Her explanation that she had been on her high school's boys' wrestling team had flabbergasted him. Of course, she hadn't been allowed to compete; she practiced with the boys to get them ready for meets. It was the saving grace of her high school years that her gym coach had seen her athleticism and got her involved in sports.

For tonight's wrestling session, she and Fillingham dragged dark blue mats onto the grass of the station's backyard. Despite her grumblings, she was glad to be occupying the evening this way. There was little to do for the last three hours of the shift, and the exercise would take her mind off her thoughts—of the missing boy, and of Hawk. She kept getting flashes of her time with Hawk: walking the boardwalk at midnight hand in hand, the dimple in his left cheek, his wide smile when he spotted her at a meeting place. She had checked her bike basket for notes and scanned Centreville for his broad-shouldered figure, but she hadn't spotted him, and he had made no contact.

And there was the strange situation of the photo of her father hanging in the Island Airport, captioned with another name. She had been pulling double shifts searching for Jacob Nowak, but Christine had caught her mom before work yesterday. Sharing a pot of tea, Phyllis had shaken her head at Christine's query, reiterating that Thomas Lane had flown for the Canadian Air Force, stationed originally in the UK. Christine was mistaken. The man in the photo just looked similar.

Her mom must be right, Christine had concluded. Maybe her brain had been fuzzy from the search, from her lack of sleep. If she had a chance, she'd go back and check the airport photo again.

But now, a fresh challenge was at hand. She exhaled slowly as she faced Fillingham in the middle of the mat. Time to thump her partner to the ground.

An hour later, Fillingham lay supine on the mat, her knee in his back. Releasing her hold, she stood up and wiped the sweat from her hairline with her forearm, her heart pounding from the exercise. She felt better—calmer. Wrestling was good for that.

She might have been too rough. She was supposed to be teaching Fillingham technique—not using him for throwing practice. But her partner didn't seem to mind. He popped up after the last hold, smiling, breathing heavily too.

"You're improving," she said.

"You pancaked me twice," he said as he grabbed one end of the mat.

She grabbed the other end. "You're hard to get a hold of."

"That's me," he said as they walked the mat toward the station's garage. "Dodgy!"

"And you're quick to learn."

He inhaled deeply, nose in the air. "Is that fear I smell, Sixteen? A queen about to be dethroned!"

Smiling as they stored the equipment, she thought about how glad she was that Fillingham was her partner. She couldn't imagine doing any of the things they did: bike races, wrestling, jogging and weightlifting, with another officer. He was like a big, energetic kid with an optimistic personality and money and charm to burn. And his ego was so big he didn't mind losing, even to a female partner. Thank God Fillingham had concluded that being an Island officer was the best way to get into the Harbor Police force. God knows what Island patrol would be like if she was stuck with Morano or Pilkington. She shuddered, not wanting to think about it.

Inside the station, they took turns showering in the station's tiny bathroom.

After changing back into uniform from her shorts and t-shirt, she exited the bathroom and inhaled the pungent aroma of percolating coffee. Fillingham always brought quality coffee—freshly ground Ecuadorian or a dark roast from Kenya. No grocery store Nescafé or Folgers for him.

They sat facing each other on the red vinyl chairs at the kitchen table. Warming her hands on her coffee cup, she stared at the small window bracketed by yellow curtains, the darkness outside making the window a mirror.

Was Jacob still on the Island? If he was hurt, could he survive five days without water? But how could he still be here? The search team had checked every building, house, shed and boat. The rest of the Island was acres of flat, open parkland. He must be in the city.

"He's not in Parkdale," Fillingham said, as if reading her mind.

"How do you know?"

"The Youth Bureau canvassed the neighbors and friends. Spoke with the local Polish families. A big fat zero."

"Who told you that?"

"I have my sources," he said, smiling, his teeth white in his tanned face.

Fillingham was a social guy—he had friends in many places, from his sailing buddies at RCYC to friends made during police training and his university days. Who did he know in the Youth Bureau? Did they contact the Women's Bureau to aid in the search for Jacob?

Julie.

Of course. He had been speaking with Julie, her friend from the Women's Bureau. The two had spent the summer flirting, despite Christine's attempt to keep them separate. It wasn't that she didn't like Julie—though her friend could be superficial and self-involved—but she always came through for Christine when it mattered, ever since they met at police college. However, Julie didn't stay in relationships for long and left a string of broken hearts in her wake.

"You on Julie's hot line?" she asked, then took a sip of coffee.

"I'm on every woman's hot line," he said.

She scowled.

"Present company excluded," he added.

"You dating Julie?" she asked abruptly.

"What if I am?" He smiled, his blue eyes looking levelly at her, his short blond hair already dry after his shower.

She shrugged. There were many reasons she could cite against her friend and partner coupling, but she wasn't going to give them a reason to run into each other's arms.

"You dating the mechanic?" he countered.

Her coffee mug halted halfway to her mouth. Fillingham had disliked Hawk from the moment they met at the amusement park.

"No," she said truthfully. She and Hawk were done. He was back in Whitefish, his reservation near Sudbury. Or would be soon, when Centreville closed.

Hawk had been willing to stay in Toronto for her, far from his family and tribe. It had been so tempting to respond, "Yes! Stay!" She wanted so much to be with this man who didn't view her as a six-foot monstrosity of a woman. In his presence, she was strong—*ogichi-daakwe*—and beautiful.

Christine placed her mug on the table with a thud. "Julie is a heartbreaker."

His eyebrows rose over his sky-blue eyes. "So am I."

She stood up. "A match made in heaven." He had been warned. As long as the couple's relationship didn't affect Christine's work and make him want to drop her as a partner when Julie got bored and dumped him, she was happy to stay out of it.

Fillingham and Julie were made for each other.

Chapter 6

The Women's Bureau patrol car, initialed with WB1 on the side, U-turned sharply on Queen Street with Julie at the wheel. Tires squealing, the vehicle pulled up alongside Christine at the curb.

"Hey baby, want a ride?" Julie shouted through the open window.

Sarah, Christine's other friend from the WB, smiled at Christine from the passenger-side window. "All's quiet on the front, Christine. Hop in the back and we'll head over to Simpsons."

Climbing inside, Christine reached to close the door just as Julie stomped on the gas pedal. "Hey!" Christine protested and lunged for the handle of the open door. After slamming it shut, Christine caught a flash of Julie's red-lipped smile in the rear-view mirror.

Julie drove a police car as recklessly as she drove her poppy-red Mustang.

The car veered onto a side street and stopped in front of a fire hydrant. Julie cranked the parking brake upright. "They'll never tow us!"

"I think I'll take the wheel after lunch," Sarah said, turning to meet Christine's glance, her short brown hair curling around her police hat.

Julie informed Dispatch about their lunch break, and the women exited the car, two in uniform and Christine in her cotton capris and a light sweater. It was Christine's first day off in a week, so Sarah had suggested she meet them during their lunch break.

"Who's up for the Arcadian Court?" Julie asked as they congregated on the sidewalk. Even in the drab darkness of the uniform, Julie looked Hollywood with her white-blond bob and the red lipstick and black eyeliner she applied when beyond range of the watchful eyes of Sergeant Baker from the Women's Bureau.

Beside Julie, Sarah was a study in freckles and naturalness. "A bit highbrow for a Tuesday, don't you think, Julie?" she commented.

Society ladies and out-of-town shoppers populated the Arcadian Court. "We're not dressed for the Arcadian," Christine said. Her sweater was pilling at the elbows, and numerous washes had left her navy capris faded. Plus, she couldn't afford the bill at the end of the meal.

"Good-looking businessmen dine there," Julie said as the trio headed north toward the entrance of the nine-story department store.

"Isn't your dance card full?" Christine said. Was Julie dating Fillingham or not?

"I'll make room." Julie tucked a strand of hair behind her ear.

Sarah said, "Head to the basement cafeteria. We may have to leave if Dispatch calls."

Walking backward so she faced her friends, Julie said, "I bought the cutest dress at Eaton's on our break yesterday. Very Marilyn Monroe!" She wiggled her narrow hips, then turned back around. Julie was compact rather than curvaceous. If anyone looked like Marilyn, it was probably Christine, with her bigger breasts and hips, a fact that added to her annoyance about her height.

The women settled at a table in the Simpsons cafeteria with their tea and egg salad sandwiches. Christine sat across from her two friends.

"I heard about the missing boy," Sarah said, addressing Christine. Julie asked, "How long has he been gone?"

"A week," Christine answered. "I've been pulling double shifts looking for him on the Island. Not a sign."

Julie said, "George Reynolds from the Youth Bureau told me they've done door-to-door interviews with Parkdale residents and checked every park, business and backyard. They're pulling blanks. It seems mysterious. Like the boy disappeared into thin air."

"They called me in to speak with the parents," Sarah said, then took a sip of tea.

"They did?" Christine shouldn't be surprised. Considering Sarah's previous job as a social worker, she was often requested in situations where citizens were in distress.

"They're a nice couple," Sarah commented. "New to the country, with some basic English. Dad is more fluent; he works at a butcher's shop. He used to be a university professor in Poland before the protests. They have friends from the Polish community helping with the search, bringing over food. The mom's brother lives a couple of blocks away."

"Where do they think Jacob is?" Christine asked.

"Mrs. Nowak is adamant that Jacob wouldn't run away from home," Sarah replied.

"Do they think he might have got homesick?"

Sarah shook her head. "He had been excited to go to the Island—his teacher had set up a baseball game against the Island school team, and Jacob was Lakeview's pitcher."

"Is she aware that Jacob wet his bed?" Christine asked.

"She was. She was surprised. He didn't do that at home."

"So what do they think happened?"

"They don't know. They're sick with worry. They wonder if someone took their son."

"But his suitcase is gone," Christine said.

Julie said, "Maybe he was heading home, and someone grabbed him on the way to the ferry."

"Anyone could have been on the Island at the time," Christine said. "Mainlanders with their own boats. Or perhaps a sailor moored in Blockhouse Bay."

Sarah laid her hand on Christine's. "How's your brother doing with all this? You said the boys are classmates."

Christine nodded. "They are, although Wayne doesn't know Jacob very well. Wayne is upset. He thinks Jacob left out of embarrassment, that maybe he's hiding somewhere in his neighborhood."

"It's difficult for children when someone they know goes missing," Sarah said. "They worry that a loved one may disappear. Or they get anxious about their own safety."

Christine sighed. "I feel slightly responsible."

"For what?" Julie asked.

"For not acting on my hunch that something was wrong with Jacob. The day before the boy disappeared, Fillingham and I gave a presentation at the school."

"I don't know why you call Geoffrey 'Fillingham,'" Julie interrupted with a laugh.

"Richie Rich is his other name," Christine said dryly.

"It is," Julie said. "What a hoot!"

Christine continued. "We found Jacob with a bloody nose. We think his roommates probably roughed him up."

"How does that make you responsible?" Julie's tone was dismissive. "You think Jacob disappeared because of a little horseplay?"

Christine shook her head. "Jacob said it was an accident, so we dropped it. I should have spoken with him longer, got the real story out of him."

Julie said, "A boy does not run away because of a bloody nose."

Sarah said. "It's hard to know the catalyst. Was it his wet bed, the roughhousing or some other factor? Kids live hidden lives. The reasons they run away are as numerous as—"

"Your freckles," Julie piped in.

The three women smiled.

"When I was working with the Youth Bureau," Julie said, "a missing thirteen-year-old was found shacked up with the forty-year-old neighbor."

"Yuck," Christine said.

"What's the dad like again?" Julie asked.

"Seemed mild-mannered," Sarah said. "Quiet. The mom's more vocal. More emotional."

"Did they seem rough at all?" Julie asked. "Maybe Jacob was afraid to come home to them."

Sarah shook her head. "I didn't get that sense...just overwhelming love and concern. They said their son was thriving in Canada. Picking up English. Doing well in school. He liked his teacher. Loved sports."

"Maybe he didn't run away," Christine said.

"That would make him a missing person," Julie said, "not a runaway, and that's never a happy ending."

"Miss Phillips!" Christine called.

Wayne's teacher propped the school door open as her students ran by her into the sunshine. She raised a hand in acknowledgement and headed over to Christine.

Donna was playing Double Dutch on the pavement with two of her friends. Her long brown hair bounced as she agilely jumped the two ropes. Wayne had headed home on his own when she told him she was going to chat with his teacher.

"Thanks for meeting me," Christine said to Miss Phillips. Wayne's teacher wore a beige and brown dress with graphic flowers that looked mod but also made her look colorless.

"I wanted to ask you about Jacob," Christine started.

Miss Phillips frowned, wrinkling her forehead. "I told the police all I know."

"I saw Jacob the day before he went missing. He'd been in a fight. My partner and I found him with a bloody nose. He said it was an accident, but I'm not sure. I feel I might have missed something—that if I'd intervened, maybe he wouldn't have run away."

Her eyes softened. "I asked him about his nosebleed and got the same response." She gave a small smile. "He's a tough cookie. Plays his cards close to his chest."

"Were you surprised he wet the bed?"

Miss Phillips said, "It happens sometimes on overnight trips, especially with the younger grades. His parents didn't mention any concerns or previous issues on the field trip forms."

"Wayne says Jacob is a talented athlete."

She nodded. "The baseball coach was pretty excited when he saw Jacob pitching at tryouts. He also made the soccer team in the spring, I believe."

"He has a Polish friend, Peter?" Christine asked.

"Police checked in with him and his family several times. He doesn't know where Jacob went; he's had no contact."

Christine could tell from her tone that she didn't want her to interview Peter, which was understandable. The boy was probably still upset about his friend's absence. She switched tack. "I know you've only taught Jacob since September, but I wonder if you had a sense of his family life."

"As far as I can tell, Jacob's parents seem nice. Dad usually drops him off in the morning. Sometimes they hold hands, even though

Jacob is in Grade 5, which is sweet. His mom made pastries for the class the first week of school."

"Any problems at home?"

Miss Phillips shook her head. "None that I heard. I asked his previous teacher about the Nowaks, and she said they are lovely—very respectful. School is important to the family—Dad was a teacher in Poland."

"Do you think Jacob ran away from home?"

The teacher's eyes looked off to the field, following the girl who was "it" in a game of tag, then looked back at Christine. "You're a police officer. Who knows what happens behind closed doors? From the few things Jacob said and wrote about his family, they seem close. And he misses Poland."

That night in the police station office, Christine said to Fillingham, "Let's keep looking for Jacob."

The Island search had been called off. Sergeant Bard said that after ten days, it was no longer a likely place to find the boy. Police didn't have the resources to continue calling in officers from 52 Division to scour the Island. Local newspapers and news stations had featured stories on the missing boy. Posters of the fair-haired child were glued to telegraph poles around Parkdale. The Youth Bureau would continue the investigation city-side, but as far as Island patrol, the case was closed.

Following her partner into the kitchen, Christine added, "After our security checks of Algonquin and Ward's, let's do another search for the boy."

Pouring himself a coffee from the pot on the counter, he said, "You think he's still here?"

"I don't know what to think. His disappearance makes little sense."

He faced her, leaning against the kitchen counter, and took a sip from his mug. "If he hurt himself, we would have found him. The search team has scoured every inch of the Island."

"If he drowned?" she asked quietly. Sergeant Bard had said the boy could not swim.

Fillingham side-stepped so she could access the coffeepot for a refill. "Drowned bodies sink first," he said, "and then they float when gasses erupt from the tissues. He would eventually wash up in a lagoon or against a dock city-side. My bet is that he's a runaway, long gone from the Island."

They faced each other, mugs in hand. "The Nowaks are adamant that Jacob wouldn't do that. And he's so young," she said.

"Nobody wants to think the worst—especially the parents."

"I'm going to look for him." She downed her half mug of coffee in three gulps. "Today, and every shift." She washed her cup in the sink and set it in the rack to dry. Heading for her locker, she added, "Do what you like."

He waited until she faced him with her police jacket on against the night chill. "Don't get your nose out of joint, Lane. What else do we have to do at three o'clock in the morning on this Island, aside from putting you in a headlock?"

She smiled, "It's called a full Nelson, you novice. And the loser cleans up the mats."

He grinned. "You're on!"

Christine pedaled the path to Ward's Island, the most easterly of the two islands that housed residents on Toronto Island. Her bike cast long shadows as she entered and exited the orbs of light from the streetlamps on the narrow path. Now that it was almost October, nights were cool, the daytime temperature dipping quickly after sunset, and she pulled up the collar of her uniform jacket.

Midnight, and the Island was hers: families tucked in bed, tourists boated back to the mainland, parks and recreation staff gone home and the ferries docked for the night. An orchestra of crickets serenaded her as she pedaled alongside the lagoon, punctuated by the reverberating twang of a bullfrog. It felt like she was the only person awake in the world—the single listener to the scratching of foraging chipmunks, the slap of waves against boat hulls and the rustle of the breeze through the poplars.

As she pedaled along, she scanned the darkness bracketing the path, looking for signs of Jacob. She knew he would not appear here, like a delivered present, but she didn't want to overlook a clue. Fillingham would check the Algonquin residences, so Christine continued past their bridge. At the Ward's Island Community Center, she rattled the door to ensure it was locked. Circling the building on foot, she checked for evidence of forced entry: scratched windowpanes or torn screens. Continuing on, she tested the locks on the adjacent lawn bowling green and tennis courts.

Remounting her bike, she headed south toward the beach and stopped at the public washrooms. She used her key to check the showers, stalls and change rooms for both sexes. Clear.

Only a handful of Ward's Island homes had their lights on. Christine checked the two houses on Third Street with absent owners, touring their backyards to ensure that Jacob or a wayward tourist hadn't bedded down there for the night. Finally, she checked Nancy Hamilton's empty house; the poor woman's daughter had been killed this past summer, and Nancy had been staying with her sister in Barrie.

Finished with her house checks, Christine coasted along Second Street. Her glance strayed to the small white cabin on her right—Hawk's house. Was he nestled in bed, planning his return trip to his reserve? Or was he thinking about her and regretting the end of their relationship? If she went to him right now, this second, and tapped on his door, would he let her in?

Indecision rooted her in front of his house. Should she climb the two steps to his door?

No. She was on the job. Even if he was home, even if he welcomed her inside, she wouldn't be able to be with him—slide her hand across his stomach, feel the thickness of the muscle underneath. Or gaze at him sleeping, the dark lines of his hair against the pillow like rivulets of drying ink.

None of that could happen. But she could still knock on the door, see if Hawk was awake, say a last goodbye. Tell him she would miss him. Miss his kindness and humor. Miss being together.

She set her bike down, strode to the door and rapped lightly on the wood, head swiveling as she checked the street for residents.

No answer. She tapped again with a knuckle.

She opened the unlocked door. Inside, the air had the stagnant smell of a sealed room.

"Hawk?" she called softly as she turned on the living room light. The old couch and coffee table remained, but the stack of LP records and the books from the wooden shelf were gone. Inside the fridge were hall-filled bottles of condiments and a box of baking soda. The house had the abandoned feel of a rental after the tenants had moved out: scratch marks on the walls and dust bunnies in corners.

In Hawk's bedroom, folded sheets sat at the bottom of the stripped bed, alongside a tidy stack of towels. Missing was the beautiful quilt made by his grandmother. She remembered Hawk gathering the blanket over her them so they could spoon, curling into each other for warmth.

A female voice said, "He's not here."

Christine jumped. Mrs. Polotov stood in the doorway of Hawk's bedroom, an ivory bathrobe wrapped around her short, sturdy body.

"Hello, dear," Mrs. Polotov said.

The old woman's hair was up in its perpetual bun, a few white-gray strands pulled loose around her face. Christine could not think of one thing to say to the long-time Island resident.

"I saw the light on," Mrs. Polotov began as they both moved into the living room. "I was heading to the bathroom and remembered that Hawk had asked me to lock up and return the key to Jan, the owner. I plumb forgot."

Again, silence.

Mrs. Polotov smiled. "How good of you to come and check that the house was secure, now that the renters have left."

Christine blinked. "Yes." She cleared her throat. "Just checking for squatters or if the missing boy found sanctuary here."

"How dutiful."

She knows. She knows about us.

Mrs. Polotov said, "I'll let Jan know the house is empty." She motioned for Christine to precede her out the front door, then turned off the light and locked the door.

"I have a few more houses to check," Christine said, heading toward her bike.

"He's gone," Mrs. Polotov said from behind her.

Christine stopped, her fingers clutching her bike handlebars.

"He caught the train this morning," the older woman said.

Christine's heart was a quarry, a pit being filled with boiling tar. So many men had left her: her first lover, the captain of the wrestling team. The karate instructor from police college. Her father, who Phyllis said had died in the war before meeting Christine. And now Hawk.

Christine didn't want to talk about Hawk with Mrs. Polotov. But maybe she had other answers.

Turning to face her friend, Christine asked, "Did you ever meet the Norwegian pilots who trained at the Island Airport?"

After a few seconds, Mrs. Polotov answered, "I did." She hugged herself in the night chill as they stood on Hawk's front lawn. "They were only here a year or so before the squad moved to Muskoka. But a handful of the men came to our barbeques and community dances. Or joined the boys and fathers playing hockey on the lagoon."

"Do you remember a Hans Larsen?"

"I remember a Hans, yes. I don't recall his surname. He used to fish off Ward's Island dock on his days off."

"What," she could hardly choke out the words, "what happened to him?"

The old woman shrugged. "I'm not sure. After training, the pilots went to England to fight in the war. I hoped and prayed that Hans and the rest of his squad made it through the war and returned home to their families."

Mrs. Polotov paused, examining Christine's face, her stillness as she held her bike. "A few Islanders received postcards from the soldiers after Armistice Day. I don't recall a letter from Hans, but I could ask around if you like."

At home, Christine had examined the photo of her father carefully: the angle of the camera, the design of the plane and the posture of the pilot. It did look exactly like the picture in the airport.

None of this made sense. Her father. Hawk. Jacob's absence.

Wordlessly, Christine climbed onto her bike.

"Bye, dear," Mrs. Polotov said as Christine pedaled away.

Christine pumped her legs as her tires bumped along the boardwalk, her breath harsh rasps as she pushed against the pedals, trying to outpace her racing thoughts.

Chapter 7

"What's got your goat?" Fillingham asked her. The ferry gently bumped the Island dock, the wooden timbers vibrating underfoot as the engine rumbled in reverse.

Christine grunted a response as they waited at the bow to disembark.

It was a Thursday afternoon in the first week of October. The *Ongiara* had only thirty people aboard as Christine and Fillingham headed over for their afternoon shift. Centreville had closed for the season, leaving a small group of visitors intent on hiking or biking the trails that crisscrossed the car-free island.

Watching the staff fasten the moorings, she inwardly conceded that she had been miserable lately. It wasn't just because of Hawk, although she still cried silently into her pillow at night, careful not to wake Donna in the twin bed beside her. Or her confusion over her photo of the pilot from the Island Airport. Christine had reexamined the picture in their living room, and it looked exactly the same as the photo of Hans Jansen, down to the plane model. She didn't know where to go with her confusion and was mulling over her next step.

The Jacob Nowak case was also affecting her mood. Since he had gone missing sixteen days ago, the boy had not communicated with his family or been sighted anywhere, on the Island, in Parkdale, at Polish businesses or cultural centers or amongst the runaways who hung around Jarvis Street.

Understandably, Wayne was still unsettled. He didn't talk about Jacob much, but his appetite wasn't the same. He went outside a lot, playing jacks or baseball with the brothers who lived in the upstairs apartment. But some nights, she could hear him tossing on the pull-out couch.

Interrupting her thoughts, Fillingham said, "No one could accuse you of being Susy Sunshine." He raised both eyebrows, smiling to take the sting out of the comment.

"I missed the chief's directive to add sunshine to your day."

"I will find that memo for you!" he said.

Her mouth twitched. Fillingham was such a goofball, always bright-eyed and bushy-tailed. He strode down the ramp to the waiting police vehicle, his gait almost jaunty. It was hard to fathom why he was the family black sheep—unless you were one of his many romantic conquests—because he was a likeable guy. Industrious. Pleasant.

Fillingham recounted that his parents were deeply disappointed about his career choice. At family functions, his older sister Beverley made disparaging remarks about policing, an employment barely superior to garbage collection. When he was eight, Fillingham had watched a Harbor Police craft come to the rescue of a family in an overturned boat, and that had piqued his interest in this career. Only his younger sister Ella, a student at Queen's University, supported Fillingham's goal of being a Harbor Police officer.

"She looks like a female version of you," Christine had commented when Fillingham had showed her a photo of Ella, a young woman with short blond curls and a pixie face. "But cute."

"I am the male version of me," he had responded. "And cute."

As Fillingham headed over to the patrol car to receive report from Sergeant Bard, a man beelined toward her as she trailed behind her partner. Tim Hawley, the teacher from the Nature School.

"Did you find Jacob?" she called, her voice tinged with excitement.

He frowned as he stood in front of her. "No."

Her whole body deflated. "I thought you had news."

She glanced over at Fillingham, who was watching her with Tim. She shook her head to show Tim did not have information about the missing boy.

"I would like to talk about Jacob," Tim said. "Can you drop by the school today?"

"Sure," Christine said with a flicker of excitement in her gut. Maybe Tim remembered something that would help in the search. "We have to check the duty log and pick up our radios. We could come after that."

"It doesn't have to be both of you," he said, hands tucked into the front pockets of his corduroys. "I don't have any hard facts. I thought if we reviewed information together, new ideas might surface." He smiled. "You could come by yourself."

Back at the station, Fillingham snorted. "Tim wants to meet with one of us. It sure as heck isn't me." He grabbed a radio from the charging unit.

She frowned. "He wants to talk about the Jacob Nowak case."

"Evidently." His tone was sarcastic.

"You can go," she said.

"I don't think I'm invited."

She gave him a look.

Fillingham added, "I've no desire to be a third wheel. Go talk to Teacher Tim, and I'll hold the fort until you return. I have to call Mrs. Clancy about a problem with her water hose."

"So now we're public works?" she asked.

"I am a man for all seasons." His hands spread wide.

"That you are." She slid a radio into its sheath on her utility belt. "I'm off, then. I'll bike over and see what Tim has to say."

At the Nature School, the secretary said that Tim was on his break, and she could find him on the beach. As Christine trudged along the shore that looked out to Lake Ontario, sand trickling into her shoes, she spotted him thirty yards away.

Was that a picnic basket beside him? Had he called her to the beach for a cucumber sandwich and a chat?

Pressing her hat to her head so it wouldn't blow off in the lake breeze, she reminded herself that her focus was on Jacob, regardless of the game Tim was playing. A memory of the boy rose: the blood smeared under his nose, the flash of his angry blue eyes, his rant in Polish directed at Roy.

She planted her legs in the sand, hands on hips, in front of Tim.

"I thought we could chat over a snack," he said. "The day is so lovely."

When she didn't reply, he sunk to his knees and pulled out a Thermos and blue tin mug from the rattan basket. "Lemonade?"

"I'm on duty. I can't stay long."

"I have dinner shift soon too," he said.

"What do you want to discuss?" she asked, extending her hand to receive the mug of lemonade.

"I thought we could review the facts."

She took a sip to stifle an impatient comment. *He* was supposed to be informing *her*.

After a few seconds, he said, "You start."

"Start what?"

"A summary of Jacob's missing person case."

"Okay." Her voice was questioning. "At ten o'clock, on the evening of September 16th, Jacob was with his bunkmates in their shared room. That's the last time he was seen."

Tim nodded.

"You were on hall duty that night," she said. "You checked that all the boys were in their beds, correct? Including Jacob?"

He nodded.

"Did you see Jacob leave his room that night?"

He shook his head and offered her grapes from the basket, which she refused.

"Did any students leave their rooms?" she asked.

"A couple boys went to the bathroom," Tim said, "but they returned directly to their rooms."

"Did they see anybody?"

Tim shook his head. "All the students were questioned that morning when we noticed Jacob was absent."

"No one got caught sneaking into another bunkroom after lights out? Girl or boy?"

"No. It was a quiet night."

"So, if a boy left his bunkroom, he would have to pass by you. Correct?"

He nodded. "I sat on a chair at one end of the boys' dormitory, near the main doors. The far exit is a fire door. The alarm sounds if opened."

"Since you saw no one, the investigators concluded Jacob must have removed the window screen, tossed his suitcase outside, then climbed out the window. Did you hear any noise from their room?"

Shaking his head, he popped a grape into his mouth.

"It's odd that the other boys wouldn't have heard him go out the window," she said. "You didn't leave your post all night?"

He shook his head.

"Were you sleepy—maybe closed your eyes for a few minutes?"

Again, he shook his head, his hair brushing his shoulders.

"You worked all day, then stayed up all night? Isn't that difficult after a busy day with students?"

"It's a double shift. I get lieu time for it."

"Do you get a break?"

"If I want one."

"When did you go to the bathroom?"

"Around midnight," he said.

"You left!" she exclaimed, her arms extending in consternation. "Did someone come and take your place?"

He shook his head. "I was gone for five minutes! It was the middle of the night. The students were sound asleep."

"Jacob could have exited through the main entrance, unseen."

"Unlikely." He reached for the thermos of lemonade to refill his glass.

"Did you tell the investigators you left your post?" she asked.

"I don't remember." He did not meet her eyes.

"Jacob could have walked out between twelve and 12:05. It's a very specific window."

He took a big gulp of his drink and placed the mug on the blanket. "It might have been longer."

"You said it was five minutes!" Gosh, was he telling the truth about anything?

"I was having stomach problems."

"How much longer?" she asked.

He leaned back on his arms, staring out over Lake Ontario as the afternoon light danced on the backs of the waves. "Twenty minutes. Half an hour at most."

Christine blew air out of her mouth. "Tim! That's a long time. Why didn't you tell this to the investigators?"

He looked at her. "I didn't want to lose my job."

"You should be able to go to the washroom when working a double shift."

"I'm supposed to wake another staff member if I have to go—and I didn't want to do that."

"Withholding information pertinent to an investigation is a chargeable offense."

"Christine." He extended one hand out toward her.

She ignored it. "Thanks for the drink." She placed her mug on the corner of the blanket.

"Wait." He burrowed into the basket with both hands. "I have figs. From Turkey."

She shook her head. "I have to get back to work."

He stood up. "Wait, please. Have coffee with me another time. I can tell you about the boys, about the Lakeview students."

She crossed her arms. "Tell me now."

After a pause, he said, "They were picking on him."

"They?"

"The stocky boy. And his freckled friend."

"Roy O'Neil? Patrick Williamson?"

"I think that's their names. The bunkmates."

"What happened?" she asked.

"At the fire pit, someone threw Jacob's marshmallow in the dirt. I caught the big boy snapping Jacob's roasting stick in two. I told the pest to sit down on the other side of the fire, and I set Jacob up with a new branch and marshmallow."

Roy and Patrick had been bothering Jacob the whole day.

"I remember Jacob because he had told us about the falcons in the woods near his village in Poland. He seemed to have experience in the wilderness."

"Do you think he could survive ten days outdoors on the Island?"

He shrugged. "Maybe. The weather's been mild."

The question was still why did Jacob leave? He had loving parents. He was smart and athletic. Did he run away because he was being picked on? Or because he was embarrassed he wet the bed? If that was the case, why didn't he go home?

"Island police continue to search the Island," she told Tim. "Can you let me know if food goes missing from your garden or your garbage looks disturbed? Or you see any signs of habitation."

"Sure." He paused. "Maybe we can go out for dinner. Off the record."

She adjusted her purse strap on her shoulder. "I'm pretty busy. I work long hours."

"Me too."

"Thanks for the lemonade." She left, wondering what Fillingham would make of Tim's confession. Did the teacher's absence on the night of Jacob's disappearance clarify or muddy the investigation?

Chapter 8

Christine saw Tim Hawley a few times over the fall. Whenever she checked in at the Nature School, she made Fillingham tag along. Tim tried to waylay her during these visits, but she stuck to her partner like a burr. Sure, Tim was cute, with green eyes and woodsy charm, but Christine was wary. He had lied. She'd had enough untrustworthy people in her life, starting with her stepfather. The eight years Eddie was around—drinking, throwing furniture and buying beer with their grocery money—were burned into her memory.

Christine had called the investigators to tell them about the thirty-minute gap in hallway supervision when Jacob could have left the school unseen. The detective responded, "The screen was off! The boy left out the window." And hung up.

She didn't trust Tim, who seemed to have his own version of events, but she had trusted Hawk. Over the last few months, she had reflected on her refusal to dine with him at Chapel House. Was her skin thinner, or was she just more realistic than Hawk?

She had been right: they could never be together publicly.

And Hawk had been right—she was a coward.

With Hawk back home in Whitefish, at least Christine hadn't been confronted with his contempt. And if he came back next summer to work at Centreville, she could avoid him. Toronto Island wasn't that small. She would have time to patch her heart, pour concrete around it and let it set so that she wouldn't feel anything when she saw him again.

The fall season had been a difficult term for Wayne and Miss Phillips's class. Two weeks after the field trip to the Island, Christine had gone to Lakeview School to watch Wayne's softball game. It was the first one scheduled since Jacob's disappearance. Before the game, the principal stood beside the baseball coach and dedicated the game to Jacob, with the ardent wish that he was safe and would play baseball for the school again. The two teams lined up on the first base and third base lines respectively, ball caps off, for the dedication. Wayne stared at the ground as the principal spoke.

When the umpire called, "Play ball!" Wayne wiped his sleeve across his eyes and headed to first base, walking past the pitching mound where Roy O'Neil was warming up.

During the principal's speech, a few sniffles had sounded, but most of the students wore blank looks, as if they hadn't sorted out what Jacob's disappearance meant. Several Lakeview students had experienced absences in their life—like Wayne and Donna, whose father had left four years ago. Other students had moved schools four or five times, leaving apartments at midnight with three months' rent owing. Some, like the Nowaks, had arrived in the neighborhood from another country and had left family and security behind.

A few students had never known their fathers—like Christine.

Since seeing the photograph of the Norwegian pilot in the Toronto Island Airport, she had studied the framed photo in their living room carefully. Did she look like the pilot in the picture? The photo was black and white, but she could tell he was fair, whereas she had brown hair and brown eyes. They did have the same muscular body and straight hair.

Seeking answers, she had pried open the frame and removed the photo. Turning the glossy picture over, she viewed the inked *Toronto Telegram* stamp on the back. Did the newspaper photograph military officers during the war? Maybe her father had gone down to the Island airport on his leave for a few practice flights. Or was this Hans Jansen, after all?

The simplest thing would be to ask her mother again, but Phyllis's dismissal of the Norwegian pilot had been so adamant that Christine needed to think about her next step. If only her mother had an old school friend or cousin for Christine to confer with. But Phyllis had been on her own since she was orphaned at sixteen, arriving in Toronto with a small suitcase and the typing skills needed to secure a secretarial job. Phyllis had moved so many times over the years, with Christine and later with Eddie and Wayne and Donna. Her mom had a few friends now, from work and the bingo parlor, but they were more recent connections.

Clearly, Phyllis was hiding information about Christine's father. Should Christine bother to pursue the truth? Did she need to or want to know her father? Eddie Williams had been her stepfather for eight years, and she hadn't liked him much. Her teenage years had been filled with the sounds of banging furniture and expletives as Phyllis and Eddie fought over money, bets, or the last beer in the fridge. Christine became the family's caregiver, hiding the rent money so it wouldn't be lost at the track or spent at the liquor store, making spaghetti because it was cheap and one of the few things she knew how to cook for her siblings, even if they couldn't afford sauce. She, not Phyllis or Eddie, had ensured her siblings were fed, washed and attended school.

Thank goodness for Fillingham. Other than her brother, Christine's goofball partner was the only male in her life, and all Fillingham wanted to do was race and wrestle and have her be a straight man to his clowning.

Over the fall, the leaves had fallen off the Island trees and the temperature had chilled as the days shortened. Now it was December, and the holiday season was fast approaching. Christine and her family were headed to the annual Christmas bazaar held in the Algonquin Island Recreation Center. Her siblings were looking forward to gingerbread cookies, hot chocolate and a horse-drawn carriage ride around the Island.

Although their teeth chattered on the ferry ride across, Wayne and Donna refused to seek shelter from the wind. Christine encouraged her mom to head for cover in the upstairs cabin; Phyllis didn't need a second prompt, since she was having difficulty lighting her cigarette in the breeze. Wayne and Donna leaned against the starboard side of the small ferry, eyes on the line of barren trees that spiked the shoreline of the Leslie Street Spit. The three of them watched the steel bow of the ferry push through the floating chunks of ice, following the fragments as they swirled counterclockwise in the boat's wake.

Ashore, Christine's siblings ran ahead of the adults toward the Algonquin Island Community Center. A gaggle of passengers trailed after, all headed in the same direction. It was quiet—the breeze that had battered them on the ferry was silenced. The sun was stretching, forcing its way out behind a cloud to light the snow that dusted the pathway. Even in winter, with leafless trees and sepia patches of dead foliage, the Island was a rugged, beautiful place.

Christmas music rang in the air as they walked the length of Algonquin Island. Residents were exiting their homes, a few waving to Christine as they made their way to the bazaar. The government was trying to evict the Islanders, shut down the two communities on Algonquin and Ward's, and turn the entire chain of islands into a public, resident-free park.

Even though they could be evicted soon, Islanders' homes were decorated with multicolored Christmas lights and spruce wreaths twined with berries.

Christine motioned Donna over. Leaning down, she whispered, "If you see something nice for Mom for Christmas, let me know."

Donna scooted back to Wayne, who had turned up the front walkway to the community center.

"Go on in," Christine called. "It's one large room—I won't lose you."

The two children went inside.

Ascending the steps to the door, Christine asked, "What's on your wish list, Mom?"

"Are things expensive?" Phyllis said, pointing inside.

Their family was on a tight budget. Christine's paycheck went toward the gambling debt that Christine's stepfather had left for them to pay, so the four of them lived on Phyllis's wages. But it would be great to buy presents from the locals. Christine knew some of the bazaar vendors by name. And Islanders were good to her, always ready with a fresh-baked scone, a cup of tea or a chat when she passed them on patrol. One family had given Christine their daughter's outgrown clothes when they heard Christine had an eight-year-old stepsister.

"We can spend a little money," Christine said. She and her mother were getting raises in the new year. A small increase, but it would add up to a few extra dollars a week. Thank goodness female officers made the same as their male counterparts. Equal pay was a primary reason Christine had signed on to policing, switching over from the civilian Records Department where Phyllis worked. There were also overtime opportunities in December supervising holiday parties and community dances, which would provide Christine with extra cash for presents.

Inside, Christine wandered off as her mother headed toward the racks of homemade jam. Silver snowflakes dangled from ceiling beams crisscrossed with white lights. The vendors' tables showcased Toronto Island artists with glass-blown ornaments, hand-sewn Christmas stockings, knitted ponchos and watercolor stationary. Between the gifts, music and cinnamon-apple aroma emanating from the kitchen, you couldn't help but feel Christmas cheer.

Wandering the aisles, Christine fondled the soft felt of a wool hat and then tried on a jade ring, even though she would never buy it for herself. The vendor came over, and they admired the deep green oval stone on Christine's long finger before Christine gave it back. Every few minutes, she scanned the room for Donna and Wayne. The community center was a safe place—she wasn't worried about that. She was more concerned that her excitable brother would swing his elbow into a ceramic vase or overturn a display case of earrings.

The merchandise was beautiful. She itched to buy a tasseled pillow for her bed or a bottle of scented hand lotion. But if she spent on herself, it meant less money for Wayne and Donna. And she had to set aside extra grocery money for the turkey and trimmings her mom had pledged to cook on Christmas Day.

"Christine!"

She turned, recognizing Mrs. Polotov's voice, and headed toward the Islander in the kitchen.

"I need to borrow your height." The old woman pointed to the serving trays on top of the fridge.

Christine said hello to the three boys placing sweet loaves on the long pine kitchen table. "I see your mothers have been busy baking."

The trio nodded. Two were brothers who lived on Ward's Island.

"No trout today?" she said in a teasing tone. The boys often fished in the lagoon near the Algonquin Bridge.

"We could catch you some through the ice," said the tallest boy, Bruce, before following the other boys out.

After retrieving the trays, Christine asked Mrs. Polotov, "What's in the punch? A secret Island recipe?"

The older lady swirled the ladle through the deep-red liquid in the large glass bowl. With her gray shawl and white hair pinned in a bun, she resembled a benevolent witch. "No secret: berries, orange slices, zest, ginger ale, juice and a healthy dose of Jamaican rum. Want a taste?"

It was two o'clock in the afternoon. Christine wasn't a big drinker. After frequently witnessing her mother and stepfather's inebriation during her teenage years, the appeal of alcohol was low. Although she was off duty, she didn't feel comfortable drinking in front of residents. "I'm okay, thanks."

"Nonsense." Mrs. Polotov grabbed a goblet, filled it with a splash of ruby liquid and held it out. "It's Christmas. Cheers."

"Okay, okay," Christine said, laughing. It was her day off. She could manage one drink. She had a soft spot for the long-time resident—and truthfully, she was glad Mrs. Polotov kept a mothering eye on her.

Christine leaned against the long kitchen counter stacked with food containers and dessert plates, sipping her punch and nodding at the volunteers who came in to gather supplies for the craft and food tables. The rum warmed her chest, and she couldn't help smiling. When she was notified of her transfer to Toronto Island from the Women's Bureau, she had been shocked and angry. Everyone knew the Island was a sleepy patrol where the inept, injured and troubled police officers were pastured. She didn't belong there. But Islanders were a creative and caring bunch, always ready to lend a hand to build a shed, bring a meal to an ailing senior or challenge each other to a baseball game. And the Island, with its beaches, willow trees, cormorants and coyotes, was like a nature center tended by the residents. The land and the people were special. That was one thing she had learned in her seven months of Island patrol.

Looking down the corridor toward the bazaar, she spied Wayne and Donna clutching gingerbread cookies. They must have wrangled the treat from the children's area or a kind vendor.

Her siblings moved out of sight, and a little girl with black pigtails came into view, her hair two dark explanation points against the powder-blue fabric of her coat. She turned to speak to the man behind her; he leaned down to listen, one hand touching her shoulder, his long braids secured with leather ties.

Hawk!

He said something that made the girl laugh. Straightening, he glanced down the hallway into the kitchen.

They locked eyes.

She clutched the punch goblet to her chest. *He's missed me. He's come back for me.*

Staring, neither of them smiled or made a move toward the other.

Behind Hawk, a young Indigenous woman approached and curled her arm around his waist under his open coat. She had the same heart-shaped face and small button nose as the little girl—clearly her mother. And obviously, by the way she touched Hawk, his girlfriend.

Christine stepped deeper into the kitchen so she could no longer see the bazaar. She gulped the rest of her punch and scooped herself another glass, drinking it in four swallows.

Hawk wasn't here to see her. He didn't journey from Whitefish to win her back. Evidently, he had moved on—as if their summer of whispered endearments and clandestine lovemaking meant nothing. As inconsequential as the cottonwood fluff that specked the Island air white in summer.

He had someone new. The rum burned her throat like the scald of her rejection. She was so stupid and naïve. As another cup of punch poured down her throat, her stomach recoiled. To Hawk, she had been nothing but a fling. Convenient. Disposable. Until Hawk found someone suitable.

And the little girl? Was that his daughter? Could that woman be his wife?

That would be the icing on the cake. First, her maybe-father had a family in Norway and now her old boyfriend shows up with a wife and child in tow.

What a fool she was! Just like she had been with the high school wrestling captain and the police college karate instructor. Every romance she started soon turned sour, ending in rejection and mortification. She was not a woman, but an ogre. Her grade-school tormenters had been right. An unlovable ogre.

She had to get out of here. She felt the burn of her humiliation on her face like a slap. But what was she supposed to do about her mom and siblings? She didn't want Hawk seeing her. Or her mother discerning the connection between them. Grabbing the ladle, Christine poured herself another cup of punch, the liquid slurping over her wrist. She drank three more glasses.

Mrs. Polotov returned with a tray of used coffee cups.

Christine grabbed the table edge to steady herself.

The older woman placed her tray on the kitchen counter and turned to Christine. "You've been drinking." Her tone was matter-of-fact.

Christine's bottom lip trembled. *No. No.* She would not fall apart, no matter how sympathetic her friend was.

Mrs. Polotov gazed at her with kind brown eyes, her face creased with fine lines. "Hawk is here."

Christine covered her face.

"So that's the way it is," said Mrs. Polotov.

Through her fingers, Christine said, "I...I can't go out there. I can't face him. And...and my family is here." She let her hands fall from her face. "I've had too much punch."

Mrs. Polotov pulled Christine into an embrace, holding her in a reassuring hug. Christine was at least a foot taller than her elderly friend—her chin did not meet the top of Mrs. Polotov's bun—so she leaned down to squeeze her back, inhaling her lavender scent.

Releasing her, Mrs. Polotov said, "I saw your mother by the Christmas tree decorations. I'll tell her you're going to stay and help in the kitchen. She can head home with your siblings whenever she is ready."

"Thank you," Christine sniffed.

Mrs. Polotov put a hand on her shoulder. "I'll be back. Stay here."

Christine nodded. For the next half hour, volunteers rushed into the kitchen to refill trays with sugar cookies and urns with hot chocolate. After dragging a chair into a corner, Christine hid behind a stack of cardboard boxes, her shoulders turned away from the hive of people entering and exiting the kitchen.

"Christine."

She turned at Hawk's voice.

He walked over to her. The width of his shoulders in his deerskin jacket blocked out the kitchen cupboards. "I wanted to say hello. See how you and your family were doing."

"What do you care?" Her words were slurred. She could feel the anger well up, unfiltered.

He regarded her silently.

"How long'd it take you to get a new girlfriend?" she asked, facing him in her chair. "A week? Two? Or did you have your little family stashed away the whole time?"

He paused before responding, his umber-brown eyes looking at her levelly. "I've been seeing Rita for a month. We're old friends." He gestured toward her with one hand. "Christine, I wanted us to be together. You know that. For everyone to see."

Her fists clenched. "I can't do that."

"Do what?"

Hawk turned at the sound of the male voice behind him.

"Geoffrey!" Christine lunged out of her chair past Hawk to greet her partner. Intending to pat his sleeve in greeting, she stumbled against him; he braced her by the elbows to keep her upright.

After disengaging from Christine, Fillingham said to Hawk, "What are you doing here?"

Hawk said, "Nothing to do with you."

Fillingham's upper lip curled. Hawk regarded him with stony silence.

"It's okay," Christine said to Fillingham, "we're done here." She turned to Hawk. "You have people waiting."

After a moment, Hawk said, "I'm glad to see you, PW Lane. Take care of yourself. And your family." He gave her a long look, then headed toward the bazaar's main room. Christine reached for the table for support.

Fillingham surveyed her, frowning. "You've been drinking? Over this guy?"

"A little punch," she mumbled.

"A little?" he said. He retrieved her coat layered over the back of her chair. "We don't want Islanders seeing you like this. Or your family. Let's head out the back door."

She pushed her arm into a coat sleeve and got tangled up. Without comment, Fillingham slid her coat off, shook it straight and held it out for her, as if he were her husband escorting her to dinner.

"Why are you here?" she asked as she fumbled with the buttons of the double-breasted jacket.

"Mrs. Polotov called me." He leaned forward, pulled her gloves out of her coat pocket and handed them to her. "Your mom's taking your brother and sister home. I borrowed a golf cart from my club; it's waiting outside. The RCYC boat taxi can take us back to the mainland; that way residents won't see you.

"I'm fine."

"You are not fine." He opened the back door. "And knowing you, tomorrow you'll be mortified." He guided her over to the forest-green golf cart capped by a white plastic roof. The Island was a car-free community, with only police and service vehicles allowed. The school and a few sailing clubs had golf carts for transportation within their facilities. With a grunt, he hefted her into the passenger's seat, and she grasped the metal-roof rod for support.

As he drove, Fillingham retraced his own tire tracks in the snow back to the shoveled pathway that led to the Algonquin Bridge.

Clasping the roof rod with both hands, Christine stared at the floor mats as the golf cart bumped along, ignoring the dizzying blur of snow-covered bushes in her peripheral vision. Her stomach turned queasily.

At the entrance to the yacht club, he hopped out of the vehicle and opened the gate with his key. He was a competitive sailor and club member. Inside the compound, they drove past locked boathouses, sheds and boats with cabins tarped blue for winter storage. He headed the cart toward the massive clubhouse rising white and majestic into the wintery marble sky.

Around the back of the grand building, the wind off the inner harbor hit them like a frigid wall, rattling their vehicle as it blew through. He parked in front of the long wooden dock and came around to the passenger side to help her out.

Waving off his arm, she stepped out of the cart, misjudged the depth and tumbled out onto her hands and knees, and then rolled onto her back.

"Whoa! Christine! Are you okay?"

She lay splayed on the snow as if she were about to make a snow angel, staring at the wisps of clouds covering the steel-gray sky like a lace curtain. "Why doesn't he love me?" she asked, her breath puffing the words out above her.

He squatted beside her. She could feel him gazing at her, but she continued to look at the clouds overhead.

"He loved you," he said.

She looked at her partner for a second and then away.

"He's moved on," Fillingham said. "He took the high road and moved on, that's all." Her partner stood up. "Let's head to the water taxi stand—it's at the end of the dock. There's a bench where we can wait."

She let him help her up and stood silently as he brushed snow off her coat and corduroy pants as if she were a child. He hooked his arm around her waist, and they lurched the length of the long dock like drunken cowboys heading into the sunset.

By the time they reached the end of the pier, Fillingham was panting with the effort of keeping them walking in a straight line; she kept veering perilously to the right toward the dock edge and freezing water below.

Leaning over, he dumped her onto the bench on her back.

She grabbed the wool lapels of his pea jacket before he could move away. "I'm lovable, right?" Her vision blurred with tears.

He gave a soft chuckle, staring into her eyes. "Yes, you sad thing," he said, his glove briefly touching her cheek. "You're lovable."

He pulled away, and she released her hold. Something pressed against her hair, lingering. Had he kissed the top of her head?

"Hey!" he called a few seconds later. "I see the *Mary Crawford*."

Turning, she looked across the harbor at the small water taxi bouncing toward them on the white-capped waves. She closed her eyes; it made her sick to watch the feisty little boat battling the waves—it reminded her of Geoffrey and the way he tackled life. And right now, she just wanted to drown.

Chapter 9

"Come skating with us," Julie commanded over the phone.

Christine surveyed the kitchen, receiver in hand. Breakfast dishes cluttered the sink, dumped by her siblings before they had headed out to church with the neighbors. Phyllis was an irregular church-goer, but she sometimes attended with the family upstairs, bringing Wayne and Donna along with her.

Not only did Christine need to tidy the apartment, but she also desperately needed a shower and a cup of tea to wash the pasty layer off her tongue.

Julie added, "It will help you get over your hangover."

Christine's knuckles whitened on the phone. Fillingham must have told Julie about the Christmas bazaar. She was going to kill him.

"Come out with us," Julie cajoled. "We're skating on the Island. The fresh air will do you good."

A pair of women's size eleven skates sat in the front closet behind Wayne's baseball gear, the white paint scratched off the toes.

"I'm not up for it."

The phone line crackled. Fillingham came on. "Lane, let's go! Shake off those cobwebs. It's beautiful outside."

"What did you tell Julie?" she said through clenched teeth. The romance between her friend and her partner was making her feel claustrophobic. And now they were ganging up on her. If Fillingham told Julie about Hawk or her tearful musings on love, she was going to throttle him. Shove his face into the wrestling mat and never let him see daylight again.

"Just a sec." He called, "Julie, can you find a Thermos for the hot chocolate?" There was a mumbled response. Julie must have gone elsewhere in her apartment. Fillingham whispered, "I didn't say anything except that you fell into the punch bowl."

Christine exhaled with relief.

"For now," he said.

For goodness' sake. "You're blackmailing me?"

"Now we're talking the same language!" His tone was cheery.

Her memory of yesterday's drunken fiasco was excruciating—and even more so given that her partner was a witness. After a few seconds of consideration, she said, "Fine! But I don't want to skate near any houses." She wondered if Islanders had seen her staggering out the back door of the community center or being tossed into the golf cart like a rolled carpet.

"We can skate on the lagoon near the filtration plant," he said. "We'll come by in twenty to pick you up." He hung up.

Individually, Julie and Fillingham could be strong-willed; as a tandem, they were impossible to combat. Christine retrieved her skates. She'd have to find her woolen hat and longer socks. And the ice had better be thick enough for her weight. She'd push Fillingham out onto the lagoon first to check.

While Christine tied her skates on the bench beside the lagoon, Fillingham was marking the bumpy gray ice with dark slashes from his skate blades. An oval of ice had been shoveled, probably by school staff, since the inner lagoons froze first. Julie stood on her skates beside Christine, her fake, fur-trimmed hat accentuating her eyes, her periwinkle sweater over black tights making her look like a Nordic femme fatale. Fillingham skated over, clasped Julie by the hands, and they began gliding in sync like ice-dancing partners, their strokes scratching rhythmically on the ice.

Of course, they'd skate well—Julie's doting parents had undoubtedly paid for figure-skating lessons. She was the single child of older parents and had been spoiled throughout her childhood. The Mustang she drove to work was a twenty-first birthday present from them. Fillingham likely had skating lessons as a youth or competed on his private school's hockey team.

Christine stood up. Her ankles collapsed inward, and she forced them straight. Her breath exhaled in streams of cloudy white air as she inched toward the ice, arms held out for balance.

Here goes! She wobbled onto the ice, her dull skates forcing her to muscle through each stroke, shortening her glide. By the time she had completed one shaky lap, her ankles were burning from the effort of holding them upright.

"Watch this!" Fillingham yelled. The pair glided by, and then he grabbed Julie by the hips and threw her into the air. She rotated half a turn and landed on one skate edge, leaning into a camel spin. He skated over to Julie, and they rejoined hands, their cheeks flushed as they smiled at each other.

Oh, for goodness' sakes. Why had she agreed to hang out with these lovebirds all afternoon? Clearly, she was a third wheel—a voyeur to their blossoming romance. She didn't want to be jealous of the duo, but she felt suffocated by their exuberance. All Christine wanted to do was hide in a closet and forget about romance and that Hawk ever existed.

She continued skating, her technique smoothing as her leg muscles remembered how to glide and the rust on her blade sanded off.

Passing the dead bulrushes circling Trout Pond, she remembered fishing there with Hawk, how they had eaten the pan-fried trout in companionable silence. And how she had kissed him in front of the open fire, her fingers entangled in his hair, breathing in his musky sweetgrass scent.

Her skates dug into the frosty layer of ice as she recalled the woman at the bazaar embracing Hawk with tender familiarity. And Hawk's look of pity as he left Christine in the kitchen.

Her humiliation pushed her to move her legs faster and faster; her foot slid as she cornered, her arms flinging out to balance herself. Two months. They had been apart for two-and-a-half months, and already Hawk had replaced her with a ready-made family.

Looping back toward the pond, she picked up speed and passed Fillingham and Julie, who had stopped to smooch. Christine's vision blurred into a horizontal band of brown and gray and white and blue—the tree trunks and filtration plant and lighthouse and sky—as her blades scraped the ice with increasing tempo, her mouth open to catch her breath, thinking only of the slap of wind on her face, the whip of her hair and the ache in her thighs.

As she turned the corner, leaning into the curve to duck the wind, her skate pick caught a bump of ice, and she went sailing into the air, arms outstretched. She landed with a thump, the air whacked out of her, and then slid ten feet along the ice into the dry stalks of bulrushes outlining Trout Pond.

A loud crack.

"Aah!" she screamed. Cold water scorched her belly as water soaked the front of her wool jacket. The ice was breaking. She was sinking.

She clutched the bulrushes with her sodden mitts, the scent of dead vegetation filling her nose. *I'm going under!*

"Spread out!" Fillingham yelled from behind her.

Christine moved her arms and legs wide, still clutching the reeds, trying to distribute her weight evenly on the cracked ice. Her breath was quick, a small moan of fear escaping with each exhale. Pond water formed a wet layer on the ice in front of her, its cold prickle now reaching her arms, thighs and seeping to her back.

She had to get out! She was going to slip through the broken ice into the water and never find her way back up.

"Don't move!" Fillingham's voice was closer now.

Fillingham and Julie shouted to each other, their words indiscernible, as Christine focused on the absolute importance of remaining motionless. Clenching her teeth, she squeezed her muscles tight—even though her torso and legs were becoming numb.

"Do exactly as I say, Lane. We're going to pull you out," he said. "I'm lying on the ice ten feet behind you."

She could hear him move.

"Julie," he said, "hand me the pole!"

"Christine," he continued. "I have the rescue pole. Don't turn around to grab it. I'm going to hook it into the back of your pants and pull you close enough so I can grab your legs, then we'll be home free."

"Uh." The metal hook whacked between her shoulder blades. Regrasping the reeds, her fingers clumsy with cold, she stared ahead into the plant stalks, snow, broken ice and gaps of open water.

"You wearing a belt?" he asked.

"Yes." Her affirmation was barely audible.

The pole poked under her jacket, pushing up her sweater and scratching a line in her skin. Closing her eyes, she prayed for Fillingham to get a hold.

The hook caught the lip of her belt, and she shifted sideways as he pulled. Something cracked.

"Aah!" She let out a scream, her eyes flaring open.

The hook scraped up to her shoulders, cold air swooping in, and returned to her waist, catching her belt again.

Fillingham grunted as he pulled on the pole shaft. She began moving slowly, inch by inch, her hands opening to unclasp the reed stems.

After she had slid back five feet, she could feel pressure on her skates, a tug as Fillingham's fingers circled the blades. Gazing at the band of open gray water in front of her, she spotted a wriggly line of red.

"Stop!" she yelled.

"What?" he said.

"Stop!" she said again. What was that red thing? Was it a shoelace? A red shoelace? Was that the rounded toe of a white baseball shoe?

"Uh!" She was whooshed backward along the ice, snow scraping into her coat, under her sweater and up into her face until she was pulled twenty feet away from the reeds where she had landed.

When Fillingham released his hold on her skates, she slowly pushed herself up on her hands and knees, teeth chattering, her hands still cupped from clasping the bulrushes.

"She's freezing," Julie said. "Her clothes are soaking wet."

"Grab her arms and stand her up," he instructed. "We'll take her into the school to dry off."

They pulled and slid Christine over to the bench. Fillingham ripped his gloves off and untied Christine's skates. Christine was shaking, whole-body convulsions, as the icy wind blew through her wet clothes, stiffening the fabric. "Sh-sh-shoe!" she said through chattering teeth.

"You mean boots," Julie said. "Here they are!" She shoved Christine's feet into her boots, and they half dragged, half carried her over to the school, one on each side, their heads under her armpits. At the main doorsteps, Fillingham ran over to the boat shed and returned with a key. The three stumbled into the empty building. It was warm, blissfully warm.

"Take her into the staff dormitory," he instructed Julie, pointing to the end of the hallway, "and remove her wet things. Check the cupboards for blankets and a change of clothes."

"No!" Christine said, pulling away from them, then stumbling onto one knee. Her shivers were so severe, it looked like she was convulsing.

Julie kneeled in front of her. "Christine, honey, you need dry clothes."

Fillingham said to Julie, "She could be in shock. We should call an ambulance."

"No!" Christine yelled. She hauled herself to her feet, staggering.

Fillingham braced Christine's shoulders with his hands to stabilize her. "Lane, what are you trying to say?"

Christine stared at him, her brown eyes wide, the tips of her hair frozen into icy points. "Jay…jay."

"J. J.?" Julie repeated. "Who's that?"

Still staring at Fillingham, her teeth chattering, Christine said, "Jay-cob!"

He stepped closer to his partner, his hands sliding down her shoulders to her arms. "Jacob? You mean Jacob Nowak?"

Christine nodded, her eyes briefly closing with relief. "Red…red…laces."

"Red laces," he affirmed.

"Baseball…shoe," Christine said. Her body was warming up from the heat inside the school. Her words were slow, but clear. "In…the…water. Where I fell." Finally, she had said it.

"You found a baseball shoe?" he asked.

She nodded, her hands clasped together for warmth.

"You think it's Jacob's?"

She nodded again, more vigorously.

Julie said, "Maybe the boy dumped his suitcase with the baseball shoes in the water before going AWOL. That's why it was never found."

"Not, not just...shoe...shoe." Christine was still shivering.

They waited.

"A hand," Christine said, her voice tremulous. "I saw a hand."

Chapter 10

"Have a good day at school." Christine held the apartment door open for her siblings; Donna gave her a quick squeeze as she went by, her snow pants making a swish-swish as she walked. The hand-me-down pants were short for her but fit her around the waist. Wayne followed Donna out the door, shoulders hunched into his coat. He had skipped breakfast and barely said a word.

And who could blame him, Christine thought. Last night, after Donna had gone to bed and Christine had changed out of the clothes she had borrowed from the Nature School, she had clicked off the TV and turned to Wayne sitting beside her on the couch. "I need to talk to you."

His eyes glued to her apprehensively as he sat cross-legged in his flannel airplane pajamas, his hair wet from his bath, looking younger than his ten years. It reminded her of all the times they had hid together when Wayne was a toddler while Phyllis and Eddie tied one on, her stepfather's voice getting louder and more argumentative as the evening progressed. Christine was a teenager then; she used to hold Wayne in her lap in the bottom of her closet, clothes sliding over their shoulders, singing songs like "Itsy Bitsy Spider" and "London Bridge" and raiding her stash of old Halloween candy she kept in their "secret fort."

"It's about Jacob," she said.

Wayne's shoulders stiffened.

Last night at the Island School, as the shadows of the trees had deepened, Christine, Julie and Fillingham had waited inside the building as the Harbor Police set up high-voltage lights around the perimeter of Trout Pond. Two hours later, the crew extracted a body.

As she sat beside her brother, Christine considered her next words. She didn't want Wayne discovering the news in the playground tomorrow, grisly rumors about how Jacob was discovered. Undoubtedly, the school would send a parent letter home and mount an assembly. But Jacob had been Wayne's classmate, teammate and bunkmate—she wanted him to hear the truth from her.

"A boy's body was found in the lagoon near the Island School," Christine said. "It's Jacob."

The color drained from Wayne's face like a pulled-down blind. Afraid that he was going to faint, she pushed his head down to his knees.

"He's...dead?" he whispered, still bent over.

"Yes," she said.

He said nothing after that, his breath loud and too quick, while Christine kept her hand on his back, trying to soothe him as Wayne covered his face with his hands.

After several minutes, after Wayne's breathing calmed, they stood up and Christine pulled out the sofa couch for Wayne. Silently, he climbed into his bed and pulled the comforter up, partially covering his face. He lay on his side, his back turned to her. She sat on the edge of the bed, stroking his leg.

The phone rang, and she rushed to the kitchen. "Hello," she whispered into the receiver.

"Christine, it's Sarah. Have you heard about the Nowak boy?"

"I found him. Julie, Fillingham and I were skating on the lagoon."

"Shoot, they never told me that. That must have been hard."

Christine remained quiet.

"Sergeant Baker called," Sarah said. "She wants us to provide support to Mrs. Nowak tomorrow."

"Who's there now?"

"The notifying officers are still there. Jacob's uncle is on the way over, as well as their parish priest. Then the officers will take their leave."

"I'm on afternoons tomorrow. What time are we expected?"

"Eleven o'clock in the morning," Sarah answered. "I'll pick you up in WB1 ten minutes before. The brass think we should attend, especially since I spoke with her before."

"She was right, you know," Christine said.

"About what?" Sarah asked.

"She said her son would never run away."

"It's a terrible thing to be right about," Sarah said.

Hanging up, Christine returned to the living room. In the dark, she could make out the mound of blankets that was Wayne, backlit by the streetlight coming in from the crack between the living room curtains. He wasn't asleep yet; she could tell. Sitting on the mattress edge, she placed a hand on his back, feeling his breath move in and out. Accidents happened all the time—she had seen terrible tragedies during her four years on the force. Gratitude washed over her. Wayne was safe. He was here, beside her, in their home. Safe.

Christine went into her bedroom and gazed at her sister, who was sprawled on her back in bed, arms flung above her head. A smile tweaked Christine's mouth. Her sister was animated—even in sleep. Christine kneeled beside Donna's bed and stroked her sister's silky hair. Christine's family was the most precious thing she had. She'd do anything to ensure their happiness and safety. Anything.

The Nowaks lived on the first floor of an older house on Leopold Street in Parkdale, a ten-minute walk from Christine's apartment. When Mrs. Nowak opened her front door to Christine and Sarah, she wailed, "I told police he did not run away!" She was short, a little thick around the middle, in her early to mid-thirties, wearing a blue patterned housedress that ended just below her knees and a thin shawl around her shoulders. Her wheat-colored hair was styled in a bob, the hairs flicking up at the end. Her face looked puffy, her gray eyes brimming with fresh tears.

Mr. Nowak appeared, eyes trained on his wife. His white-blond hair was receding in two points up his hairline. He was tall, with the straight nose and high cheekbones that Christine remembered in his son.

Sarah took a step toward the couple. "I'm so sorry for your loss."

Mrs. Nowak regarded Sarah, whose hands were clasped in front of her, eyes wide with sympathy. Although Mrs. Nowak was probably five years older than Sarah, she looked a decade older, with fine lines webbing around her eyes and a suspicious glare. After several seconds of consideration, Mrs. Nowak turned on her heel and went inside, leaving the front door open. Her husband stepped back to let the policewomen follow her through to the front parlor.

Sparse furnishings bore witness to the Nowak's recent arrival in Canada: a couch upholstered in faded mustard tapestry, two mismatched wooden chairs and a battered coffee table. A floral tapestry hung on one side of a wood fireplace, a crucifix on the other. A framed photo of the family and one of Jacob by himself were placed on the ledge of the bay window.

Sarah took the chair nearest to Mrs. Nowak, who was sitting at the far end of the couch. Christine sat in the other chair beside Sarah.

Leaning toward the grieving mother, Sarah said, "Again, my deepest sympathies for your loss."

Mrs. Nowak flinched, as if the condolence itself hurt her.

In the kitchen, cutlery rattled and a cupboard door thudded shut. Mr. Nowak entered the parlor with a porcelain tea set decorated with delicate brown and blue flowers. After placing the tray on the coffee table, Mr. Nowak poured the tea. He handed cups and saucers to each officer before handing a set to his wife.

Mrs. Nowak turned to Sarah as if continuing their conversation. "He would not run away."

"Yes," Sarah said.

"The teacher know he is a good boy," Mrs. Nowak said.

Sarah said, "I heard he is a hard-working student."

"Smart!" Mrs. Nowak's eyes blinked wetly. "So smart. In math, he is..." She turned and spoke in Polish to her husband, who provided her with the word.

"Advanced," he said.

"Advanced," she repeated.

"I heard he was a skilled pitcher," Christine said, speaking for the first time. Too late, she realized she had spoken in the past tense. Mrs. Nowak and Sarah had spoken in the present tense, as if Jacob was still alive.

The parents looked at her.

"Baseball," Christine added. "He is a good at baseball."

Mrs. Nowak nodded at Christine. "Jakub so proud to be on baseball team." She looked at her husband sitting at the other end of the couch. "Alfred buy him new baseball shoes for birthday." She looked back at Christine. "So much money they are! How he love them. Always cleaning."

Christine thought of the red laces floating in the pond, the white shoe tinted gray-green underneath the water. The parents mustn't know the details of his drowning yet.

The doorbell chimed throughout the day: Parkdale neighbors, the local parish priest, Polish church friends hefting trays of cabbage rolls, silent men in suits arriving to shake Mr. Nowak's hand, customers from the butcher shop where Mr. Nowak worked. Kitchen chairs were pulled out into the living room. Two elderly ladies in headscarves hummed prayers in the corner with rosaries webbed through arthritic fingers.

Mr. Nowak was a quiet, stoic presence, refreshing the boiling water in the teapot, responding to the doorbell peal, only the stoop of his shoulders and the straight line of his mouth evidence of his suffering. Mrs. Nowak murmured in Polish with friends—sometimes moved to quiet tears, other times sobs, wiping her eyes with her handkerchief or the edge of her shawl.

At one o'clock, the two officers rose to leave. Mr. Nowak retrieved their coats. Mrs. Nowak pushed herself off the couch and walked them to the door.

They said their goodbyes; Sarah left first to warm up the car. Christine put her gloves and coat on and turned to follow Sarah out the door. A hand clamped on her arm, halting her.

Mrs. Nowak's fingers pressed hard into Christine's sleeve. "Jakub not go in water." Her eyes bored into Christine's. "He is afraid. He cannot swim."

Christine nodded.

"Someone did this," Mrs. Nowak said.

"Everything okay here, Constable?" a deep voice said.

Christine turned, recognizing the voice; Mrs. Nowak released her hold.

Deputy Chief Darlow stood at the door in uniform, the crown and maple leaves of his rank on his shoulder board. Removing his hat, he addressed Mrs. Nowak. "Ma'am. On behalf of Chief Adams and the Toronto Police Force, our sympathies on your loss."

Mrs. Nowak looked up at the deputy's six-foot-three height and medaled chest, then lifted her chin, pulling her shawl tight around her shoulders against the cold. "Someone do this. Someone kill my son."

Deputy Darlow's glance shifted to Christine, as if she had planted this idea with Jacob's mother.

With a mumbled excuse that she was on shift soon, Christine departed with a "Sir" to the deputy and "Ma'am" to Mrs. Nowak before rushing down the front path to catch up with Sarah. A grieving mother and a superior officer were difficult conversation partners. Last summer, Christine had gotten into trouble with Deputy Darlow. The more she stayed out of his line of sight, the better.

"The preliminary report came in," Julie told Fillingham and Christine as the trio approached Lakeview Public School. It was the day of Jacob's memorial, and the maple leaf flag hung at half-mast in the school's front yard. Sarah could not attend the dedication, so Sergeant Baker had chosen Julie to represent the Women's Bureau. Christine and Fillingham asked Sergeant Bard if they could show their respects.

"Death by drowning," Julie said.

Fillingham opened the school's front door for the policewomen. "That's it? No evidence of a struggle: bruises, defensive wounds, torn fingernails?"

"None mentioned," Julie responded. "My friend Linda works at the coroner's office; she typed the report. The investigators signed off—the case is closed."

Christine released her breath. So it was an accident. A terrible, terrible accident. The boy had drowned. She wondered what the Nowaks would think of the report's conclusion.

They followed the stream of children and staff heading to the gym, everyone uncharacteristically solemn. Several boys wore ties or blazers, and many girls wore dresses. Lines creased foreheads; frowns tugged at their mouths.

It must be so frightening to have a student from your school die, Christine thought. Certainly, Wayne was shaken. This morning, her brother had dressed in his best pair of pants and a white, long-sleeved, collared shirt, short at the wrists now. Phyllis had ironed it for him, handing the warmed shirt to her silent son. Shortly after, Wayne ran into the washroom, and they could hear him heaving into the toilet. Phyllis had tucked him back in bed, a glass of ginger ale on the floor beside him to settle his stomach.

In the gym, gray metal folding chairs had been arranged in two sections separated by a middle aisle. The principal and Jacob's teacher stood at the front, guiding students to their seats and greeting the parents in attendance.

Catching sight of the officers, Miss Phillips gestured to three seats in the front row. Her expression was controlled, her lips firmly pressed together in her alabaster face.

Two seats were reserved for Jacob's parents, although Christine heard they would not be attending. Jacob's funeral, two days before, had been private—limited to friends, family and parish members. Staff, students and the police were barred from the Polish Catholic ceremony. Clearly, the Nowaks believed that the school board and the police hadn't fulfilled their duties regarding their son.

Fillingham elbowed Christine, and she turned. Staff from the Nature School were entering the gym. Tim Hawley caught her eye.

After a quick nod, Christine looked away. Tim was nice, but his geniality was manipulative. He thought a picnic lunch would buy her silence—stop her questions about the night Jacob went missing. Now that Jacob's body had been found, she wondered if the investigators would interview Tim again, check to see if anyone had seen Jacob leaving, suitcase in hand, wearing his beloved baseball shoes. Weren't the investigators curious why a child was beachside in the middle of the night? And wasn't the school board and the principal of the Nature School probing how a child died on their watch? Did the accidental drowning conclusion really close the case?

Christine frowned. Another point bothered her. She knew from Wayne that you only wore your baseball shoes on the field; other surfaces dulled the metal cleats. And baseball shoes were expensive—Christine worked overtime at a Catholic dance to buy a second-hand pair for Wayne this past September when he outgrew his old ones. Why would Jacob be wearing baseball shoes when he left the school?

Principal Seymour raised his hand; Christine's attention returned to the memorial. Speaking into the microphone at the lectern, he welcomed attendees and described the school's close-knit community where parents, staff and students supported each other. How it was upsetting when someone they knew got hurt. He noted that accidents happened, but they were rare. The tragedy of Jacob's death reminded them to be kind to each other, watch out for each other and take care of each other.

Miss Phillips replaced the principal at the lectern, somber in her navy dress with pearls at the throat. "Jacob was a student determined to succeed." Her voice was soft and husky. "He was a hard worker, always trying to improve his English, and his math skills were superlative." Her voice was stronger now. She gave a little laugh. "He was the one who helped me solve the tricky bonus question at the end of the algebra unit." She swallowed, loudly. "At recess, I'd see him out on the baseball field practicing his pitches. I only knew Jacob for a few weeks, but he was a talented and hard-working child. I knew he would do well—at school, in Canada, in life. He was a model for all students, and I will miss him." Her voice quavered on her last words, and she quickly returned to her seat.

When Mr. Seymour returned to the mike, he was holding a silver trophy with a black base. "In honor of Jacob's industry and his athleticism, we are creating the Jacob Nowak Award for most valuable male athlete of the year. This trophy will be awarded to the Grade 5 boy who demonstrates not only superior athletic skills, but also leadership and good sportsmanship." He placed the trophy on the stage behind him. Back at the lectern, he said, "We know this is a difficult time for staff and students, particularly those who knew Jacob last year in Mrs. Pine's class or this year in Miss Phillips's, so I want to remind teachers that Mrs. Elvin"—a woman in a white sweater and gray skirt raised a hand—"is a social worker who will be at school this week to support us. Teachers, please speak with her to discuss ways she can help you and your students."

The principal closed with a prayer, the "Our Father." Adult and youthful voices blended in a somber chant. Then, row by row, led by their teachers, the students left the gym. Christine wondered if Peter, Jacob's friend, was exiting the memorial, and what he would have to say about his friend's drowning.

Fillingham stood. Christine said, "We're invited for coffee in the staff room."

Julie shook her head. "I have to get back to work. Sergeant's orders."

Fillingham turned to Christine. "I'll see Julie out. Meet you at the front office."

Julie and Fillingham smiled at each other as they left the gym.

They made a cute couple, both small, blonde, attractive and fun-loving. Like matching salt and pepper shakers. Julie had confessed that they'd been going out for four months. Usually, Julie's relationships were brief and torrid—heady infatuations followed by tedium, her wandering eye soon seeking greener pastures.

But she and Fillingham had hung on. When the two had flirted in the summer, Christine had worried that Julie would break his heart, and then he'd refuse to work with Christine because of her friendship with Julie.

Fillingham was a big boy, a charmer with a flashy smile, attentive manner and old Toronto money. With his relentless optimism, he'd survive any relationship dissolution. Anyway, it was good to hear their laughter and playful banter; there wasn't enough love in the world.

Christine thought of Hawk and the woman he had brought to the Christmas bazaar. Some part of her was glad Hawk had someone, even if the idea was an icepick to her heart. Hawk would be a loyal boyfriend and a dependable parent to the little girl. The trio would make a loving family.

Shaking her head clear of thoughts of Hawk, Christine followed the stragglers out of the gym. Near the office, she scanned the hallway for the staff room where refreshments were being served. A stocky boy in a brown T-shirt and jeans bent over the water fountain for a drink.

"Roy!" Christine called.

He looked up, water dripping down his chin.

"How is it going?" she asked, approaching him.

His gaze strayed past her, as if that was the direction he wanted to head.

"Wayne's not feeling well. That's why he's not here today." She gestured to him. "How are you doing?"

He shrugged, his expression giving nothing away. "Okay."

"I know it's been difficult for your class. It's been hard on Wayne."

He waited, silently looking at her to finish.

"Any new thoughts, Roy? Things you remember about the night Jacob left?"

He shook his head. His dark hair was longer than in September, his bangs now down to his chin.

"Were you awake during the night at all?"

His head shook again.

"You didn't hear anything...a suitcase being dragged across the floor, the screen being removed? Or a door closing?" she asked.

"As I've said a hundred times, I was sleeping. I didn't hear any-thing." He averted his face. "Can I go?"

"Sure." Christine watched him walk away, and then she headed across the hall to the staff room, where she met Fillingham in front of the beverage table.

Miss Phillips came over and offered them coffee from the large aluminum urn. As she handed Christine a cup, Miss Phillips said, "Is Wayne ill?"

Christine nodded. "I'm not sure if it's something he ate or if he's upset about Jacob."

"It's been very hard on my students," Miss Phillips said.

It had been hard on Miss Phillips. Her navy dress hung loosely, as if she had lost weight, her collarbone prominent under her scooped neckline. To have a student go missing and be found dead was a tragedy that would stick to her all her life. For now, she would be reminded of Jacob every time she looked at the class photo, Jacob's artwork on the bulletin board or his last spelling test.

The teacher excused herself to speak with parents. The principal approached the two officers.

"Thank you for coming." Mr. Seymour gave a vigorous handshake to each officer.

"It was a nice memorial," Christine said. "I'm sure the Nowaks appreciate the award in Jacob's memory."

He nodded, his eyes scanning the room, touching on the Lakeview teachers with plates of cheese and crackers. It was recess, so most of the staff was present.

"The Nowaks didn't attend," Fillingham observed.

The principal's eyes returned to Fillingham. He cleared his throat. "They were too upset to come, as you can imagine."

"They are suing the school board for negligence," Christine said.

Principal Seymour's mouth thinned. "Where did you hear that?"

"Mrs. Nowak."

He shifted. "It's natural for parents to lash out in grief, even when it's a senseless accident." He placed his coffee cup on the table with a clink. "I'll leave it to the lawyers to debate. For today, I'd like to remember a talented child and focus on the students left behind." He gave them a nod, then walked away.

Fillingham snagged a chocolate chip cookie from the table. "What's up, Lane?" He took a bite, blue eyes on her. "You think the school is liable?"

"Maybe." She sighed. "How about police culpability?"

He licked a cookie crumb off his lip. "Are you feeling guilty because he was lost on our watch, or because we found him?"

Her eyes bored into his. "We saw him the day before he went missing with blood on his face. He was being picked on."

His face scrunched in skepticism. "You think we could have prevented his drowning?"

"Maybe," she said. "Yes. No. I don't know."

"A bloody nose doesn't lead to a runaway kid or someone walking into a pond. We weren't negligent."

"Was the school board?"

"Let's find out." He brushed cookie crumbs from his palms while scanning the room, noticing the sandy-haired teacher talking with a shorter man with dark hair. "Tim!" he called.

Tim turned and spied the two officers. He said something to the dark-haired man, and they both headed over. Tim introduced his companion as Derek Mansfield, the paddling instructor at the Nature School.

Fillingham said, "Lots of Island school staff here."

Tim glanced over at his peers gathered beside the coffee urn. "It's shaken us up, to be honest."

Derek added, "I've been at the school for five years—Tim, you've been, what, eight? Nothing like this has happened before."

Tim said, "Kids sneak out for a cigarette or to meet a girl on the beach, but for a child to..." His voice petered out.

"No one has drowned before?" Fillingham asked.

Derek and Tim shook their heads in unison.

Tim said, "We don't let students swim unless we have trained lifesaving staff supervising or the students put on life jackets. We're diligent about water safety."

Not so diligent about hallway supervision, Christine thought.

Fillingham addressed Derek. "Can you introduce me to the rest of the school staff? I don't think I've met them all."

Derek and Fillingham walked away. What was her partner up to, leaving her alone with Tim?

Giving her a sympathetic smile, Tim said, "It must have been hard, finding the boy."

She frowned, pushing away the image of the small gray hand beside the waving red shoelace. "It's always difficult when a child is involved."

After a pause, he said, "Can I take you out for lunch?" He gestured to the table of desserts. "I don't really feel like cake or cookies. We could talk. It might make us feel better about the situation."

Did he have something to confess—an additional detail to clarify the last hours of Jacob Nowak's life? "Okay. I have a little time."

On the way out of the staffroom, she interrupted Fillingham's animated discussion with Derek about canoes to tell her partner she would meet him at the station for their afternoon shift. He nodded and continued his conversation. Both were boatmen. They probably could talk for hours about wind direction, tacking and racing. Derek had the sailor's perpetual tan and lines around his eyes from squinting into the sun.

Nearby, a family-owned diner on King Street had reasonable prices, so Christine led them there. When they were settled in a booth and had ordered, Tim said, "It's been a tough couple of months for the school."

Christine nodded at him. She had noticed that the overnight program had closed for the fall and had just reopened this past month. "I can imagine." After a pause, she added, "It's been tough for Lakeview School, too. For Miss Phillips, Jacob's classmates, his baseball and soccer teams. They've all been affected by the boy's absence." She thought of Wayne sick in bed now and his solemnity since the news of Jacob's death.

Propping his elbows on the table, Tim said, "The superintendent has visited the school three times in the past week—examining our protocols, programming and staffing."

"That's to be expected," she said. "They're trying to identify problem areas to prevent another tragedy."

"We are careful. Our program educates thousands of students every year. Safely."

"The board has to cover their bases. The family is suing."

"They're bound to find something—minor lapses, shortcuts, violations."

The conversation stopped as the waitress delivered their sandwiches, and they spent a few minutes eating silently. After getting their water glasses refilled, Tim said, "They might close the overnight school."

"That would be a shame," she said. "It's a wonderful opportunity for children to experience the beauty of the Island."

"Or they might clean house and fire the current staff."

"That's heavy-handed," she commented.

"The superintendent is looking for a scapegoat. The lawsuit has them scrambling...eager to pin the blame on someone for Jacob's death. Not the reason he died—we know it was accidental. But how he got to be alone by the water in the first place." After a bite of his Reuben sandwich, he said. "The other month, when we had lemonade on the beach..."

She waited.

"I mentioned I had left my post for a few minutes to go to the washroom."

"Half an hour."

"I haven't—I didn't mention that to the superintendent."

She said nothing.

He reached out across the table to touch the dark sleeve of her uniform. "I was hoping you wouldn't mention it, either."

She slid her arm away and glanced out the window at a couple trudging by in winter coats and hats, scarves wrapped around their lower face. "I'm a police officer. I am obliged to tell the truth, inside a courtroom and out."

He frowned and sat back against the red vinyl seat. "It's a small favor—for my job."

She wondered if she should tell him she had already relayed this information to the investigators—who had discarded it as irrelevant.

"Why would you be fired for going to the bathroom?" she asked. "If Jacob escaped through the window, how are you responsible?"

He gave an impatient snort. "I wasn't in the bathroom."

She remained silent.

"You know Jean," he said. "Miss Phillips?"

She nodded.

"Well...we...I..." he exhaled. "Truth be told, I was in her room for that half hour."

Christine blinked.

No wonder Miss Phillips's face looked gray. She had been in bed with Tim when Jacob was escaping out of the dorm window.

Tim said, "The school was quiet. All the students were asleep. Everything was secure. We weren't hurting anybody." He leaned over the table, closer to her. "So you see, more than one job is at risk here."

Christine wiped her mouth with a napkin. "I have to go."

She insisted on paying her share of the bill, even though Tim offered to pay. She couldn't afford the dollar fifty, but she didn't want to be beholden to him.

Tim opened the door, and a swirl of snow blew inside. They stood beside each other on the sidewalk, bunching their coats tighter around themselves.

"Several students left their rooms that night," he said.

She turned to him. "You mean the boys that went to the bathroom?"

He nodded.

"The police spoke to them. They didn't see anything," she said.

"There was one more boy I saw when I came back from...seeing Miss Phillips."

"Who?" she asked.

"Your brother."

"Wayne?" Her tone was quizzical.

He nodded, shoving his bare hands into his coat pocket.

"He must have been going to the bathroom, too," she said.

"Maybe," Tim said. "Except that the boys' washroom is the other way."

Chapter 11

Snowflakes instantly flecked Sergeant Bard's dark coat as his burly frame maneuvered out of the patrol car parked by the ferry dock; Pilkington stepped out the passenger side. The men staggered as a gust blew them sideways; they hunched low against the wind as they approached Christine and Fillingham, who had disembarked from the Center Island ferry.

Sergeant Bard shoved a gloved fist at Fillingham, car keys dangling. "All quiet. Residents are hunkered down inside, as they should be in this blooming snowstorm." He nodded as he passed Christine; the two officers disappeared into the wind-sheltered warmth of the ferry's cabin.

Christine hurried after Fillingham to the waiting Jeep, glad of the long underwear under the wool trousers of her winter uniform. Even in a car, Island patrol was chilly.

Snow danced across the path to the Center Island Police Station, the late-afternoon light like a dull white beacon penetrating the blizzard. To the right was a bowl of frozen lake water, Long Pond, the basin that had hosted a century's worth of rowing competitions.

"Whoa!" Fillingham braked hard as a wall of snow temporarily blocked visibility, then slowly eased forward until they could make out the blue neon *POLICE* sign. "Hot dog, this is a crazy storm."

Christine looked over at her partner. She might suggest that they stay inside the station for their afternoon shift and catch up on paperwork or organize the attic. No doubt he'd lure her outside and ambush her with a snowball. Good thing she had an accurate throwing arm, thanks to high-school javelin training. But Fillingham was fast. And relentless.

Which was fine, she thought. She didn't want to sit around for eight hours, mulling over the impending Christmas holiday. How she was alone and Hawk was not. Or bemoaning the meagerness of her family's celebration. One of these days, after they paid her mother's debt, she'd buy her family the biggest tree in the lot. Not the straggly two-dollar balsam in their living room window, but a regal one. All the ornaments would be new—red and gold. And for breakfast, they'd eat eggs, German sausages from Andersons on King Street and pastries from Audrey's Bakery. Afterward, they'd open five big presents each.

The car turned into the police station driveway, sliding to a halt.

Fillingham clicked open his door. "Run for it!" He sprinted across the driveway, closely followed by Christine, who pulled the front door tight behind them, shutting out the howling wind. They shook themselves off like dogs and wiped their boots on the mat, mindful that they would have to mop up the mess themselves.

"Hey, a Christmas tree," Christine said.

"Pilkington's been busy," he responded. The edge of the counter had a garland of spruce and berries running along it, a tree blinked colored lights and two poinsettia plants brightened the corners of the waiting room.

Fillingham led the way into the back kitchen. "Coffee?"

She nodded. Before Fillingham, she had been more of a tea person, but her partner's habits were contagious. Plus, he was the one who always made coffee on their shift. The couple of times she had tried, he complained the brew was too strong or too watery, so she was glad to leave it to him. She selected two mugs from the cupboard above the sink while Fillingham located a box of digestive cookies. Five minutes later, they were sitting at the kitchen table with their steaming mugs.

"How was lunch with Nature Boy today?" he asked, eyebrows raised.

"It's not like that. Tim's worried about his job."

"Why?" he asked.

"Remember I told you he left his post for half an hour the night Jacob went missing?"

"Aren't the staff allowed breaks?" he asked.

"Tim was visiting Miss Phillips's room."

He whistled. "No wonder he's shaking in his boots." He tipped back in his chair, coffee mug in hand. "What does it matter, though? Didn't Jacob escape out the window?"

"The window screen was off. But he could have exited out the main door when Tim was away from his post."

"Anyone else sneak out that night?"

Tim had mentioned seeing her brother in the hallway. When Christine returned home after the memorial service and her lunch with Tim, she had asked Wayne if he had left his room that night for any reason. Wayne was lying on his sofa bed, nursing his stomachache.

Wayne was angry. "I already told you and the other officers I was in my room the whole night. Why would Tim say that he saw me? He didn't even know my name then."

Christine couldn't figure out what game Tim was playing with her. "I don't think anyone else left the building," she said to Fillingham. "All the students were questioned. No one saw Jacob, in or out of the school."

She sipped her coffee, enjoying its deep, roasted taste. "Tim said the school superintendent found discrepancies."

"Discrepancies?" He bit into a cookie.

"The school is under review because of Jacob's death. They found violations."

"What's a violation? Missing lifejackets? Improper food storage? Negligence?"

"Tim wouldn't say." The house shuddered with a blast of wind. The kitchen window was a frame of light gray as the snow fell in the darkening twilight. Turning back to Fillingham, she asked, "Could an incident with staff make Jacob run away?"

He held her gaze. As police officers, they had seen too many adults prey on children. "That would do it."

"What staff was there that night?" he asked.

She frowned. "I think there is day staff that helps with food preparation and cleaners who stay on longer. But overnight, it would be Tim, the two female staff and some of the specialty staff like the paddling coach. And the three Lakeview teachers, of course."

"Who are they?" he asked.

"Well, Miss Phillips, Miss Patterson and Mr. Ivy," she said.

"I don't see a woman for this, which leaves the male staff."

Christine shook her head. "Tim was on duty, and Mr. Ivy is quite a well-loved junior teacher." She shrugged. "But you never know. Can we interview the Nature School staff?"

He shook his head. "The investigators closed the case. We have no reason to."

"We could contact mainland schools that have attended the Nature School in previous years," she said. "See if they noticed anything funny. And interview teachers who used to work there. Check if they remember staff with anger issues or who were overly friendly to students."

His mouth turned down in disgust.

She forced herself to continue, even though she felt uncomfortable. "It happens more than you'd think: fathers, stepfathers, neighbors, babysitters, camp counselors, coaches."

"I know," he said.

"I've rarely seen charges laid. The child refuses to talk or is silenced by parents who are worried about what people will say about their child or family."

He held his hands behind his head. "So we're not buying accidental drowning?"

"He left with his suitcase, and it hasn't been found."

"It could have floated into the harbor. Or sunk."

"The divers didn't find it by the body. I also heard that his one baseball shoe was tied to his wrist." She let out a long sigh. "Why would he take his suitcase or baseball shoe into the water in the first place? His family doesn't have money to buy another pair. The only reason the Nowaks can sue the school board is because a Polish lawyer offered to take their case pro bono."

"Sad to say," Fillingham said, "but maybe it is suicide."

"Do you believe that?" she asked. "When we saw Jacob bleeding on the ground, he looked ready to take on both boys himself. From what his parents and teachers have said, he was a resilient, high-achieving boy."

"True."

"Logically, the drowning makes no sense. A boy who couldn't swim leaves the school in the middle of the night with his suitcase and walks two hundred feet off the main path to the lagoon. Why? If he's trying to leave, the docks are a fifteen-minute walk from the school."

"Ferries don't run at night," he pointed out.

"Common sense says he would walk toward Hanlan's Point dock, hunker down on a bench overnight and wait for the seven o'clock morning ferry."

"What's the point of all these 'what ifs'? The coroner filed his report. From the police perspective, the investigation is closed. The lawyers will sort out civil liability." Fillingham got up and stretched, his hands fisted above his head, then went over to place his mug in the sink.

"It's not sitting right with me," she said.

He leaned against the countertop, facing her. "Is that so? Well, while you were charming Nature Boy over soup and a sandwich, I dropped by the school office."

"What did you find out?" she asked quickly.

"Guess who transferred schools?"

"Who?"

"Patrick Williamson," he answered.

"The fourth boy in the room."

"Yup. He left Lakeview in October, right after Jacob went missing."

Funny, Wayne hadn't told her that Patrick had moved away. "Maybe Patrick's family blamed the school for Jacob's disappearance, just like the Nowaks do, so they transferred him. Or Patrick was traumatized and wanted a fresh start. Or it's just coincidence, and they planned the move."

Fillingham held up the four fingers of his right hand. "Four boys bunked in that dormitory room. Jacob is dead." One finger went down. "Patrick has moved." A second finger went down. "That leaves your brother and Roy."

She stood in front of him with her empty mug. "What are you saying?"

"The two remaining boys know more than they're letting on."

She stared at him for several seconds. "Do you think my brother is lying? He said that he didn't hear or see anything that night."

He raised both hands in surrender. "I don't know, Lane. Between the boys in the room, the Nature School, Tim Hawley and Miss Phillips, something is being covered up. You sense it too. That's why both of us can't leave it alone." He tapped on the kitchen table with his fingers r in a quick drumroll. "Lucky for us, I have connections."

"Connections?"

"Our esteemed coroner, Dr. David Putnam, will be waiting for us at the morgue after our shift at eleven thirty tonight."

"To talk about the Nowak autopsy? Wow! How did you swing that?" she asked.

His light brown eyebrows arched. "I know people," he said. He added, "The coroner's secretary is an old schoolmate of Julie's—she got us in."

"Riding on the coattails of a policewoman," she teased.

"I like the view," he responded.

"Ever been to an autopsy?" Fillingham asked as they drove along Victoria Street toward the morgue. Snow blasted around his winter car, a GM Beaumont, which kept slowing and sliding on the slushy streets. To avoid side-slamming parked cars, he was driving in the middle of the road. Thank goodness few vehicles were out, and fewer pedestrians.

"No," she replied. Autopsies were the purview of the homicide department. In her four years as a police officer, she had attended many calls regarding children, women and the elderly, which could be tragic. "I've seen a few dead bodies: an alleyway alcoholic; an old lady who got hit by a car; and a baby who starved to death. We're not here to see the boy's body, I hope." The car tires slipped as they turned onto Lombard Street, and she grabbed the door arm for support.

Fillingham wrestled with the wheel until the tires gained traction. "You don't want to see a body that's been in the water for three months."

She thought of Jacob's delicate features—the straight nose, high cheekbones and wide glacier-blue eyes. He had been a beautiful boy.

"Here we are," he said. They pulled up in front of an old stone building, snow accumulating on the narrow window ledges on either side of the double oak door. Above the door, the words *City Morgue* were carved in Roman font into the concrete.

Their heavy boots thudded softly on the snow as they climbed the steps to the front door. Up close, a light layer of grime tinged the building a darker gray. "Kind of creepy going to a morgue at midnight," Fillingham said, making a silly face. His gloved finger pushed the doorbell, and they could hear a low-timbred chime inside.

As they waited, Christine asked, "Should we be doing this?"

He replied. "Visiting the morgue?"

She gave him a stern look. "Investigating Jacob Nowak's death."

He shrugged, smiling. "It's a free country. We're on our own time."

"It's not as simple as that."

"You started this circus, Sixteen. You're the one who can't let it rest."

A foyer light turned on, and one of the heavy doors opened inward. A stout, bald man in a white lab coat greeted them. "Officers. My apologies. I was in the back."

Inside, the foyer smelled of disinfectant, like the one used to clean public bathrooms, alongside the scent of rubbing alcohol. Her eyes met Fillingham's, both thinking about the autopsy table.

Overhead hung an incongruously large chandelier, its light dimmed by dove-gray layers of dust. A tall brass tin with a single umbrella occupied one corner. The wall to the right featured a framed etching of the morgue building when it was first built.

Christine and Fillingham removed their gloves and shook snow off their sleeves.

"Dr. Putnam," the doctor said, shaking Fillingham's hand and then her own. "This way." He waved them toward a door to their right.

A large desk dominated the rectangular room, the yellowed blinds pulled low in the narrow windows.

Easing himself into the maroon leather chair, Dr. Putnam gestured to the two chairs in front of his desk. "Please have a seat. You're here about the boy who drowned."

Fillingham nodded. "Yes. Thanks for seeing us."

"My secretary said you had some questions," Dr. Putnam said. Before either of them could speak, he added, "It was a clear-cut case of drowning."

"Can I ask how you know that?" Fillingham asked.

After opening the manila file on his desk, the doctor scanned the typed text. "The water specimen from his lungs matched the sample from the recovery scene, showing he drowned at that location, not elsewhere. The foam in his trachea and the enlarged red lungs indicate he was alive before he went into the water. Although it's hard to tell for certain, as the body is partially decomposed, I detected no signs of trauma. It's difficult to determine if injuries are pre- or post-drowning, as bodies can get banged around underwater."

"What was he wearing?" she asked.

"The fabric disintegrated as the body bloated, but the material was plaid flannel, typical of pajamas."

"Pajamas," she said. "Are you sure?"

"Yes. I understand he went missing at night three months ago, which is consistent with the amount of decomposition."

"Was he wearing anything other than his pajamas?" she asked.

"He had a sport shoe with cleats with him. The investigators took it as evidence. I was told the boy played baseball."

"Was he wearing the baseball shoe?" Fillingham asked.

"No. His feet were bare, the skin loosened and scored with minor abrasions."

"What type of abrasions?" she asked.

Dr. Putnam leaned back in his chair, his dark gray tie slightly loose around his white shirt collar. "A few scratches. One deeper cut from rubbing against underwater rocks or obtained prior to immersion—say, from running outside in bare feet. Again, it's hard to tell which scenario, because of the time under water."

"If he wasn't wearing his baseball shoe," Fillingham asked, "how did he hold on to it?"

"The laces were knotted around his wrist," the doctor answered. "I would estimate on purpose. The shoe stayed with him, even when his grip loosened."

"He went into the water in his pajamas," she said, "with one baseball shoe tied to his hand. And he had no lacerations, other than those on his feet, or broken bones or bruising?"

"That is correct." Dr. Putnam glanced at his watch. "Officers, I must excuse myself. My shift ends at midnight, and I must finish a few things before the medical attendant arrives.

They stood, then shuffled in a line back out to the foyer. As she pulled her gloves on, Christine asked, "Doctor, could you tell if Jacob was healthy?"

The coroner replied, "No disease or trauma was evident, externally or internally. His height and weight would have been average for his age. He had some early tooth decay—a cavity in his back molar. No previous broken bones. I would venture he was your typical healthy ten-year-old boy who unfortunately did not know how to swim."

The police officers were silent as they returned to the car. Christine swiped snow off the side mirrors, and Fillingham brushed the rest of the car off.

As the windshield wipers scraped away a film of snow, Christine said, "It seems strange that he had his pajamas on."

Fillingham looked over at her. "He went missing at night."

"But he took his suitcase. Why would you wear your pajamas when your regular clothes, your jeans and sweatshirts, are with you? Plus, it's too cool at night in September to just be wearing PJs."

Fillingham started the car. "Maybe he wasn't thinking straight. He's unhappy, wants to leave... He doesn't care what he's wearing. He just takes off."

"But no shoes?" she questioned. "The path to the Gibraltar Lighthouse is gravel. That's hard on the soles of your feet. Who runs away shoeless? They didn't find any footwear left in his bunkroom. He had his running shoes with him." As they headed west along Lombard, she said, "He goes barefoot toward the water, we don't know why, because he can't swim, baseball shoe in one hand, suitcase in another. He loved baseball—why would he bring the shoe into the water to ruin it? And where is his suitcase?"

"Stashed elsewhere?"

"The investigators searched within a half mile of the school. Nothing."

They drove in silence for a while.

"He seemed desperate," she said. "Like he was in peril. Like he was running away from someone."

"Let's request that background check on staff from your friend at Records," he said.

"For priors?"

"Anything interesting."

When they reached her apartment, she asked, "Are we ruling out suicide?"

He shrugged. "New country, new school, new language. It's got to be tough."

"The Nowaks are Catholic. It's a sin to kill yourself."

"Maybe that's why Mom insists it's foul play. She can't accept the possibility of suicide because it goes against their creed."

Christine shook her head. "She isn't buying the conclusion of accidental drowning because she doesn't believe Jacob would go near the water. She thinks someone did this to him."

"What did they do? Push him in? Force him to go barefoot? Make him go into the lagoon with his one shoe? No defensive wounds marked his bodies: no ripped fingernails, marks on his hands, bruising or broken bones. I can't see Jacob going into the water without a fight."

He touched her coat sleeve. "We need to talk to your brother. Maybe he can fill in some gaps."

She paused before responding. "He's tired of being asked about that night. It makes him upset."

"Roy O'Neil merits a visit, too." He paused. "How about I take Wayne," he pointed to his chest, "you take Roy. Divide and conquer."

"Okay." She opened the car door. "I hope we're right, that something's amiss. Otherwise—" she paused, "otherwise, this digging might cause more pain. To the family. To us."

"Who's going to give us a hard time?" he said.

"Do you want a list?" Deputy Police Darlow came to mind. And the 51 Division investigators. She should probably add Sergeant Bard as well.

She exited the car, stepping over a snowbank to the sidewalk. The living room window of her apartment was dark, only the streetlight lighting a milky path to her door. Wet flakes pelted her face as she struggled along the unshoveled pathway. After her visit to the morgue, she'd be happy to reach the warmth of her apartment and the cocoon of her sleeping family.

Chapter 12

Inhaling the smell of pine sap from the potted Christmas trees, Christine and her siblings waited in line for Santa at the Christmas party. Every year, the police union rented out a facility to provide free rides and entertainment for young police families. Nearby, a toddler shrieked with pleasure as she clung to the merry-go-round horse, her father's hand around her waist as it went up and down.

"What's on your Santa list?" a voice asked.

Christine, Wayne and Donna turned. *Oh no!* It was Deputy Chief Darlow. And he was addressing Christine's little sister.

Donna smiled, not intimidated by the man in dress uniform. Her mouth was mustached with a brown line from the free hot chocolate, and she hugged a balloon under one arm. She launched into a description of the board game Operation, demonstrating how you pulled the bone out with tweezers. "Like a surgeon," she said to Deputy Darlow.

Please don't touch the deputy with your sticky hands, Christine prayed. What was her superior officer doing here anyway? It was a non-brass event. He must be giving a speech about the Widows and Orphans Fund.

"What's this?" Deputy Chief Darlow pointed at Donna's balloon animal.

"The clown made it for me!" Donna exclaimed, hazel eyes shining as she showed it to the deputy chief, almost hitting him in the chin with the balloon.

Christine pulled Donna's arm down.

"A monkey?" the deputy asked.

"No!"

"Elephant?" he queried again.

"NO! It's a dog!"

A small smile edged his mouth. "Of course."

A woman dressed in green leotards approached. It was a policeman's wife, dressed as Santa's elf. "Kids, Santa's ready for you."

Wayne looked from the elf to Christine, his face sullen. At ten, he was getting a bit old for Santa. "Take Donna," Christine instructed, forestalling any debate.

Donna ran alongside the elf in her red velvet dress that was a little tight in the armpits, her hair in curled sausages down her back, past the Christmas trees to the opening in the white picket fence. Santa waved them over to his knee. Wayne looked tall and uncomfortable, perched in his dress pants and white shirt. Santa turned to Donna, who launched into an animated monologue.

Deputy Chief Darlow said, "PW Lane, a complaint has been lodged against you."

Christine's head jerked to look at him.

He continued, "By Mark O'Neil. The father of Roy O'Neil—a Lakeview Public School student."

Her brows knit together. "I know him. What is the complaint, sir?"

"You interviewed his son about Jacob Nowak."

She hadn't had time to speak with Roy again, as she and Fillingham had planned. "I only spoke with Roy for a minute at the memorial—"

He interrupted. "Why are you asking questions at all, Constable? No inquest has been called. The coroner and the investigators concluded death by drowning. The case is closed. Continued interviews upset the children and their families."

She opened her mouth to list the anomalies, the reasons she and Fillingham were persisting in the investigation, but viewing the straight line of the deputy's mouth, she clamped hers shut.

"Further to that," he continued, "the school board has directed staff at the Nature School to refuse interviews regarding the Nowak case, due to litigation with the family. You spoke with a teacher, Tim Hawley, without notifying him of his rights to a lawyer or union advocate."

"It...it wasn't an interview; it was just coffee. *He* asked *me*." She cringed at the defensive tone in her voice.

He stared at her for several long seconds. "You're overstepping. Again."

Last time she had overstepped, she and Fillingham found a murderer. Deputy Chief Darlow didn't seem to remember that arrest. Why was she perpetually in trouble with this man? She'd never make it to sergeant if he was on the interview team.

She rolled her shoulders back to stand straighter and nodded in recognition of his position, of his implied directive.

He left without another word.

Donna came running back to her. "I asked for Operation and Nancy Drew and a book on rocks and some pencil crayons." She was so excited, her words tumbled together. "Is that too much?"

Christine took one last look at Deputy Chief Darlow's straight back and turned to her sister. "I'm sure Santa can manage a few items on your list...unless you've been naughty."

"I haven't!" Donna protested, hands on hips.

Bending to hug Donna's wiry body under the velvet material, Christine said, "I know." Donna was a keen learner, her report cards glowing, and an avid reader, a pile of library books permanently in a tumble by her bed. She loved school, learning facts, doing homework and drawing. Christine would have to pick up an extra shift, but maybe she could manage two or three items on her sister's list. Donna deserved it.

Wayne walked toward them, sucking on a candy cane, smiling. Santa could still work his magic, even on a ten-year-old.

Four days later, on Christmas morning, Donna searched under the Christmas tree in her red velvet dress, reading the labels on the presents aloud. "Did Daddy send me a present?" she asked.

From the couch, Phyllis said, "I'm sure he did. It must have got lost in the mail."

Donna looked at her mom. "You said that last year."

Christine frowned at her mom, who was sitting beside her. She hated the way their mom talked about her stepfather Eddie, as if he were a busy father working out of town rather than a raging alcoholic who had sent Phyllis flying across the kitchen and introduced her to race-track betting. Who had cleared out their bank account when he finally left, after Christine, as a newly minted police officer, threatened to charge him with assault.

Donna distributed the presents. Each child had three wrapped gifts: from Santa, Phyllis and Christine. Phyllis opened Donna's present to her, a snowman made with toothpicks and Styrofoam balls. Next was the papier mâché poinsettia Wayne had made his mom in art class.

Christine received warm wool socks for patrol from her mom, and Phyllis was happy about her renewed subscription to *Women's World*. Wayne loved his signed Billy Williams baseball card, the leather oil for his baseball glove and his Rawhide Kid comic book.

After putting her new book and pencil crayons in her room, Donna placed her board game on the living room rug to play. Kneeling, Christine gathered the wrapping paper, folding it so they could use it again next year.

"Tea?" Phyllis asked Christine.

"Sure."

Bing Crosby's "White Christmas" played on the radio as they sat on the couch with their tea, bellies full from their breakfast of French toast.

Thinking about her stepfather made Christine think about her father. "How many Christmases did you have with my dad?" she asked.

"One or two."

"None with me there?" Christine asked.

Phyllis frowned. "I told you this before. He came back on leave, then headed back to the front. It was after that I found out I was pregnant."

"Was he happy when he found out?"

Phyllis smiled briefly. "Yes."

"How did he know?"

"I wrote him a letter."

"Did he write you back?"

"Yes."

"Can I read that letter?" Christine asked.

Phyllis snorted in exasperation. "That was long ago, Christine. I don't keep things like that." She paused. "Why are you talking about this today?" She gestured to the Christmas tree. The light cast colored orbs on the living room walls.

"I guess because it is Christmas. You think about family." She pointed at the framed picture on the shelf across the room. "Do you have any other photos of my dad?"

Phyllis placed her mug on the coffee table with a thud. "No. We moved a lot. I married Eddie. Things got lost."

"How about a keepsake—his wedding ring, military ID tag?" Christine asked. There must be another clue about her father's identity other than the living room photo.

"No," Phyllis said.

Donna squealed as a buzzer went off in the Operation game as she tried to remove an organ with plastic tweezers.

"Did my dad have family?" Christine asked.

Phyllis reached for her cigarette package on the coffee table. "I've told you. He was an only child. His parents are dead." She lit her cigarette with a hastily scratched match, puffing deeply, her upper lip wrinkling on the filter.

"You have nothing from your courtship: a locket or dried flower?"

"No! Why are you bothering me about this?"

Donna looked up from her game at the two women.

Christine smiled at Donna to show everything was okay, then regarded her mother: circles under her eyes from shift work, the coarse, wavy hair threaded with gray, her thin shoulders. "I'm not criticizing you, Mom. You've had a lot to deal with on your own. I know that."

Her mother nodded, slightly mollified.

Phyllis was right. It wasn't the right time to hash out things about Christine's father, even if her mom was hiding something.

After she finished her tea, Christine joined her siblings on the rug, smiling as Donna screamed when the buzzer went off on her turn.

"Remind me never to let you remove a splinter," Christine said to her sister.

"Watch me," Wayne said. "I'm the master."

It was nice to see Wayne regain his old cockiness. Phyllis was right. Christine's family, the one in this room, was the most important thing, not the past.

Boxing Day meant double-time wages, so Christine had signed up for the afternoon shift at the Center Island station.

"The Island's quiet today," Christine said to Pilkington as they sipped tea at the station kitchen. Fillingham had the day off; he was skiing with his sister Ella.

"It's always like this in the winter," he responded.

"Looks like Islanders are staying put to enjoy their Christmas presents and leftover ham."

"Fine by me."

"I like the way you decorated the station," she said, trying to make conversation. "Very festive." He nodded at her compliment. Pilkington was fussy about the upkeep of the station, since he spent most of his time in the building.

"Did you see the sweet loaves on the counter?" she asked. "Should I cut us a slice?" Pilkington was tall and slim, his Adam's apple protruding in his neck. He looked like he could use a meal.

"Did you check the fridge?" he said.

She shook her head.

"Cookies, a gingerbread house, mincemeat pies," he said. "Have your pick. All baked by the residents."

"That's so thoughtful of them." She got up to have a look.

"Richie Rich gave us gifts," he said.

She turned, "Fillingham?"

He nodded. "Check on top of your locker."

She hadn't noticed anything when she hung up her coat. Checking above, she smiled as she took down the box of caramel chocolates from a Yonge Street chocolatier. She loved anything with a caramel or butterscotch flavor. Sometimes, on shift, Fillingham would pull out a package of Rolos for them to share, both jawing on the chocolate-covered toffee until it dissolved. Beside the chocolates was a smaller box. Opening it, she gazed at the jade ring—the same one she had tried on at the Christmas bazaar and put back because she couldn't afford the indulgence. How did he know? Her eyes blinked with an onrush of tears at her partner's thoughtfulness.

After a few seconds, she asked Pilkington, "What did you get?"

"Scotch. Good Scotch. Fifteen dollars a bottle. He gave one to all six of us. Pretty generous. He did the same thing last year."

All she had bought for her partner was a mug that said *Harbor Police*, since it was his dream job to get into this elite agency. And they had given it to her free when she dropped by their harbor front station.

Inside the fridge, shelves were crammed with trays and plastic containers of desserts. She looked over at Pilkington. "What's your pick?"

They chose mincemeat pies and sat back down at the table after warming the pastries. As they ate, Christine asked her colleague about his Christmas. He had visited his parents. She described her family Christmas with her siblings, including the small turkey Phyllis had cooked, and that was the end of their conversation.

After washing her teacup, she said, "I need fresh air. How about I secure the buildings while you hold down the fort."

"Sure."

Everyone knew Pilkington rarely left the station to go out on patrol. Rumor was he'd been jumped one night while walking the beat, mobbed by young thugs, then hospitalized for a month. Ever since, he had been assigned desk duty.

Police lore was that Island duty was banishment for officers who were alcoholics, injured, cowards or had a temper. Christine had never directly asked Pilkington, Sergeant Bard or the other officers how they ended up on Island patrol. When she was transferred from the Women's Bureau to 52 Division, she naively assumed she was going to work at the downtown station. She'd forgotten that Toronto Island came under the purview of 52 Division. The sergeant there quickly let her know he would never allow her in a patrol car with a male officer and directed her to the ferry docks.

Outside, Christine squinted against the brightness of the afternoon sun reflecting off the flat swathes of snow. Stomping her feet to warm up, she headed to the patrol car, her breath puffing in small, gray-white clouds. As she waited for the windshield to defrost, she clapped her leather mitts together to keep the circulation going.

It was a novelty to be driving the Jeep. Fillingham usually drove. She had her license—all officers did—but since her family didn't own a car, she didn't drive much. The Island was a good place for a novice driver, since car traffic was limited to service vehicles, parks and recreation staff, school buses and police. She doubted she'd see another car on the path today. As she reversed out of the driveway with a lurch of gears, she mentally listed the houses she needed to check because they were abandoned and awaiting demolition or because the families were away on holidays. At the end of her car patrol, she'd stop by Mrs. Polotov's, inquire about her Christmas and more than likely receive a cup of tea and plate of shortbread.

First, she'd check the far end of the Island, Hanlan's Point, and wend her way eastward. En route, she'd rattle the locks at the change room on Manitou Beach and ensure no one was illegally squatting there or at the closed snack bar at Hanlan's Point. Most of these transgressions occurred in the summer, but she always checked anyway.

Driving along Lakeshore Avenue, she spied the yard-high chunks of ice deposited on Manitou Beach like giant ice cubes, making the view seem supernatural and otherworldly. Lake Ontario never froze completely; it was too large, and the current was constantly moving. Only the inner lagoons, harbor and ponds iced over. As she approached the Nature School, she tensed, remembering skating with Julie and Fillingham. She had pressed her skate edge hard, pushing herself faster until the air-piercing crack, the shock of cold water on her skin, the fluttering panic as she realized she was sliding into the water.

Then the bright line of red lace floating in the tea-green water, the small hand silhouetted behind.

She parked in the school's driveway and climbed the snowy steps to a classroom to check that it was locked. The stairs were hilly mounds, except for the cleared steps in front of the main door. After rattling the classroom door handle, she paused, hearing youthful voices nearby.

Following the sounds, she headed toward the lighthouse, the snow squeaking under her tread, her movements slowed by her heavy police boots, thick winter pants and wool coat. When she reached the red lighthouse door, she spotted bright snowsuits on the frozen lagoon to her right. The three boys looked about Wayne's age, maybe younger. They squatted on short wooden stools around a dark circle. Three fishing lines led into an ebony hole in the ice.

As she stepped carefully onto the ice, three heads swiveled toward her. They were Island kids, often seen fishing in the lagoon by Algonquin Island. The biggest one was Bruce, one of the Lankin boys from Ward's Island; he had been at the Christmas bazaar delivering sweet loaves baked by his mom.

Walking across the same frozen lagoon where she had skated with Fillingham and Julie was making her stomach flip-flop. Her eyes locked on the ice, monitoring it for variations in color and soft spots. People drowned on the Island more than you'd think, summer and winter, Islanders and tourists alike. The Island's history was full of stories of locals pulling people from the water, including sailors whose boats ran aground during storms.

Fillingham had told her that the only reason she had cracked through the ice was because she had landed near the pond's edge where the plants had broken through the frozen water. The rest of the lagoon where she was walking was six inches thick. Safe.

Still, she carefully placed one foot in front of the other in a direct beeline to the children. "Hi boys," she said when she arrived. "Catch anything?"

Bruce looked at her from underneath his navy and red hat. "Nah."

"How long have you been out?" she asked.

"Maybe an hour," he replied.

"Who are your friends, Bruce?" She tilted her head toward the two other boys.

He pointed with his elbow. "My brother Hank."

"George." The red scarf covering his lower face muffled the third boy's voice.

"You boys being careful on the ice?" she asked.

All three nodded as they huddled on their stools, fishing rods in hand.

"Your parents know where you are?" she asked.

"They know we're fishing," Bruce responded.

"You should always tell them your location. And wrap up before dark. You must be able to see which parts of the ice are safe to walk on."

She scanned the area, the filtration plant a hundred feet away, the leafless trees huddled around Trout Pond and the gray plank-board schoolhouse. "Fishing good here in the summer?" she asked.

The boys nodded. Above their respective scarves, she spied Bruce's lean face, Hank's blue eyes and runny nose, and George's brown eyes and freckled cheeks. He must be a red head.

"Were you fishing the night Jacob Nowak went missing?"

These were Island boys. Although they did not stay at the overnight Nature School, they attended the regular day school, which occupied the other half of the building. They had to have heard instantly when Jacob went missing.

The boys avoided her glance.

Anticipation fluttered her gut. "Hank, did you guys go fishing that night?"

Hank's eyes widened. He looked over at his brother.

Christine squatted beside the boy. "Hank, tell me if you were out that night. It's important."

Bruce said, "We were fishing off the side of the lagoon."

"Where exactly?" she asked.

"Toward Blockhouse Bay." Blockhouse Bay was about five hundred feet from where they were standing.

"How far up?"

His chin pointed north. "Between here and the American boats."

In the summer, Blockhouse Bay was lined with boats leasing dock space, many of them Americans or out-of-towners.

"Did you see anything unusual?" she asked.

"No," Bruce said.

A small, rocky island blocked her view north. She asked, "Did you hear anything?"

Bruce's eyes widened.

Bingo.

"What did you hear, Bruce?" she asked.

"Voices."

"Whose voices?"

"I didn't recognize them." He looked over at Hank, who nodded vigorously in affirmation.

"What were they saying?" she asked, regarding each boy.

"I couldn't tell." Hank turned to his brother. "Could you?"

Bruce shook his head.

"It must have been loud for you to hear a couple of hundred yards away."

"When it's quiet, you can hear people over the water. And they were yelling," Hank said.

"They?" Christine squatted beside Hank, her gloves on the ice to steady herself. "How many people did you hear?"

"Two?" Hank looked over at his brother. "Three?"

Bruce shrugged. "We heard a yell. And then it sounded like a different person was talking or yelling, and it went back and forth. Then the voices stopped."

"What time was that?"

"Twelve thirty," Bruce said.

"You're sure?" she asked.

"My dad went to bed at eleven thirty. Hank and I waited until midnight to sneak out of the house. George couldn't come. We're not supposed to go out on a school night, that's why we didn't tell anyone about it.

"How long were you there?"

"We left at one thirty."

"How do you know the time?" she asked.

"I have a watch. The numbers glow in the dark."

"Did you hear anything else from twelve thirty to one thirty?"

"One boat was having a party—we could hear people laughing and music. That was from the other direction."

"None of you heard anything after twelve thirty from this area?"

The brothers shook their heads in unison.

Thanking the boys, she pushed herself up off the ice. Arms akimbo, she half-slid, half walked to shore.

Wait until Fillingham heard that Jacob Nowak was not alone the night he disappeared.

She jogged down the gravel path back to the school. The sun was low on the horizon, the chill from the ground more noticeable as she quickly checked the rest of the school.

Her steps back to the police vehicle were quick, excited. The case was breaking.

As she started the car, she checked herself. She was assuming one voice had been Jacob's. It could have been residents out for a stroll, lovers quarreling, lost tourists or kids fishing. She was jumping to conclusions, probably because she was keen to find out what happened to Jacob. Her approach had to be objective, logical. On her next shift with Fillingham, she would see what he deduced from her conversation with the three boys. But really, could it be a coincidence that on the night Jacob drowned, angry voices were heard near the lagoon?

A plane rumbled overhead; Christine looked up at its white belly. People were returning from Christmas get-togethers or heading to the airport on holiday. The Island Airport would be fully staffed today because of the busy schedule. Maybe she could pay a visit, take another look at the photo of Hans Jansen and compare it to the one in her living room. With Phyllis uncommunicative about her first husband, Christine would have to do her own poking around. Maybe Christine could find a senior employee who had known Hans Jansen and put to rest her questions about the man who looked exactly like her father.

Driving onto the dunes at Hanlan's Point Beach, she headed toward the waterline. She dodged chunks of ice and driftwood as she steered north along the beach and passed the airport's fenced boundary. Sticking her head out the open window to assess for incoming planes, Christine gunned across a runway. The air traffic controllers were probably shaking their fists at her from the control tower that topped the terminal.

Last time, the airport manager had been expecting them; he had supervised the search for Jacob Nowak. She hoped he was amenable to an unannounced police visit.

Mr. Benson greeted her in the hallway outside his office. "What can I do for you today, Officer?" He was in a suit and tie, his brown hair mussed, as if he had been running his fingers through it. His perfunctory tone showed he was busy.

"We're clearing out files at the station and came across information about the Norwegian Air Force that flew out of here in 1941."

He smiled. "I remember them well. I was a teenager doing odd jobs around the airport, learning to fly myself."

"They were stationed at the Island Airport for a year?"

"More like eighteen months. One pilot almost plowed into a ferry during an attempted landing." He shook his head. "What a jerk that guy was. The next thing you know, they were heading to Muskoka, lock, stock and barrel. It was a shame. The rest of the squad was great."

"Do you remember a pilot named Hans Jansen?"

He nodded. "I do."

"Can you tell me about him?" She itched to grab her notebook, but she didn't want to stop the flow of words.

Mr. Benson leaned against the door frame of his office. "Nice guy. Always ready to help out—wash a plane, give the mechanics a hand, offer an aspiring pilot like me a flying lesson. And good at cards. He cleared out many a pocket, playing poker."

"Did he fraternize with the Canadian pilots who also trained at the airport?"

"Sometimes. The Norwegians hung out together—they were bunking across the channel at Fort York and spoke the same language—but all the pilots got along. Most of them spoke a little English, and they got better while they were here. At Christmas, the Canadian pilots took the Norwegians home for turkey dinner, given that the Nords were on their own."

"Did Hans have a family?"

"Pretty sure he did. He always carried a stick of wood in his pocket—carving toys for kids. I remember he made a whistle for his daughter."

"Did he marry a Canadian?"

"No. He was already married. Most of the squad had wives back home, although I think families were scattered after Germany invaded their country."

"Did Jansen have a girlfriend in Canada?"

Benson's chin went in. "I don't think so. The Norwegians were fun-loving guys but staunch Christians. They carried photos of their families in their wallets and cockpits. Inside their pockets were letters from their wives or their kids to remind them why they were doing such a high-risk job."

"None of the Norwegian men dated Canadian girls?"

He crossed his arms. "The single guys attended Island dances and music clubs, but if anything started up, it was short-lived. I don't recall any marriages." He glanced at his watch. "What's the police's interest in the NAF?"

She shrugged noncommittally. "Just background."

"They were heroes," Mr. Benson said. "Did you see the photo on the main floor?"

"Yes, I did. The pilot beside the plane—is that Hans Jansen?"

He nodded. "I was here when the photographer took that picture. The *Toronto Telegram* published an in-depth article on the squad."

Toronto Telegram. The name of the newspaper stamped on the back of the photo in Christine's living room. The photo must be from the article about the Norwegian Air Force. The man must be Hans Jansen—a man Phyllis professed not to know.

"Mr. Benson. Phone," a female voice called from inside the office.

"Do you know what happened to Jansen?" Christine asked quickly.

He shook his head. "Didn't hear from the pilots after they left. Just prayed that they all survived when they headed back to the war in '42."

She bid him goodbye and went back downstairs to the main floor. Standing in front of the photograph of Hans Jansen, she stared at his wide smile, broad shoulders and fair skin. Was he still alive? Could she be his illegitimate daughter? Was her mother lying about Thomas Lane, the war hero? And everything else she had told Christine about her father.

Chapter 13

Christine pointed to the top hat on Fillingham's head, imprinted with *Happy New Year* in glittery gold script. "You're going to the party like that?"

Her partner bounded over the countertop into the waiting area of the police station, managing to keep his hat on his head. He turned back to her. "You're going like that?"

Her dark uniform over a white blouse did seem drab for ushering out the last day of 1968. "We're on duty while we're there."

"I'm sure Mrs. Polotov's guests will not be checking the crease of our pants or the shine of our shoes." He walked over to the Christmas tree in the corner and pulled off a line of bushy silver garland. Entering the office again, this time through the hinged countertop, he commanded, "Bend."

She frowned at him but slowly cantilevered forward.

"Done!" he said.

She straightened, reaching for the prickly tinsel now bordering her police hat brim.

"Much better," he said, "except for the look on your face. We're going to a party! It's got to be better than sitting at the station staring at each other as the clock ticks down to shift end."

"I'm not drinking tonight," she said.

"Glad to see you're on the wagon.

"Ha-ha," she said sarcastically.

"Take me to the jelly rolls, shortbread cookies and cocktail sausages." He tilted his head. "And the female guests dying to make my acquaintance."

"I thought you were dating Julie." As soon as the words left her mouth, she itched to recall them. She didn't want to know anything about Julie and Fillingham's romance—it was none of her business.

"I'm like honeysuckle to butterflies."

Brrrriiiing!

Fillingham groaned. It was the direct line to the station—which meant an Islander had a complaint that would need a response. He snatched the receiver off the wall. "PC Fillingham. Center Island Police Station. Toronto Police." His expression brightened, and his head swiveled toward Christine. "Yes, she is here, Lisa from Records. It sounds like PW Lane has you doing her work for her." He laughed. "No problem. I do her work at the station, too."

"You do not!" Christine strode over and snatched the phone from his hand.

"Lisa," she said. "Thanks for getting back to me. Anyone at the Nature School show up in your search?" She listened for a minute. "Derek Mansfield." She looked at her partner.

"The paddling coach," Fillingham said.

"For assaulting a minor," Christine repeated, eyes widening as she met Fillingham's glance, "but the charge was withdrawn." She covered the phone receiver with her palm. "Do we want her to dig deeper? Check juvie records for Mansfield and the other staff?"

He nodded.

"That would be great, Lisa," Christine said. "I know it will take a bit of time. No problem. Let me know if you find something." She hung up.

He said, "I don't see Derek for this."

"Why? Because he's a sailor, like you?"

He shook his head. "Just doesn't seem the type." He headed toward his locker, where his coat hung. "Let's head out before anyone else phones."

Two minutes later, they were in the Jeep heading toward Ward's Island. "I play a mean Pin the Tail on the Donkey," he said.

"Your talents are endless."

He gave her a big smile. "It took seven months, but you're finally getting me."

An hour into the party, Christine glanced around the packed living room. People sat crammed four to a couch or two to a chair. Younger adults sat cross-legged on orange-tasseled pillows on the living room floor. Fillingham was chatting by the bookshelf with Mary Leonard, the old lady who grew marijuana in her herb garden. Christine could tell Mary was cracking him up. Women of all ages liked her partner—his appeal was universal. In another corner, an argument erupted about which Island baseball team had won the most season trophies. "Ooezes!" one man said.

"No way!" another guest countered. "The Dingbats have won the past three years in a row!"

In the kitchen, Mrs. Polotov filled the kettle with water. The room smelled like sugar. Christine spotted the round trays of desserts on the kitchen table.

"Is it against house rules to have a second butter tart?" Christine asked.

The older woman smiled as she placed the kettle on the burner of the antiquated stove. "Have three, love, if you like. You're a growing girl."

"Let's hope not. I'm already six feet." Christine leaned over the table and chose a tart.

"I would have asked Hawk to join us tonight," Mrs. Polotov said.

Christine turned toward the Islander, hand clutching the dessert.

"But he went back home after the Christmas bazaar." Mrs. Polotov crossed her arms; her red and silver shawl slid down her shoulders to her elbows.

Voices from the living room were singing an off-key version of Nat King Cole's "Happy New Year."

"Is…is there work for him on the Island in the winter?" Christine had to raise her voice to be heard above the singers.

Mrs. Polotov shook her head. "Nothing until Centreville opens in late spring." The old woman's veiny hand touched Christine's sleeve. "He was crazy about you, love. You said no. He had to move on." With a pat, she moved out of the kitchen.

Christine waited by the kitchen table until she regained her composure. She promised herself that she wouldn't fall apart or drink like a madwoman, like she had at the bazaar. It had been months since she and Hawk were together. She was the one who had ended their romance, more or less, when she refused to make their relationship public. She would make the same decision today.

Dumping the rest of the butter tart into the garbage, she pasted a smile on her face and returned to the living room, her eyes searching for Fillingham to signal it was time to leave. It was ten thirty, and they were catching the eleven o'clock ferry back to the city. She'd had enough of this party. And of 1968. It was time to welcome a new year.

"You're awfully quiet," Fillingham said as the police vehicle headed toward the Center Island ferry dock.

She shrugged, not answering, as she stared at the cottony snowflakes illuminated in the twin beams of the Jeep's headlights. When they arrived at the dock, Fillingham parked close to the ramp;

few people would exit the ferry at this time, aside from their replacement, Pilkington.

"The ferry's late," Fillingham said as they waited in the car. "My New Year's Eve party started three hours ago, and I still have to change into my tux."

After a pause, he asked, "Any plans for tonight?"

"As I said before at the station—no."

"Why don't you come with Julie and me to the RCYC party on George Street?"

"No." Her tone was definite.

"C'mon. It's New Year's Eve."

"I'm fine." Squinting through the passenger window, she searched for the ferry lights in the inner harbor.

He tapped her shoulder; she turned to look at him.

"I know how to cheer you up," he said.

"How?"

"I have good news."

She waited.

"I paid off your debt."

She sat up straight. "You what?"

"George Ray. I cleared your account with him."

"What are you talking about?" Her voice was loud.

"Sixteen, relax." He gave a wide smile. "It's good news. You don't owe that blood-sucking loan shark anything. You don't have to pay his exorbitant interest or the principal anymore. I've covered it for you."

After a few ticks of her watch, she stepped out of the car and slammed the door so hard, the vehicle shuddered. She stomped off toward the dock.

"Christine!"

Fillingham's police boots thumped behind her on the shoveled path.

She spun around so he almost ran into her. "How dare you!"

"What?" he asked, arms wide.

"How dare you interfere with my life!"

"By interfere, you mean save you from financial penury?"

"That's not the point."

"Lane," he said, his voice quieter, "the guy was taking you and your family for a ride. That one-thousand-dollar loan was going to cost you four, five, maybe ten times that amount by the time Ray finished with you."

"That doesn't matter!" She stepped forward, towering over him. "The loan is *my* problem—not yours." She thumped her chest with a mittened fist. "You had no right!"

"I have no right to help you? You'd rather live hand-to-mouth, constantly worrying that the brass will find out about your mom's gambling and your illegal loan from a Montreal syndicate."

"I am in charge of my family. Me! Not you!"

His face was mottled red. "I am trying to help you and your mom, but you're too stubborn to realize it." His finger jabbed the air. "You will never get out of debt with the interest Ray is charging. Your sister will never go to university. Your brother will never get elite baseball training. And you'll never move to a bigger apartment."

She flinched at each of his points. "That's my problem."

"No, it's your family's problem."

The mournful bleat of the ferry interrupted them; they turned to look at the boat chugging toward them, blue and white lights twinkling its arrival.

Christine swallowed. She had to tamp down her emotions. Between her resurgent feelings about Hawk and her anger at her partner, she felt completely unstable.

She waited a few seconds. Then, in a calmer tone, she said, "I don't want to be beholden to you. To anyone."

He looked at her, his mouth an angry line.

She continued, "I don't want to owe you anything. I don't want you to expect anything from me."

"Expect anything!" he yelled. His hands briefly touched his head before extending into the air. "What the hell would I expect from you, Christine?"

She crossed her arms. "I'm not owing you."

"Jesus Christ. What do you think I'm going to do—make you my slave for the day? Ask you back to my place for a nightcap?"

"I...I don't know what you'd ask me to do."

"Do I look like I need to pay for companionship?" he roared. He walked several steps away, then quickly came back and stood in front of her. "Do you think I paid the debt so I could make you my personal call girl? Is that how warped your thinking is? After being partners for the past year, almost getting killed last summer and solving Ginny Rogers' murder, this is your conclusion about my character?"

He was making her feel ridiculous. "No. Not when you put it like that."

The ferry's engine whirred in reverse, followed by a clink as the gate unlocked and the metal ramp lowered onto the dock.

"You know what," he said, "pay me back, don't pay me back. I don't care!" He threw his hands up in the air. "From the moment I met you, you've been a burr in my side."

"That's because—"

"Because what? Men have been assholes to you? Well, welcome to the real world where men and women act like jerks. Most of us get over it and move on."

"Geoffrey," she said softly.

He glared at her, his arms twitching by his side.

"I've set up my life," she said, "so that I am not dependent on a man. Especially after my stepfather. That's all."

"How's that working for you?" Fillingham turned and hailed Pilkington, who was heading toward them from the ferry.

Christine waited until her partner had boarded before she headed onto the ferry and entered the warmth of the inside main cabin. Fillingham was elsewhere on the boat, freezing himself outside or maybe up with the captain, since he knew all the ferry staff. She sat on the wooden bench, staring at the lines of orange life jackets hanging from the ceiling like rows of pillows. Her partner thought he was being kind. She understood that, but her finances and her family were none of his business. Like a high-and-mighty savior with deep pockets, he had swooped in without asking her what she thought, just like he had bought her the expensive jade ring; he expected gratitude, like a lord with his subjects.

When the ferry bumped to a stop, she trudged the length of the cabin to the lowered ramp outside. The ferry worker slouched against the bow, waiting for her to disembark, mumbling "Happy New Year," as she strode off the boat.

Fillingham was long gone, roaring away in his Beaumont to his tony party.

Heading across the parking lot to the streetcar stop, she tried to quash her self-pity. So what if she was by herself on New Year's Eve, abandoned by Hawk and a disgruntled Fillingham, heading home on her own to a darkened apartment. Maybe her mom and Wayne would still be awake when she arrived home, watching the countdown at Times Square on the television.

"Christine Lane!" a deep voice growled.

Christine jumped, startled. A bulky figure in a parka stood thirty feet away, face shaded by the lowered hood.

"You need to back off," the voice said.

"Who are you?" she asked, her hand unlatching her purse, where she kept an extra billy.

He walked toward her, imposing with his six-foot height, broad shoulders and large girth. They faced each other in a shadowy corner of the parking lot, a hundred feet from the road.

She scanned the area for partygoers or lovers heading toward the warmth of a restaurant before the midnight countdown. No one.

The man pulled down his hood to reveal a jowled, unshaven face with tousled hair. It was Roy's father, Mark O'Neil. What was he doing here?

"You've been pestering my son." His voice was flat and accusatory.

She thought back to the memorial, to Roy's sullen face, his glance refusing to meet hers. "I..." The word came out as a squawk. She cleared her throat. "In what way?"

"You've been asking him about that Jacob kid."

She wanted to respond, "So?" but she could feel the menace emanating from him. She had to be careful—she had no backup. "Mr. O'Neil, we've been asking all of Jacob's classmates questions to help with the investigation."

"What investigation?" His arms opened widely. "The kid drowned." He sounded like Deputy Chief Darlow.

"We are making sure we have all the bases covered so we understand what happened."

His heavy galoshes thumped forward several steps until he was ten feet away. "You're not covering the bases with my son. I never gave permission for you to interview him."

"It wasn't an interview."

He came closer. "My son is under eighteen. You need a parent in the room if you talk to him. I checked." He pointed at her. "If I hear that one of you pigs has talked to him again, I'm calling the newspaper to report how Policewoman Christine Alexandra Lane is illegally picking on my kid."

He knew her middle name. The hair on her arms rose.

O'Neil said, "Stop trying to dig up dirt on Roy. Keep poking around and you're going to find something you don't like. Ask your brother Wayne what I'm talking about."

"What do you mean? Why do I need to talk to Wayne?"

Without answering, he turned and headed toward a row of parked cars.

She quickly headed in the other direction, her heart pounding, away from the isolation of the parking lot toward the road. Heading up Bay Street, she hunched her shoulders against the wind, constantly checking behind her for a husky man in a parka. Groups of raucous celebrants made their way to parties in pairs and straggling groups. Christine prayed that the King Street streetcar would be waiting at her stop.

It wasn't. As she stood there shivering, she reflected on her disastrous night. First, Mrs. Polotov's remarks about Hawk, then Fillingham's grandiose payment of her mom's debt. The icing on the cake was O'Neil's threats. And she would probably celebrate the first minutes of 1969 alone in a streetcar.

And what the heck had Roy's father meant? *Ask your brother what I'm talking about.*

"Happy New Year, Mrs. Bowler," Christine said to Lakeview School's secretary, handing her a cyclamen plant that Christine had received from an Islander. It was Wayne and Donna's first day back after the Christmas Break.

Mrs. Bowler stood up, smiling. "You didn't have to do that, Christine." Lakeview's secretary was a plant fanatic. The office looked like a tropical plant exhibit from Allan Gardens; every available surface greened with spider plants and blossoming cacti. "Such a lovely color." Mrs. Bowler gazed at the fuchsia petals as she found a place for the plant on a window ledge.

Christine said, "I'm having a small party for Wayne's birthday, and he wants to invite Patrick Williamson. But I don't have their new number since they moved."

"They didn't move, dear," Mrs. Bowler said. "They're in the same house." The phone rang, and she raised a finger for Christine to wait as she answered. After she hung up, she added, "Patrick transferred to St. Vincent de Paul."

"On Roncesvalles?"

The secretary nodded.

"Do you know why they left?" Christine asked.

Mrs. Bowler shrugged. "Some parents think Catholic schools have more discipline."

"Isn't Holy Family closer?"

The phone rang again. Mrs. Bowler nodded in response to Christine's question and answered the phone. She waved as Christine made her way out.

Why would Patrick go to a Catholic school farther away? Holy Family was around the corner. And why transfer in the first place? As her boots crunched the salted sidewalks, Christine considered heading over to St. Vincent's. Maybe she could find Patrick in the crowd of children ambling home and have a chat with him as they walked. It wouldn't be an interview. She'd just ask him one question: Why had he left Lakeview Public School?

Christine exited the school through the front door and headed home. The hulking figure of Mr. O'Neil flashed across her mind. Would the Williamson family complain if she spoke to Patrick without their consent? She had to be careful—Deputy Darlow was keeping tabs on her.

The bunkmates in the Nature School were the key. She just had to figure out how to get them to talk. Christine had already spoken to Wayne again. At first, she wasn't sure whether she should mention her conversation with Mark O'Neil, but when Wayne grew irritated at her questions, she told him what happened in the parking lot.

"I know something about Jacob?" Wayne had said incredulously as she sat across from him at breakfast, his eyes wide. "That's what Roy's dad said?"

Christine nodded.

He pushed his cereal bowl aside. "I was at the Island for one day! One day! I hardly knew Jacob. He didn't sit near me in class. I just knew him from baseball. On the Island, I didn't even see him until we went to bed."

"So you don't have any information about Jacob?" she asked.

"No!" His tone was emphatic.

"Did you see any of the staff talking to Jacob? Singling him out?"

He frowned. "I told you. I didn't see him. We went for a hike and then a canoe ride and then had a fire. He wasn't even in my group."

"Why would Mr. O'Neil say that you knew something?"

"Maybe to get you to stop bugging everyone."

After the conversation with Wayne, Patrick and Roy were next on the list to be interviewed. Right now, Roy was a no-go. She didn't want another visit from the deputy or O'Neil. But maybe Fillingham could speak to Patrick. A friendly hello. He could pretend he was visiting the school for a safety talk or say he recognized Patrick from the Island school visit. Fillingham would interview Patrick if she asked, now that he was no longer mad at her. They'd made up since their fight on New Year's Eve.

Fight wasn't the right word—it hadn't been a lovers' quarrel. At first, she had been furious at Fillingham, then upset that they had disagreed, then enraged all over again at her partner's presumption that he could butt into her life. All New Year's Day, she considered his payment of the debt, turning it over in her mind. She concluded she had a right to be offended; her family was her business, and she didn't need to be rescued. But as the day went on, a trickle of hope dribbled into her thoughts. With George Ray's loan repaid, she could reimburse Fillingham at a normal bank interest rate, instead of Ray's exorbitant fee. The debt would be paid in a fraction of the time. Her family could move out of their cramped apartment before her siblings reached high school. They could set money aside for Wayne's sports training and an education fund for her siblings.

As a peace offering, Christine brought an apple pie that her mom had baked the previous day in to work. Phyllis had always been good in the kitchen. On her own at sixteen, she had learned rudimentary cooking skills. Baking was something she did for relaxation or if she was in a good mood when they had enough money for the ingredients. One of Christine's fondest memories was baking chocolate chip cookies with her mom and Wayne, Donna in her highchair nearby, a rare moment of familial fun during the tough years with Eddie.

Christine wasn't as adept at baking as Phyllis, but she had joined her mom in preparing the pie. Phyllis rolled the pastry while Christine mixed the filling. Shaking cinnamon over the sliced apples, Christine told her mom that Fillingham had paid the gambling debt.

"What?" Her mom froze, hands clutching a ball of flour-dusted dough.

"He paid the loan to George Ray," Christine repeated.

"All of it?" Phyllis asked.

Christine nodded.

Phyllis grabbed Christine's hands, her fingers slippery with butter. "The debt is gone? Completely gone?"

"We have to pay him back."

Her mom waved her hands in the air. "I know. I know. But George Ray." She shuddered. "He's a frightening man."

Grabbing the rolling pin, Phyllis said, "Let's make this pie for Geoffrey. Such a wonderful man." She rolled the ball of pastry flat. "What a considerate, lovely, lovely man. Bless him. God bless him."

The next day, Christine took the apple pie into work and placed it on the kitchen table in front of Fillingham. He had been quiet on the drive to the station from the ferry—not angry or surly—but she could tell he was still miffed.

"For me?" he said.

"Yes," she said, gesturing to the strips of lightly browned pastry crisscrossing the top.

"Did you make it?"

"With my mom."

He crossed his arms, regarding her. "Isn't that a tad tradition-al...making food for a man?"

He wasn't making this easy. She pressed her lips together to keep silent.

"You're okay with pandering to me in this way?"

She felt a flare of anger. He had been out of line, and here she was making amends. She felt like taking the pie back, or even better, throwing it in his face. But she thought of Phyllis, humming last night as she washed the dishes. And how good it would feel to stop her biweekly visits to that dumpy Yonge Street bar to hand her wages to George Ray.

"My mom and I thank you for what you did," Christine managed, her voice low and controlled. "We will pay you back, every payday, with interest."

He said nothing but leaned over the pie, inhaling its cinnamon-apple scent.

"I know you are being kind," Christine said in a speech she had rehearsed that afternoon. "You didn't have to use your money on us. You didn't have to get involved with someone like Ray. So thank you. You're a good person."

His blue eyes regarded her. "Too good for you, Lane." Then, as if the knob of an oil lamp had been turned up, he brightened. "Let's put the pie in the oven to warm and come back after target practice to eat." He had hammered a wooden circle to a tree in the station's backyard, the bull's eye painted black, encircled by a ring of red, then blue.

A wave of relief rushed over her. He wasn't mad anymore. She couldn't stand Fillingham's cold treatment. His perpetual sunniness was needed to get her through the day. Clearing her throat, she said, "How many times do I have to hit the bull's eye with my snowball before you concede I have better aim?"

His finger pointed into the air. "There's a new game in town, Sixteen!" He went to his locker, banged around inside, then held up a small ax by its wooden handle. "Ta-da!"

"You're chopping wood?" she asked.

"We're throwing axes at the target," he said as if the answer was obvious.

"An ax?" she parroted. "Like they do in the circus?"

"You're thinking of knives, Sixteen. And in the circus, you aim at people, not a wooden bull's eye. What I have in mind is more like a lumberjack competition." He threw the axe in the air and caught it by the handle. "Five throws each. Three rounds. High score gets the biggest piece of pie."

She shook her head in wonder at her partner's idea and then placed the pie in the small oven. Fillingham was always game for a little competition: a bike race, wrestling match, target practice or a snowball fight.

But Fillingham was in for a surprise. Her throwing arm was strong and accurate, not from baseball training like Wayne, but from shot-put and javelin. She had come in third in the city javelin championships in eleventh grade. Sure, a seven-foot spear wasn't the same as an ax, but when you had both power and technique, she was definitely securing the biggest slice of pie.

Chapter 14

"AAAAAAAAAAH!" Donna's scream came from outside the apartment.

Christine galloped down the front hallway, threw open the door and stumbled as she hopped over the motionless, furry thing on the doormat.

Wayne and Donna huddled together by the stairwell, faces pulled into horrified expressions. The dead rat at Christine's feet stared at her with sightless black eyes above two protruding yellow teeth, arms and legs frozen in half-extension.

"I opened the door," Donna said, voice squeaky with alarm, "and it was there! Dead!"

"How did it get into the building?" Christine wondered.

"It was put there," Wayne said, voice flat.

"Who would put a dead rat at our door?" Christine asked.

He didn't respond, just turned toward the staircase.

"Wayne, what's going on?"

He took a step down the stairs.

"If this is your friend's idea of a joke," she said, "it's not funny."

He took another step down.

"Wayne." She walked over to him. "Do you know how the rat got here?"

"I don't know," he said, gaze down. "We're going to be late for school."

Shaking her head, she let her siblings leave. Back in the apartment, she pulled on rubber washing gloves to dispose of the rodent. Why was a rat around in winter? It must have survived by raiding garbage cans and apartment dumpsters.

And why would Wayne say someone put the rat at their door? Could a tenant have placed it there? The occupants of their three-story apartment building included two elderly couples, several female office workers, married couples and then the Derringer and Shultz families. Christine and her mom were on polite terms with all the residents.

It couldn't be the landlord. It wasn't his style. Plus, he knew she was a police officer. And what would be his motivation? She paid the rent punctually the first of the month. After spending her childhood sneaking out of apartments at midnight to avoid paying the overdue rent, she was diligent about paying it on time. And it certainly wasn't a message from George Ray. Fillingham had paid their entire debt.

Did Wayne know the culprit? Was it the Derringers' boy, Tommy—had they had a falling-out? Or the twins? Could it be Roy from Wayne's class—or worse, his father? But she hadn't gone near Roy since O'Neil cornered her in the harbor parking lot.

Was the message for her—someone from her past she had arrested? A person who didn't like the police? Who didn't like policewomen?

Or was it simply that after living outside all winter, the rat had sneaked inside the apartment and died due to age, disease or hypothermia?

After disposing of the rat in the outside garbage bin, Christine decided Wayne needed a break—they all did. Her siblings were always game for fun: a circus, a parade, a visit to a playground. This weekend, she would take them to see *The Love Bug* showing at the

Parkdale Theatre and splurge on a tub of popcorn for them to share. Her wallet had a few more bills in it now that George Ray was out of the picture. They could use the distraction of watching a loveable white Volkswagen race its competition and, despite being the underdog, win the day.

"They wouldn't talk to me," Fillingham said as the patrol car ascended the Center Island Bridge.

"Who?" she asked.

"The kid—Patrick Williamson—and his mother."

Christine sat up in the passenger seat. "Where did you see them?"

"You told me he attended St. Vincent de Paul, so I hung around before school this morning until I spotted him."

"You remembered what he looked like?"

"Sure." He parked in the station driveway and cranked the emergency brake. "That morning when we saw him with Jacob, he was trying to act cocky like Roy—but he couldn't pull it off. He's a follower, not a ringleader."

"What happened?" she asked.

"I wasn't in uniform, so he didn't recognize me until I introduced myself." He pushed his door open. As she followed him into the station, he said over his shoulder, "He was okay. It was his mother who reacted. As soon as I said I was following up on the Jacob Nowak case, she yanked Patrick by the collar, said, 'We have nothing to say,' and hauled him into school."

They hung their coats in their respective lockers. He continued, "I waited for her to come back out, thinking that she didn't want to talk in front of Patrick, but she must have exited the school through a different door."

"Are they afraid of the police?" she asked.

He headed over to the fridge with a paper bag stamped with the logo of a Front Street restaurant. "They're scared of something. I'm not sure it's us."

After forty-five minutes of routine jobs—checking the log, filing incident reports, sweeping the floor, phoning an Islander back about a shed that had been damaged—Fillingham sat down in a desk chair. "I forgot to tell you. I spoke with the complainant who charged Derek Mansfield, the paddling coach."

Christine was sitting diagonally from her partner at the second office desk. "What did the complainant say?"

"I got an earful. This guy says Mansfield tried to kill his kid at canoe camp."

"Really?" She turned her chair to face him.

"The father says Mansfield abandoned the boy overnight on an island in the middle of the lake. So he got 'Mansfield's ass fired,' and that's a quote, from his camp job. The dad called the police. The camp director persuaded Dad to drop the charges to avoid the hassle of court and gave him a full refund for the camp."

"Do you think Mansfield said or did something to Jacob to make him leave?" she asked.

"Why would he do that?" he asked.

"Why would he leave a child in the middle of a lake?" She paused, then answered her own question. "It could be negligence. Or maybe he just forgot the kid. Or...or maybe he did something to the boy. Maybe he did something to Jacob, too."

Fillingham's eyebrows went up in disbelief.

"The Island boys were fishing that night," she continued. "They heard voices down by the lagoon near the lighthouse. More than one voice. It could have been Mansfield and Jacob."

He opened his arms wide. "The paddling coach is a serial child killer, is that it? Or a guy who messes with kids?"

"Possibly," she answered. "You've got a soft spot for Mansfield."

"Tim works his charm on you," he said.

She shook her head. "Hardly. We could verify Tim's story with Miss Phillips. I have a suspicion she will confirm his alibi. Although we don't know what he did the rest of the night."

"We need to talk to Mansfield," Fillingham said.

All these people to interview, except she and Fillingham were supposed to be minding their own business. They did their inquiries in their off hours or during slack time on shift. Still, her stomach had a permanent knot of worry, tightening with each new action in their investigation.

"I made a few phone calls myself," Christine said.

"And?" He pushed his foot against his desk and sent his chair rolling across the wooden floor, braking with his heels in front of her.

"We have to be careful," she said. "We're not supposed to be asking questions about the Nowak investigation."

"In for a dime, in for a dollar." He tilted his head. "Who'd you call?"

"Photos of previous staff are in the school's foyer. I spoke with three teachers who used to work at the Nature School. They were very positive about the outdoor program."

"Did they mention Derek Mansfield?" he asked.

"Two of them worked with him. Said he was great. Tim got good reviews too, although one said he flirted too much with visiting teachers, which wasn't surprising."

"Keep your man in line, Lane," he teased.

She ignored him. "They said nothing about staff being too friendly with students—were horrified when I hinted at it."

"Anyone get bad press?"

"No one had anything nice to say about the principal, Mr. Albany. He's out of sync with the staff, more focused on his career. The Island School is a stepping stone to bigger and better things for him. Teachers complain he chews them out publicly, which doesn't endear them to him."

"Maybe that's why he's forbidden staff from talking to us—he's covering up something," Fillingham surmised.

"With a lawsuit pending, Albany's directive is not surprising," she said.

He stood up. "Let's go over to the school right now."

"And do what?"

"Something fishy is going on. We have to sniff out the source of the stink."

She stayed seated. "I'm not sure that's a good idea."

"Why not?" he asked, heading to the back. He reached into his metal locker and retrieved his wool police jacket.

She stood up. "Staff is not supposed to speak with us. It could look like harassment."

His eyebrows pushed together in disbelief. "Who are we harassing?"

Her hands went to her hips. "The people we've interviewed could accuse us of interfering; we could get in deep trouble. If Patrick's mom complains like Mark O'Neil did, we'll be in the doghouse. And not just with Sergeant Bard. I told you, O'Neil was waiting for me on New Year's Eve. He wants us to back off. He's not a fun guy to meet in the dark, and I don't want a repeat. Plus, Deputy Darlow personally told me to back off the case."

"Your points reinforce my conclusion that the situation stinks. There *is* dirt to dig up, or we wouldn't be getting these reactions from the different parties."

"I, for one, would like to keep my job." She crossed her arms. "Principal Albany will be suspicious if we ask questions, as will the investigators from 52 Division." The lead investigator, Fenwick, with his close-set eyes and thin mouth, did not like anyone messing with his cases. She found that out the hard way in the Ginny Rogers' homicide when he almost broke her wrist.

Fillingham pulled her navy wool coat off the hook of her open locker and held it out to her. "How about we visit your good friend Tim at the school. A social call."

She groaned. "Why?"

"Just a friendly chat. Maybe we can offer to teach a winter safety lesson. Ice safety. Nothing to do with Jacob Nowak."

"I went through the ice, remember?" Christine said.

"Fine. I'll lead the discussion."

"What are you hoping to find?" she asked.

His arms opened wide. "Something. Anything. How about an explanation as to why a kid who doesn't swim ends up in the water at midnight with a baseball shoe tied to his wrist?"

When the partners arrived at the school, students were returning from a hike, voices grumbling about the taste of the bitter bark tea they had made in the bush.

Fillingham sighted Mansfield in a Shetland sweater and a gray wool toque. "Derek!"

Mansfield smiled in recognition, moved away from the stream of children ascending the main entrance stairs and headed toward the two officers at the picnic bench.

"It's better if I speak with him alone," Fillingham said to Christine.

"I'm staying," she said.

Derek greeted them, his cheeks above his black stubble pinked from the fresh air. "What's up?" he asked. He swiveled to watch the last chain of students enter the building.

"Tell us about Samuel Goldrich," Fillingham said.

Derek's head snapped back toward them.

"We've been doing background checks on staff," Fillingham said.

"If you checked up on me," Derek said, "you know I don't have a criminal record."

Christine nodded. "True."

"I'm a good teacher," Derek said.

"That's what other staff say," Christine commented.

"So what happened with Samuel Goldrich?" Fillingham asked again.

"The kid was a spoiled jerk," Derek said.

The officers waited.

Derek gave a long sigh. "Samuel was a twelve-year-old signed up for a two-week paddling camp. God knows why. He had no interest in the outdoors. He wouldn't do anything: make a fire, set the table for meals, play games. He avoided swimming because he didn't like getting wet. Even though it was a canoe camp, he refused to paddle. So he sat in the boat with his arms crossed while everyone else did the work. Nothing was good enough: the food, weather, showers, outdoor toilet or the group activities. Even the campers got fed up with him."

"How did he end up in on an island by himself?" Christine asked.

Derek looked at her.

"I spoke with the dad," Fillingham said.

Derek snorted. "He's a piece of work, too." He paused. "It's five days into camp, the middle of July. About twenty-five of us, campers and leaders, paddle to this island to pick blueberries to make blueberry cobbler back at the kitchen. While the kids are in the bush filling their pails with berries, Samuel is sitting on a rock. As usual, he's refusing to take part. After an hour, groups start paddling back to camp, and there's just one canoe left. Samuel refuses to get into it—says he wants one with a padded bench. My canoe's the last one on the island—and it doesn't have upholstered seating. I spend an hour trying to convince him to come—begging him, bribing him—but he just sits on the rock, cross-legged, shaking his head at my suggestions, expecting me to paddle back to camp to get the other canoe and come back for him. It was a twenty-minute paddle, one-way. Eventually, I lost my patience and told him to haul his ass into the boat. He told me he didn't take orders from the help."

Derek exhaled, shaking his head. "And that was it. I'd had enough. It wasn't right, but I told him that if he didn't get in my canoe, the last canoe returning to camp, then he could stay where he was. He said, 'Fine,' and I left him there."

"For how long?" Christine asked.

"Overnight."

Fillingham snorted a laugh. "I guess he enjoyed that."

Raising his eyebrows, Derek said, "The bugs got him pretty bad." He put one booted foot on the bench seat of the picnic table. "I was wrong, of course, to leave him. No matter how much the kid deserved it or was an asshole. I was younger then—more hot-headed. The director fired me. The dad came screaming into the parking lot in his Mercedes to pick up his son. I went over to apologize. He jabbed a finger in my face and said he's calling the police, that he was going to sue my ass and the camp's ass."

"Did he?" Fillingham asked.

"In the end, he dropped the charges, because it was going to cost him ten grand in lawyer fees to prove negligence, and I guess his kid wasn't worth it." Derek shrugged. "Who enrolls a kid in camp when they know he'll hate it?"

"When did you start at the school board?" Fillingham asked.

"I got a job with another camp and then came down to Toronto to work on the harbor tour boats. I got hired by the Toronto Board about five years ago."

"Did you have any interaction with Jacob Nowak when Lakeview School was at the Island?" she asked.

"I looked at the photo provided by the police. I don't remember him. There were sixty kids that week. A group of them were out for a short paddle that first night; we take them in turns. I don't recall speaking with a child that looked like Jacob. He didn't paddle in my canoe or with my group." Derek tilted his head toward the sheds east of the school. "If that's all, I have to head out. I'm on wood-chopping duty for tonight's fire."

The officers went inside the school to look for Tim. They checked the meeting room where students sprawled on bean bags and extra-large pillows, then headed toward the office. Letting her partner pull ahead, Christine perused the photos in the long hallway: school groups paddling on Lake Ontario, three boys sticking their heads out of a red pup tent, two girls catching maple tree sap in a metal pail. Incredible learning happened here, she reminded herself. Jacob's drowning made you forget that.

Fillingham cleared his throat; she looked over. He was halfway down the hall, in front of the caretaker's work closet. He jerked his head for her to join him.

"What's up?" she asked when she reached him.

"Step inside." One arm gestured to the caretaker's room.

She followed him into the small room housing a double sink, metal pails, brooms, mops and other cleaning equipment. It smelled like washroom disinfectant.

He pointed to the right. "Look behind the drapes."

Pulling the striped curtain aside, she stepped into a shelved closet with stacked soap bars, toilet paper and paper towel rolls. She was about to let the drape fall when she spied cardboard boxes behind the detergents and paper products. Flashlight in hand, she stepped deeper into the space. Inside these boxes were cigarette cartons, candy, chocolate bars, potato chips and stacks of *Playboy* magazines in individual plastic sleeves.

Quickly, she joined Fillingham in the hallway.

"What's the story?" she asked. "Is he stealing?"

He shook his head. "He's selling the stuff to the kids."

Closing the door to the janitor's room, the partners continued to the office with the unspoken agreement to keep their find to themselves, for now.

The principal wasn't in, thank goodness. He might have shooed them away. The secretary said they could find Tim in the cafeteria, prepping for dinner. Retracing their steps down the hallway, Fillingham said softly, "Quite the contraband stash."

"Does it connect with the Jacob Nowak investigation?" she asked.

"Don't know."

"Just like we don't know if Derek Mansfield's temper makes him a suspect."

Fillingham said, "The janitor's stash hasn't been discovered, or they would have fired him. Let's see if we can use that to our advantage."

In the large cafeteria, a handful of students were setting cutlery and dishes on the rectangular wooden tables. Christine spotted Tim setting out bins of water glasses.

Fillingham said, "Wave at your boyfriend. See if he knows anything about Patrick Williamson or about the goodies in the caretaker's closet. I'll go look for Mr. Black Market himself."

Tim greeted Christine with a small smile, his brown hair pushed flat at the crown from wearing a toque, rugged-looking in his sweater and cargo pants. He was attractive, she had to admit, even if he was a smooth operator.

"Two minutes before the hungry horde arrives," he warned.

"Just a friendly visit," she responded, making herself smile widely. "How are things?"

He hauled a yellow tub of rattling ceramic bowls onto a table. "It's going," he said. He began distributing the bowls in a row along the table's length. "As you know, it was slow in the fall because schools canceled. And there's been mutterings about closing the program and reassigning staff." He glanced briefly up at her, then returned to his task. "But things have picked up."

"Any new thoughts about Jacob Nowak?" she asked, her tone light. She wasn't supposed to talk to Tim about the case, and she was being too direct, but she only had him for another minute.

He opened a cupboard on the side wall and extracted a tray of mugs. "What's there to say?" His back was toward her. "The kid left the building. He went into the water. He couldn't swim. He drowned. It was a terrible accident." He glanced over at the students setting the tables, ensuring they were out of earshot.

He faced her with his tray of mugs. "It's all very sad, Christine, PW Lane, but I have nothing to say. I've been told not to speak about the case because of legal proceedings with the board. I'm moving on. I suggest you do the same."

A crowd of students waited by the cafeteria entrance, and he gestured them in.

Shouldering her way through the mass of ten-year-olds, she exited the cafeteria. Down the hallway, she spied Fillingham speaking with a slim man in his late thirties who was wearing blue overalls and leaning on a mop propped in a metal bucket.

When Christine reached them, Fillingham introduced her to Sal Bagni, a staff janitor. His front teeth were crooked, angled into each other, and his hair was receding. Fillingham described the stash he had found in the caretaker's closet. Bagni sputtered his ignorance until Fillingham threatened to speak to the principal about his discovery.

Motioning them into the janitor's closet, Bagni confessed to a side business of selling gum, candy and assorted vice items like cigarettes and men's magazines to interested students. But no drugs or alcohol—he was adamant about that. And he never looted the school's inventory; he bought the products himself.

Fillingham said he was only interested in the week that Jacob Nowak went missing. Bagni nodded enthusiastically and said he made a few sales on that day. He remembered, because the rest of the week was a bust as the students went home the next day and the school was empty for the next two months because of cancelations.

A trio of girls had bought gum and chocolate. He sold cigarettes and a copy of *Hustler* to two boys—he doesn't know their names, but they were in the same room as the boy who disappeared.

Christine wondered if Wayne had purchased anything, but Bagni's physical description sounded like Roy and Patrick. Plus, Wayne hadn't brought money on the trip.

On the night Jacob left, Bagni had been on the three-to-eleven shift. He met Patrick and Roy in the boys' washroom at nine forty-five to deliver their items and take payment. At eleven, Bagni was on the last ferry home. This had been verified by ferry staff. When he returned the next day on afternoon shift, Jacob had been missing since that morning.

"Did you hear or see anything on your way to the ferry that night?" Christine asked.

He shook his head. "I drove the golf cart to the ferry. I leave it at the dock for the day shift janitor. No one was around. A few sailboats on Blockhouse Bay had their lights on, but I can't hear anything over the cart engine."

"Any students near the lighthouse?" Fillingham asked.

Bagni said, "Didn't see anyone, but wasn't particularly looking."

"Do you remember seeing Jacob Nowak at the school?"

Bagni shook his head. "Lakeview had only been here one day. I don't get to know the students. My job is to clean up after them. Even the kids I sell to, I don't ask their names, just tell them what I have, my price and the meeting time if they want something."

"Was Jacob with the two boys you met in the washroom that night?" Christine asked.

"No. The first time I saw what the kid looked like was when the principal showed me a photograph. Then his picture was all over the newspapers and television stations."

The next morning was laundry day. In her apartment, Christine folded clean sheets, thinking about the Nature School's caretaker. It didn't sit right with her that Bagni was selling contraband to children. She had a duty to report him to his employer, to stop more ten-year-olds from rotting their teeth and staring at centerfolds. But Fillingham had convinced her that the janitor could be their inside source regarding the school and its staff. No point in throwing away a key informant. They could deal with his low-level profiteering later.

Back upstairs in the apartment, Christine tucked the clean sheets around the corners of Wayne's sofa mattress. She doubted Sal Bagni would contribute relevant information to the Jacob Nowak investigation, since he had left that night at eleven and returned the next afternoon. But he might have a few observations about the people who worked at the school.

If only they could get Patrick Williamson to talk to them—he was their best option for information on what happened that night.

Finished making Wayne's bed, she lifted the bottom bed legs, folded the mattress on itself and tried to push the mattress into the sofa frame. Darn thing wouldn't close. Christine gave it a gentle shove with her thigh and still met with resistance. What was the problem? The sofa couch was acting finicky lately and showing its age. The mattress sagged in the middle. Wayne was heavier now; the mattress wouldn't last through his teenage years. Maybe they could buy a new sofa bed next Boxing Day, when the sales were on, now that they didn't have a loan shark breathing down their neck.

Kneeling beside the couch, she peered up into the bed's metal skeleton, searching for a stuck pillow or sock in the hinge. Something white was wedged in the frame. Geez, was that a shoe? Why was Wayne's shoe in the couch? Footwear was stored in the front closet.

Bum in air, she reached under the bed, extending her arm to touch the shoe heel. Good thing she had long arms. With a bit of wrangling, she curled her fingers around the heel and wriggled it free. Sitting back on her heels, she regarded it.

A white baseball shoe with metal cleats and red laces.

Chapter 15

The apartment door clicked shut. Christine strode down the front hallway as her siblings slid their knapsacks to the floor. "I need to talk to you, Wayne!" Christine said.

Her brother's head jerked up at her angry tone, one boot off. Donna's eyes flicked quickly from Christine to her brother and back.

Christine grabbed Wayne by the coat shoulder and pulled him along the hallway.

"Hey!" he said, stumbling out of his other boot, his stocking feet slipping along the wooden floor.

Christine pulled him into her bedroom and slammed the door shut behind them. She shuffled him toward her bed and pushed him onto the blue comforter.

Sprawled on his back against the faded floral fabric, his expression was a mixture of surprise and wariness.

Hands clenched at her side, her breath coming in big huffs as if she had run a race, she made herself wait. Her anger was so consuming, like a white searchlight, blanking out thought. She needed to pause and follow her rules for disciplining her siblings: no screaming, swearing, hitting or pushing. There had been enough of that when her stepfather was around, especially after he had drained a whisky bottle. Wayne was only six when Eddie left, but he remembered hiding in the room the three siblings shared, a pillow held around his head to block out his parents' argument over who had smoked the last cigarette.

After counting to ten, Christine's anger had been tamped down. She opened the top drawer of her night table and took out the white, cleated shoe with red laces.

The color drained from Wayne's face. "I didn't do it," he said, scrambling away from her until his back pressed the wall.

"Didn't do what?" she said, instantly angry again.

He looked away from her furious gaze, staring unseeingly at the books on Christine's shelf: the *Ontario Highway Traffic Act*, the *Ontario Criminal Code*, the *Toronto Police News and Views*.

"Teeny?" Donna's voice sounded outside the closed bedroom door.

"What do you want, Donna?" Christine asked curtly.

"Can I come in?"

"Wayne and I are just talking right now."

"I want to read on my bed."

The doorknob turned. Christine quickly walked over and held the door open a crack, the shoe hidden behind her back. "Donna, we'll be done in ten minutes."

"What's wrong?" Donna moved, trying to see around Christine in the doorway.

"Nothing. I'm just talking to Wayne," Christine replied.

Donna looked reproachfully at her sister. "You were yelling. Did Wayne do something bad?"

Christine ignored her sister's question. "I'll try to talk softer." She pasted a smile onto her face. "Why don't you get yourself a snack? There's crackers beside the cereal. Peanut butter in the cupboard."

"With jam?" Donna asked.

"I think there's strawberry jam in the fridge door." She gave her younger sister a tight smile and closed the door.

Turning back to Wayne, she said through gritted teeth, "Do you know who this shoe belongs to?" She waved it at him.

He nodded.

"What is it doing in your bed?" she asked.

"I don't know." He stared down at the comforter.

"You don't know!" Both her hands raised. "A dead boy's shoe is in your bed, and you don't know why?"

Silence.

She kneeled in front of him. "Where did the shoe come from, Wayne?"

"I said I don't know!" he howled, then covered his face with his hands.

Placing a hand on his leg, she said, "Wayne, I'm going to ask you one more time how this shoe got into our apartment. And I don't want to hear, 'I don't know.'"

He pulled his hands down, showing his anguished brown eyes, eyelashes wet with tears. "Somebody put it in my backpack."

"Who?"

"I don't know."

"When?" she asked.

"I found it when we came back from the Island trip."

She got off her knees and sat down beside him on her bed. "You've had this since September?" Her voice was calmer now.

He nodded, tears streaking his cheeks. "It was in my bag when I unpacked. I don't know how it got there. I knew it was Jacob's, and he had run away, so I didn't want anyone to know I had it."

"Why didn't you tell me? Or the police?"

"I didn't want to get in trouble."

"Why would you be in trouble?"

"Because—"

"Because what, Wayne?"

"I didn't want anyone to think I was mean."

"Mean?"

"Take his stuff...steal his baseball shoe."

Christine moved so her leg pressed against her brother's. "Wayne, what's going on? What do you know?"

"I don't know anything," he said, shaking his head, his tone frustrated. "I've told people that a hundred times. Jacob bunked in the same room as me, that's all. And then he was gone, and he never came back."

"Did Jacob put his shoe in your bag?"

Wayne frowned. "Why would he do that?"

"For safekeeping?"

His expression was confused. "One shoe?"

"Could someone have hidden it in your knapsack as a joke?"

"It wasn't in there when I packed—and Jacob was already missing."

"Who would do this?" Christine pointed to the shoe in her lap. "Who would frame you for stealing the shoe?"

Wayne averted his face. "I don't know."

"One of your roommates?" she asked. She wouldn't put it past Roy. Or Patrick. Or maybe it was one of the staff trying to divert suspicion.

He turned to his sister. "Before we left the Nature School, we put our bags on the driveway. The driver was going to load them onto the bus that was taking us to the ferry."

"Anybody could have slipped the shoe in your knapsack? A student, staff, people walking by?"

He nodded, his expression miserable.

"Wayne, I'm going to be straight with you. Jacob was found near Trout Pond holding his other baseball shoe."

His body stiffened beside her.

She continued. "So whoever put this shoe in your bag may have information about the drowning. Did you see Jacob that night after lights out?"

"No." His voice was quiet but firm.

"Did anyone see him that night by the pond?"

"I don't know anything!" he wailed. Another tear trailed down his cheek to his chin and dropped onto the collar of his winter jacket.

"Hello!" a female voice called from inside the apartment. It was Phyllis, back from work.

Christine returned the shoe to the nightstand drawer, hiding it under a pile of papers. Turning back to Wayne, she said, "I'll tell Mom you're not feeling well, and you're resting in here where it's quiet. Don't say anything to her, okay?"

He nodded emphatically. Phyllis ran hot and cold in the discipline department. Wayne had been on the receiving end of her spanks and had his TV time taken away for his transgressions. But if Phyllis was tired, or in a good mood, she would let the kids stay up late or eat too many cookies. Christine wasn't sure what her mom would do if she thought Wayne was involved in the Jacob Nowak investigation; Wayne didn't want to find out either.

At the dinner table, Christine explained that Wayne still wasn't feeling well after returning from school with a stomachache.

Phyllis said, "You don't look so great yourself."

Christine pushed away her half-eaten eggs. "I'm not hungry."

After they cleaned up, Christine sat on the couch with the police union newsletter, trying to behave normally in front of Phyllis, her stomach clenched with apprehension, rereading the same paragraph about one-person versus two-person vehicle patrols. Her mind swirled with thoughts about Jacob's shoe. Did she believe her brother's story? Did it matter, since the case was closed? Was the shoe in the backpack suspicious? And who would do that? Roy? Patrick? A staff member covering his tracks?

The acids in Christine's stomach gurgled. To follow police protocol, she should deliver the shoe to the investigators at 52 Division. Investigator Fenwick would ask her how she came into possession of the shoe. She could imagine his response when she replied that her brother had withheld it for three months.

Would the investigators reopen the case? Most likely not. But two issues nagged her. First, did the shoe implicate her brother in Jacob's death? Or was it totally unrelated—a product of kids' shenanigans? Maybe someone had taken it and dumped it with Wayne after Jacob went missing. Her second concern was that she was withholding evidence—a chargeable offence under the *Police Act*.

When Phyllis went into the bathroom to run a bath, Christine called into work. Pilkington answered the phone at the Center Island Station. Christine told him she had the stomach flu and wouldn't be in for her shift the next day. Pilkington complained about finding a replacement on such short notice; Christine said thank you and hung up.

That night, Donna, Phyllis and Christine watched *Hee Haw* on television together, Donna erupting into laughter at the slapstick comedy. Christine smiled automatically, not really listening to the punchlines. When Donna went to bed, Christine found Wayne asleep on her own comforter, his winter jacket tossed on the parquet floor, his face so relaxed she didn't have the heart to wake him and guide him to the pull-out couch.

By eleven o'clock, Phyllis was in bed and Christine lay bundled in the sofa bed. The apartment was quiet now, the only noise the screech of a passing King Street streetcar. The sheets twisted around her legs as she tried to find a comfortable position while she sank into the center of the soft mattress. Maybe she should talk to the investigators after all. It wasn't a murder case; the autopsy conclusion was drowning. The discovery of the second shoe was incidental—maybe a case of theft—but had nothing to do with Jacob's death. Or did it?

Why would another student have Jacob's shoe? Had that person seen or been with Jacob before he drowned? Was her brother part of this, whatever this was?

In the morning, her insomnia and accompanying nausea meant she didn't have to pretend when she told her mother she was too sick for her afternoon shift. At eight thirty, Donna and a subdued Wayne headed to school.

Phyllis had the day off—which was a strain. Every time Christine encountered her mom in their small apartment, she had to smile and act normal while her gut twisted with worry. Her mom made her a ham sandwich and heated a can of tomato soup for their lunch, trying to tempt her appetite.

As they spooned their soup at the kitchen table, there was a rap on their apartment door.

Christine frowned. It annoyed her when people didn't use the entrance intercom. Not only because of safety concerns, but because it was usually a salesman pitching magazine subscriptions or vacuums.

"I'll get it," she said. In her tense mood, she would dispatch the seller quickly.

"Fillingham?" she said after opening the door.

Her partner stood in casual pants and a short wool coat. "You don't look sick."

Closing the door behind her, she whispered, "I'm not feeling well. I won't be at—"

"You're healthy as an ox," he contradicted. "Plus, you have an overly active work ethic."

"What's your problem?" she said in an aggrieved whisper.

He smiled. "You tell me the problem."

She frowned. Couldn't he let her be? "I'm taking the day off. Officers do it all the time."

"Why?"

He was so intrusive—always in her business. She should slam the door in his face.

As if he were reading her mind, he said, "I can knock on your door all day."

"You're on shift in two hours," she said.

He crossed his arms. "Actually, I'm not. Family emergency."

Christine glared at her partner and his affable smile. He was like a bulldog who wouldn't release a bone. She eased the door open behind her, stuck her head inside, and called, "Mom. I'm going to check if the washing machine is free."

Brushing past Fillingham, she led the way down two flights of stairs to the basement laundry room. Below a narrow horizontal window, a pine table was pressed against the cement brick wall. Across from the window, a battered washing machine and dryer sat under a sign with faded black script: *25 cents a load.*

He followed her in and closed the door. "What gives, Lane?"

"Why do you have to know everything? Why can't you let me be?"

He sat up on the laundry table, legs swinging over the edge, and waited.

It was bad enough she owed him money—that her family's gambling debt had been revealed. No way she was telling him about Wayne.

"What's happened?" he asked, his voice low and quiet.

"I... I don't want to tell you."

"Try me."

"I don't want your help."

He made a face. "Tell me something I don't know."

She exhaled. "It's not good for you to know. I need to work it out myself."

"Like I said, try me."

"It will compromise you."

"I like being compromised." He gave a suggestive wiggle of his eyebrows.

"This is not funny!" She moved away from him to pace the room, her chest heaving as if she had run around the block.

"Why isn't it funny?" he asked gently, as he followed her movements back and forth across the cement floor.

"Because...because...." She stopped in front of him. "It's about Wayne!" she exclaimed.

"Wayne? Is he hurt?"

She brusquely wiped a tear from her eye with the back of her hand. "You want to know everything. You think you can handle it. Stay here. I'll be right back."

She threw the door open, ran upstairs to her apartment and returned in one minute to the laundry room. "Here!" she yelled. She shoved the baseball shoe into his chest.

He looked down at the shoe he was now clutching. "Is this the shoe they found with Jacob's body?"

"It's the other shoe!"

After a moment, he said, "Where did you get this?"

She faced him. "In my brother's bed."

"Wayne? Wayne had Jacob's shoe?"

She nodded, struggling to hold back the tears, then covered her face with her hands. She heard his shoes tap the floor as he jumped off the table.

His voice was near her when he said, "What's your brother's explanation?"

Dropping her hands from her face, her cheeks wet with tears, she said, "He said someone put it in his knapsack on the Island. He found it when he unpacked."

"Do you believe him?" he asked.

"What choice do I have? If he's lying, then he is a thief or is involved with Jacob's drowning."

Placing the shoe on the table, he turned back to her. "We were right."

"What do you mean?"

"Jacob's death wasn't accidental—as Mrs. Nowak's been saying all along."

She bit her lower lip. "What if my brother is at the bottom of it?"

"Do you think that's the case?"

"No. No, I don't."

He smiled, gesturing toward the door. "Let's find out who is."

As they climbed up the steps from the basement, a flash of blue passed above them, heading up the stairs to the second floor. "Wayne?" she called as she reached the main landing. He froze at the top step to their floor, body swiveled, face frightened. Caught.

"What are you doing home?" she asked. "It's only one thirty. You should be at school."

Wayne looked behind Christine and saw Fillingham. "I thought you were at work."

"Why are you home?" she asked again.

"I'm not feeling well," he said.

"Hey, Wayne." Fillingham waved with his free hand.

Wayne spied the baseball shoe in Fillingham's other hand. His mouth pinched. "You told him!" he yelled.

"I...he's helping us," she said.

"You told him!" Wayne repeated.

"Wayne, a boy died," she said.

"You think I hurt him?" Wayne asked his sister.

"No, I don't—"

Wayne flew past them, exploding out the side door with a whoosh of chilled air.

"I'll get him," her partner said, handing her the shoe.

After waiting several minutes on the main landing, Christine went outside and scanned the street, her arms crossed against the January chill. No Wayne or Fillingham in sight. With a shiver, she returned to her bedroom and placed the shoe back in her nightstand.

Her mom's bedroom door was closed, which meant she was lying down, thank goodness. Phyllis often napped on her day off; shift work left her perpetually exhausted. Christine didn't know what to say to her mother about Wayne, the baseball shoe or Fillingham's presence. How was she to explain what was going on when she didn't know herself?

For half an hour, Christine wandered the apartment, doing two-minute chores: putting away the dishes in the rack, straightening the front closet, dumping ashtrays, lining up Phyllis's magazines on the coffee table. She couldn't stop moving, as if she needed to match her frenetic thoughts with action. As she dusted the living room shelf, she regarded the framed photo of her father. Wayne was not the only person keeping secrets in her family.

The floorboard creaked. "Hey," Phyllis said, shuffling into the living room, her wavy hair tousled from her pillow.

"Who is this man?" Christine held up the framed photo.

Phyllis stopped in her tracks.

"I saw the exact photo in the Toronto Island Airport," Christine said. She didn't know where she was finding the courage to speak. Maybe it was from her rising anger, the exasperation that caused her fingers to tremble as she held the photo out to her mother. "This is a Norwegian pilot named Hans Jansen. This photo was published in the *Toronto Telegram* with an article about the Norwegian squad training on the Island."

Her mother's eyes widened.

"Islanders remember him," Christine continued. "He had a family back home. A couple of kids, too."

Without a word, Phyllis headed toward the kitchen.

"You have nothing to say?" Christine's voice was not quite a yell, but it was loud. She stepped in front of her mother, forcing her to stop by the kitchen table.

Phyllis's brown eyes looked into hers. Then she sidestepped Christine and headed toward the stove. "I'm not talking about this."

"You're not talking about this!" Christine shouted at her mother's back. "You're not going to tell me if this man is my father—and not Thomas Lane! Or someone else?"

At the sink, Phyllis filled the metal kettle with water.

"AM I A BASTARD?" Christine hollered.

The apartment door clicked closed, followed by the thump of approaching footsteps. Wayne appeared in the kitchen, followed by Fillingham. Had they heard her question?

"Everything okay in here?" He looked from Christine to Phyllis, who remained at the stove.

Christine nodded curtly. Her humiliation in front of her partner continued.

Fillingham placed his hand on Wayne's shoulder. "Wayne and I went for a drive."

Her brother looked up at Fillingham, then at Christine, a small smile on his face. "He drives a GM Beaumont. The seats are real leather."

Christine tried to smile. "Yes, I know. Very cool."

Phyllis continued to make tea as if nobody else were in the kitchen, pouring hot water into the teapot, then swirling the tea bag around with a spoon.

"Christine?" Fillingham pointed his chin toward the front door. "We should head out."

"Okay," she said hesitantly.

Phyllis poured herself a cup of tea, her back to the three of them.

Christine gave herself a shake. Her father's identity was secondary. Wayne and the Jacob Nowak case were urgent priorities. Maybe Fillingham had been successful at teasing the truth out of her brother.

Buttoning her winter coat, she followed Fillingham outside to his car. Did it really matter who her father was? Hans Jansen? John Lane? John Doe? Family was the most important thing, the one she lived with daily, not an imaginary parent she had never met. Whoever he was, she had done fine without him for twenty-four years.

What she really needed to know was: What was going on with Wayne?

Settled in the car, Fillingham said, "Sarah is waiting for you at Mrs. Nowak's. Ask Jacob's mom about his baseball shoes."

"Okay," she responded hesitantly.

The engine roared to life. "You need to ask about Jacob's school life—who his friends were and who was bothering him." He drove north to the stop sign.

"What happened with Wayne?" she asked.

Fillingham turned onto Queen Street.

"Fillingham!" Her tone was urgent. "What did Wayne say?"

He glanced over at her before returning his gaze to the road. "He was there."

"Where?"

"At the lagoon edge."

"What!" she shrieked.

"They were all there."

Yanking his coat sleeve, she yelled, "Pull over!"

The car swerved. "Jesus, let go of me!" His free arm pressed down on her arm to force her to release him. "You're going to get us killed." He steered to an abrupt stop in front of a pawnshop.

She turned to him. "What are you talking about?"

"All four boys went outside."

"Which boys?"

"Jacob, Roy, Patrick...and Wayne."

"When?"

"After lights out."

Between gritted teeth, she said, "Tell me exactly what Wayne said."

"Roy and Patrick were bugging Jacob: walking on his bed with their muddy shoes, scuffling with him during the game of Predator and Prey. At lunch, they put a bug in his sandwich. Stupid stuff like that."

"What has this to do with Wayne?

He motioned her to wait with his hand. "Wayne said Jacob was trying to ignore their pranks. Then Miss Phillips announced that Jacob, not Roy, would be the pitcher in their friendly game the next day against the Island Day school team."

"Roy was mad?"

"Roy snuck Jacob's baseball shoes out of his suitcase. Sometime after lights out, he threw them out the window."

After a few seconds, Christine said, "It's a seven-foot drop from the windowsill to the grass, right?"

Fillingham nodded. "Jacob can't leave the building, because students are supposed to be in bed, and they know Tim is monitoring the hallway. Neither is Jacob a tattletale. So he climbs out the window and drops to the ground to retrieve his shoes."

"Is that when he ran away from the school?" she asked.

"The rest of the boys followed him out the window."

She frowned. "That doesn't make sense. If they all went outside the locked school, how did they get back in?"

He briefly touched her sleeve. "I'll come to that. After the boys climbed out the window, Roy grabbed one of Jacob's shoes from him and took off with it, Jacob in full pursuit."

"Toward the lighthouse," she said, her voice flat.

Fillingham nodded.

"What did Wayne and Patrick do?"

"They followed the racing pair past the lighthouse and down the trail to the water. When they reached the lagoon, they saw Roy holding the shoe high over Jacob's head; Jacob was jumping, trying to get his shoe back."

Christine's stomach flipped queasily. "What happened next?"

"I don't know."

"You don't know?"

"Wayne had had enough. Roy was being mean—a bully. Your brother didn't want any part of it. He knew they'd be in big trouble for breaking curfew and going outside—maybe even sent home by Miss Phillips."

"What did Wayne do next?" she asked.

"He went in the school. He couldn't get back in through the window—it's too high to reach on your own, so he tries the main door. It's unlocked. Inside, he expects a staff member to bawl him out, but the hallway was empty. So he scoots back to his room, pulls the cover over his head and hides."

She thought of Tim Hawley visiting the bedroom of Miss Phillips. "When did the other boys come back?"

"Wayne said he was awake for the next fifteen minutes, but no one came. He thought the staff had caught the boys outside, or that Jacob was telling Miss Phillips about Roy taking his shoe. Wayne fell asleep. The next morning, he wakes up. No Jacob."

"How did Roy and Patrick get back in?" she asked.

"Wayne doesn't know."

"Why didn't any of the boys tell the teacher that they had gone outside that night?"

He rubbed his hand through his short, blonde hair. "Roy showed Wayne and Patrick a hunting knife he had brought on the trip. The threat was explicit."

Roy's tactics made her sick. How could one child wreak such havoc? The car's windows fogged from their warm breath, the people walking by reduced to charcoal shadows. Turning to her partner, she asked, "Why didn't Wayne talk to me? I'm his sister. He knows I could help him. I'm a police officer."

He sighed. "After the students returned to Lakeview, Wayne saw Roy talking to Donna in the schoolyard."

"Why would Roy do that?"

"Roy started playing with Donna at recess, tossing the ball with her, playing tag and Frisbee. Donna was having a blast with Roy. The threat to Donna was implicit, so Wayne kept quiet."

No wonder Wayne had looked gray these past months. Christine covered her face with her gloved hands. Roy, like his father, was intimidating, a bully who threatened anyone who challenged his authority.

Christine felt a quick double pat on her shoulder from her partner and then heard Fillingham shift the car into gear.

"The first step," he said, "is for you to talk to Mrs. Nowak about what she knows about Roy and Patrick."

Her hands dropped from her face. "What are you going to do?"

"Have a chat with Patrick Williamson. He was with Jacob and Roy when Wayne went back inside the school. He knows more of the story."

Shaking her head, she said, "Patrick wouldn't say anything before. And his mom will stop him if he tries to speak."

The car pulled away from the curb. "Nothing a little Fillingham charisma can't wear down."

When she raised a skeptical eyebrow, he added, "Or I'll bluff and say based on new evidence we're taking her son into the station for questioning regarding Jacob Nowak's death. That should get us some cooperation."

Chapter 16

Mrs. Nowak handed a teacup and saucer to Sarah, who was sitting beside Christine on the mustard couch. Christine received the next cup. Mr. Nowak was at work at the butcher's shop.

Seated across from the officers, Mrs. Nowak sat in a high-back chair in a dark skirt and white cardigan, her flaxen hair pulled back from her face with a wide cotton hairband. She looked calm but faded, as if the energy had been pressed out of her, leaving just an imprint.

The policewomen hadn't been sure that Jacob's mother would let them in when they rang the doorbell. After opening the door, Mrs. Nowak asked them what they wanted.

Sarah had answered, "If it's okay, we would like to ask you a few questions about Jacob."

Mrs. Nowak had given them a suspicious sniff but motioned them inside.

Mrs. Nowak took a sip of her tea, then looked at them expectantly.

Christine started, "Can you tell us again about what Jacob was like?"

She gave a little sigh but quickly said, "Jakub learn English fast. He does the chess, math, soccer, baseball. So good. So good at many things." She frowned, as if trying to contain her emotions.

"Coming to Canada must have been hard for him," Sarah said.

Mrs. Nowak addressed Sarah. "Jakub a good boy. Smart. Not trouble." Her lips thinned as she glared. "Not run away."

"Miss Phillips says he was doing well at school," Christine affirmed.

"She very nice," Mrs. Nowak said. "Jakub like her."

"Did he like all his teachers?" Christine asked.

"Baseball coach he love," Mrs. Nowak replied.

Christine smiled. "My brother Wayne is on the team, and he loves Coach Watson, too." After a second, she asked, "Did you talk to Jacob when he was on the Island trip?"

Mrs. Nowak shook her head. "Teacher say no phone call on trip. I wish he call." She looked down, her expression forlorn.

Christine wished he had called, too. They might have more insight into what Jacob was thinking and feeling. "Did he have friends at Lakeview School?"

Frowning, Mrs. Nowak said, "At first, it is hard. Jakub doesn't know English. The children make fun—his clothes, his words."

"What kids?" Christine asked.

"Big boys."

"You mean older boys?" Sarah asked. "Do you know their names?"

"Jakub not say." She shrugged. "Maybe he tell Mariusz."

"Is that Jacob's older cousin?" Christine asked. The teenager had helped with the search when Jacob went missing.

Mrs. Nowak nodded.

Sarah asked, "Did the big boys do anything else to him?"

Mrs. Nowak glared. "They take his lunch." She looked at Christine. "Not to eat—to throw on ground. Call it pig food. He come home with nothing in belly. I know they do more—but he stop saying."

"How do you know there was more?" Christine placed her cup and saucer on the wooden table.

"His shirt has hole." She pointed to her knees. "His pant dirty, here. He said from soccer, but I no believe."

Sarah asked, "Did this happen this year in grade five?"

Mrs. Nowak said, "I only see last year."

"Did these boys graduate from the school?" Lakeview only went up to grade six, then students attended middle school.

"Jakub not say."

"Were they on his soccer or baseball team?" Christine asked.

"Jakub not say." Mrs. Nowak added, "I never know names. Maybe tell Mariusz." She took a sip of tea.

Christine said, "Do you think we could talk to Mariusz?"

Mrs. Nowak frowned. "Why?"

"He might know about Jacob's friends and schoolmates."

"So?"

Christine didn't know what to tell Mrs. Nowak, given that the investigation was clandestine.

Mrs. Nowak waited her out.

"I want to make sure we got the complete story about Jacob's disappearance and death."

She stared at Christine for a few seconds, then abruptly got up and went into the kitchen. The policewomen could hear her talking in Polish on the phone.

Christine and Sarah exchanged a glance.

Mrs. Nowak returned to the living room. She reached for the teapot and topped up Sarah's cup. Sitting back down on the coach, she said, "Mariusz come now."

"Here?" Christine said.

"Five minutes," Mrs. Nowak responded.

"So the two cousins are close friends?" Christine asked.

Mrs. Nowak squinted, as if trying to figure out how to express her thought. "Mariusz like big brother for Jakub. He been here for two years." She held up two fingers. "He know more."

"So he could help Jacob get used to living in Toronto," Sarah said.

Mrs. Nowak nodded. "Also," she smiled, "play baseball, go to park and do a game with other boys. It fun for Jacob."

Christine said, "It sounds like he practiced baseball all the time, just like my brother Wayne."

"He love baseball—always throw ball against side of house."

Christine said, "You bought him new baseball shoes for his birthday?"

Mrs. Nowak gestured with both hands. "My husband found on sale. Jakub so happy. He sleep with new shoes first night. Keep so clean." She smiled at the memory.

"What would Jacob do if a person tried to take his baseball shoes?" Christine asked.

Mrs. Nowak shook her head. "He no let them."

Christine swallowed, thinking of the white shoe with the red laces in her nightstand drawer.

"Why did he have shoe?" Mrs. Nowak's eyes searched Christine and then Sarah. "They no tell me why."

"We don't know," Christine said. "We don't know why he left the school or went into the water."

Mrs. Nowak said, "He is scared of water. Since little. One time he fell out of boat, almost die. He not like after that."

Sarah said, "Would he try to swim on his own—practice in case his class went swimming?"

Jacob's mother shook her head vigorously. "He afraid of water. Afraid of big boat to Island."

"The ferry?" Sarah asked.

Mrs. Nowak nodded. "He no go in canoe. He told teacher. She said it okay."

"Why do you think he went into the water?" Christine asked.

Mrs. Nowak shook her head. "He not go. He never go. Someone make him. Someone put him in."

"Who?" Christine asked. "Who would do that?"

"Where is other shoe?" Mrs. Nowak asked.

Christine's stomach dropped.

A quick rap came from the front door, then the sound of it opening. Mrs. Nowak called out in Polish, and a teenager entered the living room. He had the same wheat-colored hair as his aunt, growing shaggy around his eyes and ears. And the physique of a boxer, muscular and compact. His glance went from Mrs. Nowak to the two women in the room.

Mrs. Nowak gestured to the chair cushion beside her, and the young man sat down.

"*Policja*?" he said to his aunt.

She nodded.

He looked back at the policewomen with the same direct stare as his aunt.

Christine introduced herself and Sarah and explained they wanted to know about Jacob's experiences at school.

"Why?" he said, just as his aunt had.

Mrs. Nowak spoke to him in Polish, and he frowned but turned back to the officers. "He like school this year."

"He didn't like it before?" Christine asked.

"When he first come to school, they laugh at the way he speaks. Push him. Call him stupid Polack," he said.

"Why didn't he tell the teacher?" Christine asked.

He frowned. "He is not a crybaby."

Sarah said, "Was Jacob upset about the bullying at school?"

He nodded. "Yes, when he first go to school in Canada." His arms gestured wide. "But now he know he's smart. Can play sports. Good at school. Maybe university. He knows those other kids dumb."

"So he got bothered less, or he was just able to ignore it."

Mariusz shrugged. "Both." He smiled. "Also, I say I take care of problem."

"What do you mean?" Christine asked.

"If someone bugging him, I come. Then, no more problem."

"Did you threaten any of the students from Lakeview?" Christine asked.

He shook his head. "No. No problem this year. Then Jacob went on trip and then he gone."

Sarah and Christine met Fillingham at a diner on Queen Street for dinner, the two women settling into the red booth opposite him. With a nod from Christine, he told Sarah about the discovery of Jacob's baseball shoe in Wayne's backpack. Christine hadn't been able to tell Sarah, even though she had been with her at the Nowaks. It was too raw.

After they were served their meals, Sarah asked, "What do you think happened after Wayne left the boys by the pond?"

Fillingham said, "That's the hundred-thousand-dollar question!" He took a big bite out of his cheeseburger.

Christine had ordered chicken noodle soup, not just because it was cheap but because her stomach was flip-flopping with anxiety.

After swiping the ketchup off his mouth with a serviette, he added, "I tried to talk with Patrick Williamson today, but the mom wouldn't crack open the door—even when I said it was police. She asked if I had a warrant. When I said I didn't, she wouldn't budge."

Sarah pointed a French fry at Christine sitting beside her. "No one at the school has a criminal record, correct?"

"The janitor's got a thriving black-market business going with the kiddies," he said.

"Does that make him a killer?" Sarah asked.

"Maybe Jacob found out about Bagni's clandestine business and was going to tattle," Christine hazarded.

He shook his head. "Jacob's no rat. And what's his motivation to expose Bagni? Plus, it was Roy and Patrick who bought stuff off Bagni. There's no evidence Jacob met the janitor."

Sarah said, "Even if Jacob blew the whistle, would Bagni drown him? A child? Isn't that extreme?"

Fillingham said, "The ferry staff remember seeing Bagni on the last ferry to the city. So he alibi's out."

"Anyone else with a history?" Sarah asked.

Christine said, "The paddling coach has anger issues. He was charged regarding an incident with a child."

Fillingham frowned. "The charges were dropped. And that's in the past."

Sarah said, "Is it?"

"People change," he said. "Grow up. Mature."

"*You* don't," Christine said with a smile.

"Peter Pan, at your service." His head tilted in a mock bow. He forked a French fry. "If Jacob was outside on his own, any of the staff could have waylaid him."

"If an adult hurt Jacob," Christine said, "it's not limited to school staff. Any person on the Island could have met Jacob after the other boys returned to their room: a boater from Blockhouse Bay, a passer-by from Hanlan's Point Beach."

He shrugged. "If it's a crime of circumstance, it will be difficult to catch the perpetrator. But again, it's hard to believe Jacob wouldn't defend himself against a stranger or resist going into the water. He had no broken bones, contusions or deep bruises."

Sarah sighed, putting her hamburger down on the plate. "Maybe he just drowned. Children are bullying him. His beloved baseball shoe is stolen. He wet his bed. He doesn't want to go back to his room, so he wades into the water and goes in farther than intended."

Christine turned to her friend. "You heard Mrs. Nowak. He would never go into the water."

Fillingham took a swig from his glass of milk. "That's the conundrum. Why was he in the water with his shoe tied to his wrist? And where is the suitcase? Why wasn't it found in his room?"

Sarah summed it up. "So his three bunkmates returned to their room. Jacob was last seen near the lagoon by the lighthouse in his pajamas, without his suitcase."

"Maybe Jacob went back inside the school later when everyone was asleep and retrieved his suitcase," Christine ventured.

He shook his head. "And then he returns to the water's edge and accidentally walks in with his suitcase and a baseball shoe? If he wanted to get off the island, he'd head to Hanlan's Point dock."

"Roy or Patrick could have the suitcase," Sarah suggested. "Maybe they stole it to bother Jacob."

Fillingham shook his head. "They couldn't have taken it home with them. The teacher would have checked the room for Jacob's belongings. Everyone knew Jacob had a tan leather suitcase. It was all over the news. Although the boys could have trashed it and dumped it in the shrubbery."

"Or maybe the staff or stranger who grabbed Jacob took it," Christine said. She leaned back in her seat. Too many possibilities.

Fillingham added, "The Harbor Police said the suitcase could have floated away from the body into the inner harbor before sinking."

"Do we have enough evidence to speak with the investigators from 52 Division?" Christine asked. "Get permission to interview the boys?"

Sarah placed a hand on Christine's arm. "What evidence? Two boys were in the company of a boy who later accidentally drowns. What's the criminal charge?" She removed her hand. "And they're ten. The *Youth Delinquent Act* doesn't apply to them."

He pushed away his plate, leaving a few French fries. "Jacob must have been coerced into the water. Maybe he was more afraid of the person than he was of the water. The people who may know something are Roy, Patrick, a school staff member or the mysterious stranger." He blew air out of his mouth in a long breath. "Patrick's not talking. And Roy sure ain't."

Christine's eyes widened in alarm as she looked at her partner across the table.

His hands opened in apology. "Yeah, I spoke to Roy."

"I told you to leave him alone," Christine admonished. She turned to Sarah. "Roy's father complained after I spoke with his son—said I was harassing the boy."

Mark O'Neil's ambush on New Year's Eve had scared Christine. Since that night, she constantly looked over her shoulder after disembarking the ferry. If it was dark, Fillingham waited until she walked up to Bay Street before leaving in his car; sometimes he dropped her off at her streetcar stop. If Roy was a dangerous bully, then his father seemed even more threatening.

Fillingham shrugged. "I thought I could talk to him, man to man, athlete to athlete. Roy let me walk home with him. We chatted about baseball and how he pitched for a league playing out of Christie Pits. He said his dad might want to talk to me." Fillingham shook his head. "As soon as we arrive at his house—it's a dumpy bungalow at the end of Virtue Street—he takes me to this large, dilapidated shed in the backyard. His dad's inside."

Christine remembered Mark O'Neil's intimidating bulk, his hostile stare. "What happened?"

"He tells his son to go inside the house so we're alone. Picture this shed," he said, arms in the air. "It's as big as a garage, but instead of a car inside, you have stuffed animal heads and pelts mounted on the wall. A rack of BB guns sits at the back beside a locked rifle cabinet."

"Legal?" Sarah asked.

"I asked him if he registered the guns," he responded. "He said they're hunting rifles. They don't need registration."

"Did you see what was in the cabinet?" Christine asked.

Fillingham shook his head. "I asked him what he liked to hunt, and he looks me in the eye and says, 'Anything I want.'"

"He's threatening you," Sarah said, her brown eyes wide.

"No kidding," he said. "And that's not the worst of it." His voice had become quiet.

Christine and Sarah leaned in. The diner was only half-filled with empty booths on either side of them.

Continuing, he said, "The guy takes a crossbow off the wall and cleans it with a rag. It looks like a tool for harpooning whales. And all the time he's doing this, he doesn't say a word. Finally, I ask if he has anything to say about Roy or Jacob Nowak. He continues to clean the bow."

Sarah said, "Yikes!"

"I decide to leave, but I was worried I'd get an arrow in the back."

"What happened next?" Christine asked.

"When I'm halfway down the yard, he calls out, 'Stay the fuck away from my son.'"

Sarah's eyebrows rose. "He sounds charming. What was he doing the evening of Jacob's disappearance?"

Fillingham answered, "I checked. He went to work, came home, had dinner, then watched TV all night with his wife."

"Does that exclude him as a suspect?" Sarah asked.

Christine said, "Why would O'Neil be on the Island that night? How would he know Jacob would jump out the window to retrieve his shoes? Or that Roy would take Jacob's baseball shoes in the first place?"

"Howdy, partners!" Julie walked toward them in a lavender hat that matched her wrap-around coat. She sat down beside Fillingham and leaned to give him a kiss on the lips, laughingly wiping away a lipstick smudge before turning to Sarah and Christine. "What are the three of you plotting on a Friday night? You better not be talking shop." She slid her coat off to reveal a tight white sweater accented with a thin silver necklace and black narrow pants.

Sarah said, "We're still trying to figure out what happened to the boy that drowned on the Island."

Julie pouted candy-red lips. "Don't you guys give it a rest? It's the weekend, for goodness' sake." She leaned into Fillingham, wrapping her arm around his back. Christine thought she looked like a Cheshire cat licking her lips before dinner.

Sarah looked at her watch. "I should head out. Don's off. I want to spend time with him before we both head in for our night shifts."

"Why don't we go to the Riverboat for coffee and the first set?" Julie asked. Addressing Sarah, she added, "Then you and I can head out to the WB for work."

Sarah shook her head, smiling. "I'll see you at eleven, Julie." She pulled several bills out of her wallet and left them on the table.

Julie turned to Christine. "How about you?"

"I need to go back—check in with my brother."

"You're such a Mother Goose, always taking care of the goslings," Julie said. "Quack, quack, quack." Her head bobbed with each utterance.

"Thanks for the invite," Christine said evenly, trying to keep her voice light. Julie's jabs got under her skin.

"Just you and me, lover boy," Julie said, turning to Fillingham.

"How'd I get so lucky?" Fillingham replied, smiling down at his girlfriend.

Walking back to her apartment from the diner, Christine was exhausted. This day seemed like an eternity—beginning with Fillingham showing up at her apartment, Wayne returning home early, the argument with Phyllis, the visit to Mrs. Nowak and finally dinner with her pals. When Christine arrived home, she'd make sure that Donna was bathed and tucked in bed and that Wayne was wrapping up his TV time. As for Phyllis—Christine had little to say to her mom about her father or any other topic. The day had leveled her. She'd be glad to pull on her pajamas, slide under the covers and call it a night.

Chapter 17

Entering the apartment, Christine heard the sound of the television in the living room. From the hallway, she spied Phyllis on the couch, arms crossed, a line of cigarette smoke trailing upward from her hand. She looked so solitary; Christine felt a pang of regret. Her mom had really tried over the past four years. She drank less with Eddie gone. And she no longer bet on horses. She had a steady job at Records. Even when things were dismal, when Phyllis was dirt-poor and scrounging to find a roof over their heads, she never gave them up. She never stopped caring for them. Really, did the name of Christine's father, dead or alive, matter?

"Hey, Mom," Christine said, joining her mother on the couch.

Phyllis scanned Christine's face. Her expression looked relieved at her daughter's calm tone.

Christine said, "All quiet on the home front?"

Phyllis mashed her half-finished cigarette into the ashtray, a sign she was upset. "Donna's in bed. Wayne's not home."

"Not home? It's nine o'clock? Where is he?"

Phyllis sat back against the couch. "I'm not sure."

"Is he with the twins?" Wayne was friends with two eight-year-olds in the building.

Phyllis shook her head.

"The Derringers?"

Another shake of her mother's head.

"So where could he be?"

"I'm not sure." She turned to Christine, her faded orange lipstick visible in the cracks of her lips. "I was in the bathtub. He yelled that he was going to see an old friend, and then he left."

"What time was this?" Christine asked.

"Five o'clock."

"He's been gone since five?" Christine's tone was surprised.

Phyllis nodded, her forehead wrinkling as she frowned.

"He didn't have dinner with you?"

"No. It was only Donna and me."

Wayne liked his food. He also knew to come home for dinner if he was playing with a friend. That was a house rule.

"Where have you checked?" Christine asked.

"I called the twins' place. I talked to the Derringers. I checked up and down the street."

Christine looked out the living room window, her image reflected in the glass. It was pitch black, a windy, wintery night, only five degrees and getting colder. Not a night that the neighborhood kids would be out. "I'll check outside again." She retrieved her coat and boots from the front closet.

Gosh, it was cold. She pulled her mittens out of her coat pockets and circled the perimeter of her low-rise building, calling her brother's name. The lamp overhead bathed the parking lot and mounds of snow in yellow light as she peered behind cars and around a shed. Could Wayne have hurt himself? Wouldn't his friend go for help if he had?

Out on the sidewalk, she intermittently called for Wayne as she checked the grounds of the apartments, low-rises, rooming houses and detached houses nearby. Maybe her brother had walked down to King Street to buy a jawbreaker at the convenience store.

King Street was relatively quiet at this time of night. The meat market, fruit stand and typewriter business were closed. A few stores were boarded up. Neon signs advertised restaurants and variety stores, and a few cars were parked in front of the open businesses. Christine entered the shops and eateries, did a cursory scan for Wayne and walked out again.

Her brother was a typical, irresponsible ten-year-old boy, but he wouldn't skip dinner or go to King Street without telling them. It wasn't like in the summer, when the neighborhood kids ran a bit wild. But even then, the children knew to come in when the streetlamps came on.

It was the dead of winter—cold and dark by five o'clock. Wayne knew their neighborhood wasn't always safe: alcoholics, drug addicts and troubled people surfaced at night. He was thoughtless but not stupid. And lately, he had been more of a homebody, staying in to watch TV or play board games with Donna.

Maybe he was still upset because Christine had been so angry with him about the discovery of Jacob's shoe in his bed. But after confessing his story to Fillingham, her brother seemed calm. Wayne knew that she and Fillingham believed him. He had been fine when she and Fillingham left her apartment.

Where else could Wayne be? When Christine was younger, the cool kids hung out at the school, puffing on cigarettes purloined from their parents, ducking out of sight when the janitor came outside to shake out doormats. Turning south, Christine checked out Lakeview School. The yard was eerily quiet, the baseball diamond and hopscotch pad devoid of children, dark shadows stretching over the pavement of the running track.

Heading back home, Christine bent her head against the wind that made her eyes water, lifting her head to scan the street for Wayne. Back at the apartment, she called out, "Any news?"

Phyllis met her in the hallway, shaking her head when she met Christine's gaze.

"Mom, Wayne said he was going out with a friend."

"An old friend."

"Who could that be?" Christine asked, gesturing with her hands. "Do you think he meant one of his school buddies—Paul, Sam, or Jack?"

"I don't know," Phyllis replied, her voice hoarse, probably from chain smoking.

Rummaging in the kitchen drawer, Christine retrieved her address book and began calling Wayne's school friends. Apologizing to the parents for calling so late, she made her way through the list.

Fifteen minutes later, she hung up the receiver on the kitchen wall, her shoulders slumping. No luck. His schoolmates hadn't seen him since this afternoon in class.

Would Patrick Williamson be an option? He had moved away, but Wayne had never buddied around with him. It would be a stretch to call him a friend.

Two years ago, a family had moved out of the apartment across from Christine. Wayne used to play with the eldest boy, Kevin. She had only called the Walshes once since they moved, but she phoned Allison Walsh anyway. Allison hadn't seen Wayne but wanted to catch up. Christine didn't want to tie up the line and promised to call another time.

Trying to calm herself, Christine joined her mother at the kitchen table for a cup of tea. While working at the Women's Bureau, Christine had seen too much tragedy to ignore her rising concern. Sure, police or neighbors found most lost children in a couple of hours, but those weren't the calls that stuck in her mind. She remembered the toddler who had opened the front door and stepped out in the freezing weather in his diaper and bare feet, the eight-year-old who had run away and hid behind his school, his face swollen from the lashings from his father's belt, the teenagers who went joyriding in a stolen car until it crashed into a tree. Kids out late at night courted trouble.

Christine dialed Fillingham's number.

"It's Lane," she said when he answered the phone. "Wayne hasn't come home." There was a tremor in her voice.

"When did you last see him?" Fillingham asked.

"At five o'clock. He told my mom he was leaving to meet a friend, and he hasn't returned. I've called his school buddies and friends in the building; I checked King Street and his school, and I searched the neighborhood. It's not like him to miss dinner or be out so late—especially in the winter."

"He could be watching TV at a friend's place and lost track of time," he said.

"Maybe." Her voice was hesitant. It was after ten. Wayne wouldn't be out this late without permission.

"You tried all his friends?" he asked.

"The ones I know," she said.

"How about friends from the baseball team? Did you call their families?

"Do you mean the school team or the summer league?" she asked.

"Both. I'd start with the school."

"Okay."

"While you're phoning, ask your mom to knock on each of your neighbors' doors in your building to see if anyone has seen your brother. Call me back in an hour if he hasn't come home. I'll swing by, and we can look for him together."

She felt better after she got off the phone with her partner—she had a plan now. Phyllis headed out the door to check with neighbors. Christine sat down at the kitchen table and started dialing. She called Wayne's baseball team—at least those with known phone numbers. Two families didn't pick up. She dialed Patrick Williamson's number.

"Wayne's not home?" Mrs. Williamson asked, her voice rising.

"He told our mom he was going out with an old friend. I've called his schoolmates and checked the neighborhood. It's not like him to be out so late. I thought he might be throwing the ball around with Patrick or another teammate."

Mrs. Williamson inhaled a sob. "It's him."

"Who?" Christine asked.

"Like with Jacob."

Panic fluttered Christine's throat. "What do you mean?"

"First Jacob, now Wayne." She hung up.

The black receiver buzzed with the disconnection. The skin on Christine's arms rose in goosebumps. What was Mrs. Williamson talking about? Christine redialed but got a busy tone.

Don't panic, Christine told herself. Mrs. Williamson seemed paranoid—which was probably why Patrick had changed schools.

Dialing Fillingham back, her finger shook in the holes of the rotary phone. She repeated her conversation with Mrs. Williamson.

"Damn," he said. "She knows something. She's always known something. I'll pick you up in ten minutes." He hung up.

Phyllis returned, shaking her head. Christine told her she was heading out with Fillingham to look for Wayne and would check in with her later. As Christine waited outside for her ride, she walked up the street, calling her brother's name, until she heard the rumble of Fillingham's sedan. Lowering herself into the passenger seat, she asked, "Where are we going?"

His blue-eyed gaze was intense. "Mrs. Williamson is going to come clean, once and for all. No more duck-and-weave. If she has information about Wayne's disappearance and Jacob's drowning, she better speak up, or I'm arresting her for obstruction. I also made a call into One Division. They're sending a patrol car to your neighborhood; they'll keep an eye out for Wayne."

Fillingham's resolve calmed Christine. People were looking for Wayne. Her brother would be found. Hopefully, by midnight, he would be tucked safely into bed.

The Williamsons lived near Queen Street on a better block than Christine's. Most of the houses were single-family dwellings, not apartments or rooming houses. A shovel leaned against the brick house by the Williamsons' front porch, the walkway and driveway brushed clear of snow.

On the third doorbell ring, the lace curtain covering the door window eased aside. Mrs. Williamson appeared, alarmed blue eyes framed by long, curly brown hair.

Fillingham rang the doorbell one more time for emphasis.

The door creaked open.

"Toronto Police," Fillingham said, holding up his badge.

"What do you want?" Mrs. Williamson said.

Fillingham stuck his foot in the wedge of the opened door, then shouldered it open to step inside.

Mrs. Williamson staggered back a few steps, eyes wide. Christine followed Fillingham in.

Before Mrs. Williamson could speak, Fillingham said, "We talk here, or at the station. Take your pick."

As Mrs. Williamson regarded them, Christine said. "May we sit?" She pointed to the living room, where Patrick Williamson sat on the couch, the glare of the television yellowing his face.

Mrs. Williamson gave a terse nod.

"A little late for a kid to be up," Fillingham commented as he stood on the edge of the oval carpet.

Mrs. Williamson walked into the living room and turned off the television. "I let him stay up late when my husband is away for work. He's a truck driver." She sat beside Patrick on the couch. The gray cushions were stiff, as if the furniture was new. Her husband's trucking business must do well.

Although Mrs. Williamson was heavy-set, the similarities between mother and son were visible: the same deep-blue eyes and apple cheekbones. Mrs. Williamson crossed her legs at the ankle and then pressed the floral fabric of her dress flat on her lap.

Christine sat down in the blue velvet wingback chair facing the couch, the teak coffee table between them.

Fillingham grabbed a dining room chair and placed it across from the Williamsons. "We can't find Wayne. It's almost midnight. He's a ten-year-old kid who had been gone for seven hours." Addressing Mrs. Williamson, he said, "We need you to tell us what's going on."

"Patrick's a good boy," Mrs. Williamson said, glancing at her son, whose head was bowed.

"Okay," Fillingham said, his tone encouraging.

"He—" she choked, "he can pick the wrong type of friend."

Christine and Fillingham waited.

"He likes to have fun, too much fun," Mrs. Williamson said. She looked down at Patrick beside her. His shaggy hair fell onto his face; he did not meet her glance.

"Mrs. Williamson. Patrick," Christine said, getting impatient. "Do you know where Wayne is? I'm worried about him. It's late. And it's cold outside. I want to make sure he's safe."

Mrs. Williamson shook her head, her chapped hands clasped.

Christine said, "You said on the phone, 'First Jacob, now Wayne.' What did you mean by that?"

Mrs. Williamson's face pinched as if she was trying not to cry.

Fillingham inched his chair closer. "If something is going on, Mrs. Williamson, you need to let us know. If someone has Wayne, or you know where he could be, tell us. Now."

"I can't," she choked out, shaking her head.

Fillingham leaned over and touched her hand. "You're obstructing justice and putting a child at risk, especially in this weather. Could you live with yourself if Wayne is harmed?"

"We were there," Patrick said in a strangled voice. He looked up briefly through his bangs at the officers, light brown freckles smattering his pale skin.

Fillingham turned. "Where?"

"Wayne, me and Roy. By the water. With Jacob." He looked over at his mother. Tears were shining on her cheeks, but she didn't stop him.

Christine said, "Wayne told us that Roy threw Jacob's baseball shoes out the window."

Patrick nodded.

"What happened next?" Christine asked.

"We were just bugging him," Patrick explained, his voice teary. "It was just for fun. Roy liked to pick on Jacob. Because he was new. Because of the way he talked."

"What happened after Roy tossed Jacob's shoes out the window?" asked Fillingham.

It was the same story Wayne had told Fillingham. The boys had run down to the water near the Gibraltar Lighthouse.

Fillingham prompted, "What happened when you reached the lagoon?"

Patrick's hand went to his eyes, covering them, as if he could block out the memory.

Mrs. Williamson turned to the officers. "Maybe we need a lawyer."

Fillingham responded, "Patrick is under twelve. We cannot charge or arrest him."

Her entire body deflated with resignation.

The boy's hands dropped from his face onto his lap. Looking down, he said quietly, "Roy ran to the water with Jacob's shoe. Wayne and I followed them to the lagoon. Roy was holding the shoe in the air and Jacob was jumping, trying to get it back."

"Where was the second shoe?" Christine asked.

"Jacob had it," Patrick answered. "Then Wayne left." He turned to Christine. "I thought he went to tell a teacher. I thought a teacher would come!" he wailed, his blue eyes anguished.

"What happened after Wayne left?" Fillingham asked.

Patrick looked away, staring at the blank face of the TV for a few moments. "Roy is strong." His bottom lip quivered. "And big. He kept the shoe away from Jacob."

Patrick paused. "Roy yelled, 'Come and get it!' and threw the shoe into the water. I could see it floating on top like a fish, thirty feet away." He looked at his mom, who placed a hand on his knee.

"Then what happened?" Christine asked gently.

Patrick's face scrunched as if he were trying to stop himself from crying. "Jacob went into the water to get his shoe."

Fillingham's hands spread wide. "But he couldn't swim."

"I know!" Patrick said, his eyes blazing at Fillingham. "Why would he do that? Why would he go in?" His voice ended in a sob.

The officers waited.

After a minute, Patrick continued. "Jacob tied his baseball shoe to his wrist—he didn't want Roy to take that one too." Patrick wiped his nose with his hand. "Then he went into the water with one arm in the air to keep his shoe dry." Patrick swallowed. "The water was up to here," he indicated his shoulders with the edge of his hand, "when Jacob grabbed the floating shoe and turned to come back. Suddenly, he slipped, like maybe the ground was bumpy or dropped off deeper and he...went...underwater."

Patrick was crying now, the tears wetting his freckled cheeks. "Jacob came to the surface, and his arms and legs were thrashing around as he tried to stand up. But...but it must have been too deep, and he couldn't touch bottom. He went underwater again and then came up for air. He was choking. He couldn't catch his breath. And he kept moving farther away."

Looking at Fillingham, then Christine, Patrick cried, "I tried to help him! Honest, I did. I went into the water to help him, but..."

"But?" Fillingham asked.

Patrick's blue eyes turned flat. "Roy stopped me."

Mrs. Williamson handed her son a tissue from the pocket of her housedress, and he blew his nose. He blew his nose again and wiped his eyes with a fresh tissue. He continued. "Roy was holding my arm tight with both hands. I pulled and pulled and hit him with my other hand, but he wouldn't let me go in. I could see the top of Jacob's head; it was bobbing on the water. Then there was nothing. He wasn't there anymore. After a few minutes, the baseball shoe floated in, but Jacob didn't come out of the water." Patrick sniffled for a few seconds. Addressing Christine, he cried, "Why didn't Wayne come back with a teacher? Why didn't he get help? From Miss Phillips. Tim. The principal. Anybody." The tears flowed, wetting his cheeks, snot trailing from his nose. "No. One. Came."

Mrs. Williamson gathered Patrick into her arms, staring at the officers while her son sobbed on her shoulder. After a few minutes, Patrick's tears were spent. He moved away from his mom, pushing the hair away from his damp face with his hand.

Fillingham asked in a soft voice, "What happened next?"

"We went back inside the school." His voice was flat, drained.

Fillingham said, "How'd you get inside?"

"Through the window. I gripped my hands together and gave Roy a foothold up. Once he was inside, he grabbed Jacob's suitcase and handed it to me through the window."

"Was Wayne in the room then?"

Patrick nodded. "Roy said he was asleep. Then we both walked along the path for a while and dumped the suitcase into the bay. We watched it sink. Then we came back. I boosted Roy inside, and he reached out the window and pulled me up and in. Then we went to bed."

Christine said, "You told no one what happened?"

He shook his head.

Christine said, "And how about the wet bed? When did you notice that?"

Patrick said, "I smelled it in the morning when Tim woke us up and lifted Jacob's blankets, looking for him in bed."

"Did Roy urinate in Patrick's bed?" Christine asked. "Or did Jacob, before he left?"

Patrick shrugged. "I don't know."

"Did Roy show you a knife?" Christine asked.

Patrick nodded. "He said it was for skinning deer. But I knew what he meant."

After a few seconds of silence, Mrs. Williamson said, "Are we done?"

Fillingham said, "Patrick, do you know where Wayne is?"

The boy shook his head.

"Could Roy have anything to do with Wayne's disappearance?" Christine asked.

"Roy does whatever he wants," Patrick said, his stare flat.

Mrs. Williamson said to Patrick, "Go upstairs and get your bag. Uncle Tommy is coming in a few minutes."

Patrick slipped off the couch and hurried upstairs, head bowed as he passed the police officers.

Mrs. Williamson turned to Christine. "Where have you looked for Wayne?"

"The neighborhood, our apartment building. King Street. The school. I've called his friends from school, from the apartment building, from his baseball teams."

"If Wayne's gone, Patrick's next," Mrs. Williamson said, her voice cracking.

"You think Roy is coming after Wayne and Patrick?" Fillingham asked.

She stood up. "We're going to my brother-in-law's for a couple of days while my husband is on the road. He's a cop. I'll feel safer there."

Fillingham got the brother-in-law's contact information from Mrs. Williamson. "I'll check in with you there later."

Mrs. Williamson nodded.

Fillingham said, "If you feel the need for protection tonight, I can have a police car swing by."

She shook her head. "We're already packed. We're being picked up in twenty minutes." She turned to Christine. "I will pray for Wayne. You need to find your brother."

Christine practically ran down the front walkway to the sidewalk. *Damn. Damn. Damn.* The conversation with Mrs. Williamson hadn't cleared anything up. Patrick's recounting of that night by the lagoon had ignited Christine's worry like a stick of dynamite. Something was wrong. Terribly wrong.

Did Roy have Wayne? Why? To silence him? If that were the case, why wouldn't Wayne grab Patrick, who knew the complete story? It didn't make sense.

"I need to check in with my mom," she said as she passed Fillingham's parked car and hustled toward Queen Street, mindful of the ice on the sidewalk lit silver by the three-quarter moon. "Maybe Wayne's back home."

Behind her, Fillingham's said, "Could Wayne be doing something he shouldn't be doing…smoking with older kids, having a drink or two in a parking lot?"

She looked back over her shoulder at her partner. "He's ten. He doesn't do those things." Immediately, she thought of the calls to the Youth Bureau regarding kids who were high or drunk or had got caught breaking and entering. Some parents were shocked at their child's criminal behavior. Others shrugged as if they had given up on their child and the possibility of rehabilitation.

No. Her brother wasn't like that.

She needed to talk to Phyllis and confirm that Wayne had returned home safely. Then they could all chuckle at Mrs. Williamson's preposterous theory that their boys were in danger.

The houses Christine and Fillingham passed were dark, residents settled into bed on this wintery night. A few living room windows glowed yellow-white as people stayed up to watch the news or the Friday night movie.

Reaching Queen Street, she spotted a phone booth in front of a restaurant and called home. "Is Wayne back?" she asked.

"No."

Christine's stomach plummeted. She shook her head at Fillingham standing outside the booth. "Mom, tell me exactly what Wayne said when he left."

"I told you, Christine. I was in the bathroom. He said he was going to see an old friend, and he'd be back soon. That he was going to Dodge or Rodge."

"What was that last part?" Christine clasped the phone tighter.

"I couldn't make it out." Phyllis's voice sounded strained but sober. Christine worried that her mom might have a few drinks if she was stressed.

Phyllis continued, "I thought he was making a joke—he was getting out of Dodge—but maybe he was saying Roger? Or lodge?"

Wayne didn't know anyone named Roger. "Was it lodge?" Christine asked. "Did he say he was going to a lodge?"

A slow exhale of her cigarette smoke. "I'm not sure."

"Could it be Colborne Lodge—in High Park?" Christine said quickly.

"I don't know," Phyllis said. "It could be. I wasn't paying attention."

"Mom, remember we took Wayne and Donna there to make Christmas crafts. And he went on a school trip. It's that old Victorian house owned by the couple who gave their property to the city."

"I don't know what he meant." Her voice caught. "I don't know where he is."

"Stay there in case he comes home," Christine instructed. "I'll call you in an hour after I check High Park."

"It's after midnight."

Phyllis worked in the Records Department of the police force. She had typed quite a few missing children reports, and not all of them had happy endings.

"I know, Mom." They had to think positive. "The police are patrolling our neighborhood, keeping an eye out for Wayne. If he's in High Park, then he's not far. Maybe he went tobogganing with a friend and lost track of time."

Christine said goodbye and pushed open the sliding doors of the booth.

"To Colborne Lodge?" Fillingham asked.

She nodded. "It's a long shot, but if he said a lodge, Colborne Lodge would be it. We go to High Park in the summer to swim in the pool. In the winter, we take a piece of cardboard and slide down the hills. So he's familiar with the area."

"What would he be doing there in the dark?" he asked.

Christine's shoulders slumped. "I don't know what to think—about the lodge or Roy or Mrs. Williamson."

"Let me make a couple of calls first," Fillingham said.

She could hear his conversation inside the booth. He asked Dispatch to notify Julie and Sarah that they were checking High Park for Christine's missing brother. He also gave Dispatch an address on Virtue Street.

As he exited the booth, she asked, "Was that O'Neil's address?"

He nodded. "I asked for a car to check in with them. See if Wayne was there."

"I called the O'Neils before, but no one picked up."

Exiting the booth, he said, "If we don't find Wayne in High Park, we'll request an all-district alert. Get more eyes looking."

She nodded, relieved that he was taking the lead. She was having a hard time figuring out what to do. Some part of her was incredulous, unbelieving. Wayne was missing! *Wayne.* Her baby brother. She remembered him as a toddler—curly chestnut hair, big brown eyes. He couldn't get enough tickling or roughhousing or games of peek-a-boo. His laugh was glorious.

Fillingham interrupted her thoughts. "Julie said they'll check with Dispatch to see if Wayne has been sighted in Parkdale or at O'Neil's. If not, they'll swing by High Park to help us with the search."

"Julie is great. You're all wonderful," Christine said. She felt weepy, so relieved that her friends and her partner were helping. Without them, she would be desperate, too frazzled to figure out what to do.

"We *are* wonderful," Fillingham confirmed as they headed back toward his car, "and that's exactly why we will find your brother—safe and sound."

Chapter 18

Fillingham's flashlight beam lit the carriage house beside Colborne Lodge, illuminating the two feet of snow pressed against its white octagonal doors. He had parked his Beaumont in a lot north of the lodge, and they were searching the area on foot.

"Wayne!" she shouted. "Wayne, it's Christine!"

"No one's been here lately, that's for sure," he said.

They trudged through the knee-high snow around to the back of the building and then headed toward a shoveled pathway leading to the lodge.

"He could be sledding on a hill," Christine said tentatively.

"It's dark." He looked around. "And the hills nearby are heavily treed."

"Maybe he came here with a friend, and they got lost on the way home."

"I thought you said you've been here before," Fillingham said.

"He has. With school and my family. With adults around, he probably didn't pay attention to the route."

"After we survey the park, we'll check the bus stops on the Queensway and up at Bloor."

"I don't think he has streetcar fare," she said.

"How long would it take him to walk home?"

"An hour, maybe. If he knew where he was going."

Fillingham headed toward the front porch of the lodge. Their flashlight beams crossed as they lit the bushes hugging the outside of the old brick house, branches powdered with snow like icing sugar.

"Wayne!" she called as her boots thudded onto the wooden planks of the porch. "It's Christine. Come out. I'm not mad; I just want to know you're okay."

Fillingham pressed his face against one of the narrow parlor windows. "Can't see a thing," he said. "Curtains are closed. Lights off."

"Do you think Wayne is inside the lodge?"

He pushed himself away from the window. "If he got lost or hurt, maybe he got in and is hunkering down for the night."

"Let's check around—aah!" Christine grabbed her leg. "Ugh!" A thud in her back.

"Get down!" he cried.

A zing near her shoulder. They crouched in the far corner of the fenced-in porch, flashlights clicked off, hearing *ping, ping, ping* as bullets hit the brick wall above their heads, dust and small chips of clay falling onto their head and shoulders. The light above the front entrance made them easily visible.

"Someone's shooting at us with a BB gun," he said, pushing her toward the porch railing. "Head to the back of the house"

They crab-walked along the far side of the house, trying to keep low as they tromped through the snow in the shadowy darkness. For a moment, Christine felt relief—they had escaped the gunman. A shot hit the bricks above them with a pinging sound, and Fillingham swore. A few more pellets thudded softly into the snowdrift beside them.

"He's following us. We're sitting ducks," he said.

"We can get into the lodge through the greenhouse," she said. She took off, hunched over as she moved along the side of the building.

The greenhouse was a later addition to the house, attached to the back kitchen. They regarded the diamond-shaped window of its locked door. Abruptly, Fillingham swung the butt of his flashlight into the pane, his other arm raised to protect his face from the glass shards that tinkled to the ground. With two more swings, he had the glass cleared, and he reached in the open window to unlock the door. *Ping.* "Ow!" He grabbed his neck, then quickly opened the door.

Bending low, she followed him in. Together, they pushed a heavy wooden cupboard over to block the door, the bowls on its shelves rattling.

Christine led Fillingham past the rows of plants and pots to the main floor kitchen. From her visits before, she knew the bedrooms were upstairs; servants' quarters and an office were below in the cellar.

In the kitchen, she pulled drawers open in the dim light, shuffling the content through her bare fingers. Gray-white light from the outdoor lamp came in through the single square window.

"Look," Fillingham said. He held up a knife—no—a letter opener.

Tossing away a wooden spoon, Christine ran to the fireplace built into one wall. A black metal cauldron hung from a hook over the empty fireplace pit. She pawed along the base of the pit, looking for something she could use as a weapon.

No luck. Beside the fire, she saw the dark outline of logs. Reaching out, her knuckles rapped against something hard and smooth. A handle of an ax.

She grabbed the small kindling ax. "Upstairs," she called to Fillingham over her shoulder as she headed out of the kitchen.

Ascending the circular staircase, she listened for the sound of BB gunshot or the tinkle of a broken window.

In the main bedroom, she strode past the high bed and stove to the window. Carefully leaning out from the window frame, she spotted the pathway from the carriage shed to the front door that she and her partner had walked. "I can't see anyone," she said to Fillingham, who stood on the other side of the window, letter opener held in his hand like a stubby dagger.

"We need backup," he said. "Does this place have a phone?"

"Maybe in the cellar office." She wasn't keen on getting trapped in the basement if the shooter broke in. "I hear nothing. Do you think he's gone?"

He peeked out behind the curtains to survey outside, then leaned back again. "I don't know what the hell is going on."

They listened for several minutes, taking turns looking out the window, scanning the yard that was lit by the front entrance light, the shadows deepening farther from the house.

"Could a kid be trying out his new BB gun?" she asked.

"It's not your brother, is it?" he questioned.

"No." Her tone was exasperated. "He wouldn't do that. Plus, he doesn't have a gun."

"Teeny!" It was a child's scream from outside.

Christine pressed her face and palms against the window. There—a figure off to the right in the front yard. "No!" she said. Mark O'Neil, Roy's father, held a BB gun in one fist and Wayne in the other.

"Wait!" Fillingham said.

Ignoring her partner, she sprinted out of the room and threw herself down the staircase, shoving the ax up her sleeve handle first. Reaching the main floor, she ran through the parlor and flung open the front door.

A BB pellet hit the soft wool of her coat. "Ugh!" Then she was on her hands and knees, tackled by Fillingham, the ax sliding out from her sleeve onto the porch.

"Do you want to lose an eye?" her partner growled as he pushed her away from the light haloing the entrance. She retrieved the ax as he shoved her behind the bushes that lined the side of the house.

Sitting with her back against the brick, knees up to her chin, ax in hand, she turned to her partner in the dark shadows. "He has Wayne." She stood up.

"Sit down!" He jerked her down by the elbow. "You're going to get us both shot."

"He has Wayne," she repeated, her voice quavering.

"I know, Christine." His voice was soft, sympathetic. "So let's get him back."

"I'll go first," she said.

"No. You're too slow. He'll get in a hundred shots before we get near. We have to get close enough to disarm him. There are two of us. That's our advantage. And we're armed."

Several shots rang out. Snow and small chunks of bricks fell onto their shoulders.

"He's getting closer," Fillingham said. "I'll run out and head south, distract him, and you close in while he's focusing on me. Tackle him and secure him to the ground."

Before Christine could respond, he stood up and ran out of the bush. Immediately, shots rang out.

Christine crawled out from under the branches, her bare hands dirty and wet. Fillingham sprinted across the snow to the fenced-in cenotaph where the original owners of Colborne Lodge rested. Gosh, he was fast. He hurled himself at the black iron fence, scaled the six-foot rods, and threw himself over their pointed tips.

Barking at Wayne to walk ahead of him, O'Neil approached the stone monument, rifle held high as he took aim, bullets ringing out when they hit the metal fence.

Fillingham rolled behind a monument and disappeared from sight.

He'd gone so fast, Christine hadn't time to close in on O'Neil. She stood at the corner of the lodge, frozen with indecision. She had to rescue Wayne. And stop O'Neil from shooting at Fillingham. But the moment to apprehend O'Neil had passed. *Damn!* As soon as she approached him, he would have sixty feet of warning of her presence.

She tried to think, push down the surging emotions of fear and fury that urged her to charge out screaming and wrest the rifle from O'Neil's hands. He was too far away, and she was too slow. She forced herself to crouch low and follow the bushes back around the side of the lodge to the carriage house, shoulders hunched in case O'Neil spied her movement. She could hear shots coming from the cenotaph, O'Neil barking that cops were cowards.

She continued on the path northward to a group of maple trees. The plan was to cross the road to the hill that sloped toward Grenadier Pond, wend her way through the saplings toward the cenotaph and surprise O'Neil from the other side.

On the count of three, she sprinted across the asphalt road, eyes on the columns of birches lit white by the half-moon, afraid to look left in case O'Neil spied her and put a bullet in her eye. Reaching the forest, she crunched through the trees, her boots cracking on dry twigs, slipping on the uneven terrain of snow, rocks and dead leaves. She slowed down, trying to muffle her footsteps, cursing her weight and her clumsiness—she sounded like a thrashing buffalo.

Slowing, she threaded in and out of trees as she headed toward the lodge, one hand pushing branches out of her way while the other squeezed the ax head in her palm.

Spotting the roof of the lodge silhouetted in the lamplight, she began ascending the hill. At the top, she paused behind a large oak, listening. She could hear her hurried breath, the hum of distant cars on the freeway and the rattle of dry branches in the breeze.

Where was Wayne? Was he still with O'Neil by the cemetery? Leaning out, she scanned the area in front of the lodge over to the cenotaph. No one in sight.

Her back pressed against the oak tree, she waited five minutes. Where were they? Where was Wayne? She counted sixty more seconds. Nothing. Head down in case O'Neil shot at her face, she stepped out of the foliage. When nothing happened, she jogged over to the cenotaph, hunched over, her gaze sweeping left and right for her brother.

Crouching at the metal fence, she called in a low, urgent voice, "Fillingham."

She heard rustling, and Fillingham appeared. He looked behind her, then pulled himself over the fence.

"Where are they?" she asked. "Where's Wayne?"

"I heard footsteps crunching through the forest. I think they went down the hill toward Grenadier Pond." He pointed toward an entry point in the trees.

Taking the lead, she headed back into the shrubbery. The first twenty feet were manageable, the forest lit with the golden light from the lodge porch. As she went deeper into the trees, she was enveloped in brown shadow. Her hands extended to feel for tree trunks and grasp at branches, while her feet stepped gingerly to find solid footing. Her partner followed behind, his steps quieter than hers.

O'Neil had Wayne. The thought pulsed in her head, constricted her throat. Roy's dad had her brother, and it was all her fault. O'Neil had warned her that something bad would happen if she continued the investigation. Her curiosity, her questions, her pigheadedness had made Wayne a target. Now she, Fillingham and her brother were in O'Neil's trap, playing some terrible game.

Shivering with fear, with adrenaline, with the night cold, she continued down the hill. The slope evened out, the trees and bushes thinning, backlit from below. She positioned herself behind the biggest tree and peered out. At the bottom of the slope was a concrete walking path that ran along the perimeter of Grenadier Pond.

"Come out, come out, wherever you are!" a male voice yelled.

O'Neil! He was somewhere north of her location. She took a few steps toward the voice.

"Wayne, ask your sister and her little sidekick to come out," O'Neil said.

"Christine," Wayne sobbed. "Help me, help—!" His plea changed into a squeal of pain.

She ran down the rest of the hill, stumbling over tree roots and rocks, her right fist squeezing the iron ax head in her sleeve so it wouldn't fall out, until she reached the flatness of the shoveled sidewalk. Off the path to her right, beside a trio of thick trees, stood O'Neil, BB rifle held in his left hand, Wayne's coat sleeve clenched in his other fist.

"Wayne!" Christine called. "It's okay. I'm here." She approached them from thirty feet away, hands in the air, the ax sliding down her sleeve so that the handle nudged her elbow. She did not know where Fillingham was, but she couldn't wait for him to create a distraction. Wayne was in peril. Now. If she could get close enough, she would tackle Roy's dad or club him with the ax.

O'Neil's unshaven face smirked as she neared. Under his open plaid lumber jacket, he wore a dirty white t-shirt. A knapsack hung over his back.

Wayne was wearing his winter coat and boots, hatless and mittless. His eyes were wild with fear.

Christine met her brother's glance, trying to calm him, to signal that everything would be all right, although her own body was rigid with fear.

She called out to O'Neil, "Let Wayne go."

O'Neil said, "Do you know that Jacob kid sent his pitbull cousin after my son?"

Christine frowned. "Do you mean Mariusz?"

"No one threatens my kid. Ain't that right, Wayne?" O'Neil shook Wayne like a manic puppeteer, making the boy's teeth clatter.

"Stop!" Christine said. "This has nothing to do with Wayne."

"Oh, this has everything to do with Wayne," O'Neil said. "Doesn't it, boy?"

Walking closer, her arms still in the air, she said, "He's a child. Let him go. The adults can work this out. No one needs to get hurt." If she could get her brother to move three or four steps away from O'Neil, she would attack.

O'Neil cocked his head. "Your brother should have thought about that before he shot his mouth off at school, telling everyone my son's a murderer."

Shaking her head, she said, "This is a misunderstanding, Mr. O'Neil. If you're talking about Jacob Nowak, he died by accidental drowning."

O'Neil nodded. "Some big-mouth blabbed that Roy was there when Jacob drowned."

"It wasn't me!" Wayne cried, looking at O'Neil and then at Christine. "I was only there for a minute. I left! I didn't see anything!" He ended on a protracted sob.

"Blaming Patrick, are you?" O'Neil said, looking down at Wayne. "That's convenient."

O'Neil looked quickly back at Christine, motioning her to stop with the hand holding the rifle.

She was ten feet away. Too far. "Mr. O'Neil, sir," Christine said, "no one's coming after Roy." Her arms widened. "It was the unfortunate drowning of a boy who didn't know how to swim. We know that. The coroner's report confirms it. The investigation is closed. Let Wayne go and we can all go home." She glanced at the forest behind O'Neil. Where the heck was Fillingham? She needed the distraction—now.

"Yeah, right. Like that's going to happen," O'Neil replied. "You're after my son, which means you're after me." He took a step closer to her. "I told you to back off. I warned you, but you wouldn't listen. You're a stupid bitch who doesn't do what she's told."

"Mr. O'Neil," her tone was placating as she shuffled a few steps forward, "none of the boys are in trouble. Even if they were present when Jacob drowned, Ontario has no Good Samaritan law. No one expects a person to go into the water, endangering themselves, to save another person—and we certainly can't expect that of children."

He was listening.

Maintaining eye contact as she inched forward, she tried to focus her thoughts on O'Neil and not Wayne's terrified face. "Juvenile court starts at twelve years old. You cannot charge a ten-year-old with a crime."

He loosened his grip on Wayne's arm.

"Roy is free of all charges and wrongdoings," she said, "as are all the boys. It was an unfortunate accident. That's all."

Please listen. Please let go of Wayne. Let it end here.

They waited, their silence filled with the sound of the rattling branches, the scurry of a small animal through dead leaves and the hum of car tires from the Queensway a quarter mile south.

O'Neil nodded, as if to himself. "Wayne," he turned to look at the boy, "take a walk." He shoved Wayne so that the boy staggered a few steps onto the path before he stopped, half-crouched, ready to bolt.

Thank goodness. Christine took a step toward her brother.

O'Neil raised his BB gun two feet from Wayne's head.

Christine halted.

"If a pellet hits you in the head, boy," O'Neil said, "at this close range, it will go right through your skull to your brain, since it's still nice and soft."

Wayne stared up at him with wide, horrified eyes.

"Take a walk onto the ice," O'Neil said to Wayne, his chin indicating Grenadier Pond.

"It's not safe," Christine said. A few days last week had soared above freezing, making the ice thickness unpredictable. The oval pond shone like a silver disc, lit on the east side from the pathway lamps and on the west by the house lights bordering the park's boundary.

"Looks safe enough to me. Walk!" O'Neil ordered.

"Wait!" she said, her hands in the air to stop him. "I'll go instead. Let Wayne go, and I'll do whatever you want."

"Hmmm," he said, head tilted as if in contemplation. "How about calling your partner out?"

No! Don't make me choose between Wayne and Fillingham.

O'Neil lifted his gun to his shoulder and shot Wayne five times, each shot making a *phht* sound. Wayne screamed in pain, clutching his leg, and then his back. He fell to one knee, then collapsed flat on the ground.

"NO!" she cried, stepping toward O'Neil.

"Touch me," he warned Christine, "and I'll shoot him in the head."

"Stop!" Fillingham's voice rang out. "I'm here!"

All three turned toward the voice coming out of the bush. After a few seconds of crackling twigs, Fillingham stepped out onto the pathway ten feet away.

What was Fillingham's plan? He was too far away for her to read his expression. Should she charge at O'Neil and risk Wayne getting shot in the head? Would Fillingham jump O'Neil when he got close? Or stab him with the letter opener?

Christine lowered her hands a few inches, feeling the ax head slide down toward her palm.

O'Neil swiveled to look at her; he strode over and grabbed Wayne by the coat collar, yanking him close. Wayne yelped.

Christine raised her arms in the air again.

The nose of O'Neil's rifle pressed into the back of Wayne's head. "I've changed my mind," he bellowed. "Both of you," O'Neil indicated Christine and Fillingham with his chin, "get out on the ice."

The police officers looked at each other. She didn't want to move away from her brother. She had to keep him near.

"Now!" O'Neil yelled.

"Mr. O'Neil," she said. "No crime has been committed. Roy's not in trouble. Nobody's been hurt. Please let us go."

"Move!" O'Neil commanded.

"The ice is dangerous," Fillingham said. "It's not completely frozen."

O'Neil's lip curled. "Then maybe you two shouldn't have been fooling around on it...or gone out to rescue young Wayne here."

Christine said, "Wayne doesn't have to come with us. We'll go." She edged toward the frozen lip of the pond, her eyes on Wayne and O'Neil, thoughts racing, trying to decide what to do, what choice would save Wayne.

As Fillingham stepped slowly toward the pond, their eyes locked. She squeezed the hard blade of the ax. Now. Should she rush O'Neil?

As if reading her mind, O'Neil raised the rifle to Wayne's temple—the soft, vulnerable spot in the skull—a small smile on his face as if daring her to lunge. "Move," he said again, his tone almost sounding polite.

Christine and Fillingham shuffled backward onto the ice, taking the smallest steps possible. Christine tried not to think of her own sprawled body by Trout Pond, the cracking sound as the ice splintered and the shocking cold water on her body.

O'Neil continued to prompt them with, "Move! Move! Move!" until they were thirty feet offshore.

Grabbing Wayne by the arm, with his rifle slack in his other hand, O'Neil escorted the boy to the frozen edge of the pond. With a shove, he pushed Wayne onto the ice.

Wayne skidded, fell on his knees, stood up again and ran and slipped toward Christine.

Christine grabbed her brother in an embrace, arms around his wiry body, her hand pressed against his warm face that was wet with tears, her eyes still on O'Neil.

"Run south," Fillingham said. "He can't get us all."

"Take Wayne," she said. "You're faster."

The trio angled toward a landing point three hundred yards south of where O'Neil was standing. Christine trailed behind the two males, feet skidding on the ice, her eyes on O'Neil.

O'Neil slipped the brown knapsack off his shoulder and placed it on the ground. From the bag, he extracted a long bow and a shaft of arrows. Quickly, he notched an arrow in the bow and aimed at the trio. "Stop!" he roared.

"Geoffrey!" she screamed. "Get down!" O'Neil had a clear shot at them, their bodies backlit by the lights from the bordering houses.

A tremendous *Bang! Bang! Bang!* erupted from the treed hill two hundred feet north. All of them turned. Twin light beams bounced around inside the darkened thicket, moving down the hill like an out-of-control sled. After a metallic screech, the two circles of light swiveled to look at them and started moving south down the narrow walking path.

It was a police car, slamming trees and bumping over rocks as it careered toward O'Neil, pinning him in its headlights. As it neared, she saw the lettering on the side—WB1—the Women's Bureau.

Julie! Sarah!

"Run!" Christine told Fillingham.

"Julie's in the car," he said.

"I'll take care of her," she yelled, waving him away. "Take Wayne and get help."

The patrol car continued its rollicking route, slowing down when its long metal snout scraped a tree trunk. It picked off a garbage bin, which rolled away with a deafening rattle. The car's wide carriage was too broad for the pathway, boxed in by shrubbery on one side and Grenadier Pond on the other.

There was a roar of acceleration. O'Neil scrambled up the hill, disappearing into the shadowed security of the tree trunks.

The car hit a large rock with a thunk, then steered toward the pond. The driver overcorrected, and the car veered sharply toward an oak tree, slamming into it with a grinding shriek of steel as the car hood accordioned and the front tire collapsed inward.

Julie! Sarah! Christine slid and jogged toward the vehicle, praying she didn't step on any soft spots on the ice, trying to judge the hue of gray under the snow-smeared pond and walk on the thickest part. In her peripheral vision, she saw Wayne and Fillingham nearing the shore.

Sarah appeared in the open passenger window, reaching up to the roof to pull herself out of the wreckage. The door must be wedged shut. Suddenly, she disappeared from sight.

O'Neil! He had reappeared on the path and was advancing toward the patrol car with his BB gun raised to his shoulder, heading toward the passenger window.

No! Not Sarah. She was a sitting duck in the crumpled patrol car.

"Hey!" Christine yelled, waving her arms above her head. O'Neil spotted her.

Squeezing the ax handle, she headed straight for O'Neil. She lost her footing, falling hard on one knee, but pushed herself up, slowly gaining speed. She ran toward him, the ax handle clutched in her fist as she pumped her arms, praying she didn't break through the ice before reaching land.

O'Neil dropped to one knee, hauled the rifle up to his shoulder and took aim.

"Uh!" BB shots thudded against her wool coat—her abdomen, then her shoulder, the flesh of her leg. She cried out when a pellet hit her cheek and the next skinned her ear. Her free arm raised to block her face, but she forced herself to continue her momentum. She would stop this man who was threatening her friends, her partner and her brother, and take him out if this was the last thing she did.

When she was thirty feet away, O'Neil dropped his rifle and reached for the bow. As he slotted an arrow into the notch, Christine made herself continue running—closer, closer—until she was near enough to take aim at the white shirt under the open plaid jacket, envisioning it as the wooden target on the tree in the station's back-yard. Arcing the ax behind her head like she had when playing against Fillingham, she threw it with all her strength, yelling as it released.

Something hit her leg, and she stumbled to her knees, and then sprawled onto the pathway on her back. The long shaft of an arrow stuck out of her thigh, as if it were pinning her to the concrete.

She pushed herself up on her elbows—O'Neil, had she stopped him?

O'Neil sat propped against a tree where he had fallen back, eyes wide with shock, face so white his grizzled beard looked black, the ax embedded in his left shoulder.

From behind the patrol car, Julie appeared, walking in a slight crouch toward O'Neil. In his dazed state, he paid no attention to her. As she stepped into the forest behind him, she pulled out her billy club. The club came down on the back of O'Neil's skull with three quick raps. He slid sideways down the tree, unconscious, the wooden ax handle still embedded in his shoulder.

A child's voice cried out, "You killed my dad!"

Julie turned. Roy O'Neil stood ten feet away, mouth pulled back in an anguished grimace. He had picked up his father's bow and arrow. He raised the bow into the air, arrow taut, and pointed the weapon at Julie.

A figure catapulted out of the trees, tackling Roy. The two bodies rolled together, bow and arrow flinging into the air. Fillingham! He wrestled the boy flat until he had Roy prone, digging his knee into the child's back and pressing his shoulders down with his hands.

"Stop struggling!" Fillingham commanded. "Your dad's not dead."

Sarah appeared from behind the patrol car, handcuffs in hand. "The radio's still working. I called in a 10-87. Dispatch is sending fire and ambulance." She kneeled beside Fillingham to handcuff Roy.

"My dad will get you!" Roy said, angling his head to look up at them. "You're dead meat—all of you!"

Fillingham cuffed Roy's head with the heel of his hand and then leaned down to face Roy. "If you don't shut up, I'll make sure your dad is the last person, the very last person, to get medical attention. In fact, why don't I drag him into the bushes right now and leave him there."

Roy glared at him but said nothing.

Fillingham looked over at Christine. "Jesus, you're hurt!" He got off Roy and ran over to her.

While Sarah handcuffed the unconscious O'Neil, Julie hurried to get a first-aid kit out of the car trunk.

Kneeling beside Christine, he examined the arrow sticking out of her right thigh.

"Where's Wayne?" she asked, clutching Fillingham's sleeve. An ambulance siren wailed in the distance.

"He's safe. He's hiding in the lodge in the cellar. I'll get him in a minute."

A dizzying wave of relief washed over her.

Sarah said, "I'll go get Wayne." She turned and headed up the hill.

"What do you need, Geoff?" Julie asked, holding up the metal box with the red cross.

"Give me a minute." He gently pressed on Christine's shoulder to get her to lie down on her back.

She could feel him pull at something—he was ripping the fabric of her pants—and then the cold air on her thigh. She propped herself on her elbows, looking at the wooden shaft with the white triangle of feathers protruding from her leg. It didn't seem real. It was as if her body belonged to someone else.

"Ow!" she said as he pressed down near the wound. She felt an instant wave of dizziness.

"It's not bleeding much," he called over his shoulder to Julie. "The arrow plugged the wound. We need to leave it there until she gets to the hospital."

Julie kneeled beside O'Neil to press a wad of gauze around the embedded ax. "This guy's hemorrhaging like a stuck pig, but I think it's just a shoulder wound." She pressed both hands on either side of the ax. "Thank God he's still out cold."

"That's quite the technique with the billy," Fillingham said.

Julie addressed Fillingham. "Better mind your manners."

Another siren joined the first—a fire engine. "How are they going to get down here?" he asked.

Julie arched her eyebrows. "I made a path for them with WB1."

As Julie and Fillingham bantered, Christine let her elbows slide underneath her. The police car, the trees, her friends' jackets blurred into shimmering lines of silver and gray and black.

The burning in her leg had gone; now, it felt numb. She lay on her back, gazing up into the dark bowl of sky dotted with constellations, the wind stirring the top of the snow around her so a few flakes melted on her face and caught in her eyelashes.

Everyone was safe: Wayne, Fillingham, Julie, Sarah. All the people she loved. The relief washed over her like a balm, her partner's anchoring presence beside her. Pressure on her inner wrist meant Fillingham was checking her heart rate. Her gaze found the pulsing brightness of the North Star directly above her, its light warming the surrounding stars, and she stared at it until the ambulance arrived.

Chapter 19

Julie leaned her head on Fillingham's shoulder, her blond bob spilling onto his navy sweater, her two hands clasped in his. She was still in her uniform, minus the hat. The pair sat side-by side on the empty bed next to Christine's hospital bed. Mascara was smudged under Julie's eyes and an oval bump rouged her forehead, but her lips sported a fresh application of tangerine lipstick.

Fillingham looked like Fillingham—alert, twitchy, even at four in the morning. Just the occasional droop of his eyelids showed he hadn't been to bed in thirty hours.

Sitting in a visitor's chair on Christine's other side, Sarah tried unsuccessfully to muffle a yawn. Her short brown curls were mussed, and she blinked sleepily. Her husband Don had already swung by the hospital in his patrol car to check on her after hearing her radio call of "Officer down" and request for medical and fire. He'd be back shortly at the end of his shift to pick her up.

After Christine's trip to X-ray, the surgeon concluded the arrow had missed the major blood vessels and sent her to the operating room to have the shaft removed. Now she sat in the four-bed police ward, wound stitched, woozy from morphine.

Smiling at her friends, Christine surveyed the room. Maybe it was the painkillers, but it felt like her body had exhaled its tension in one long breath, starting from her center, down her limbs to her fingertips and toes. Sure, she was wounded, and the pellet marks stung, but Wayne had been found, her friends were safe and the truth about Jacob Nowak's death had been revealed like an onion finally unpeeled to its core.

"You still with us?" Sarah asked. Her fingertips touched Christine's wrist.

"A bit groggy," Christine replied, smiling.

"You're so mellow," Julie said to Christine.

"You should see her when she's drinking," Fillingham said.

"Hey," Christine protested, but the word came out more like a salutation than a protest.

Julie stretched her arms above her head. "It's almost morning. We should get some shuteye."

Shaking Julie's shoulder gently, Fillingham said, "You need to stay awake until Dr. Jim discharges you. Make sure you don't have a concussion."

Julie's arms came down. "I don't know what all the fuss is about. I didn't bump my head that hard on the windshield."

"The lump is the size of a lemon," Christine said.

Julie glared at Christine. "You have a hole in your leg, and you look like you've come down with chicken pox."

Fillingham said, "It's not a competition, ladies."

"Julie," Sarah chided, staring at her friend from across Christine's bed, "she's just out of surgery."

Julie rolled her eyes.

"And," Sarah continued, "her chicken pox is from the BB pellets meant for us. O'Neil was going to riddle us like Swiss cheese."

Julie pressed one hand to her chest. "Did you forget I saved Christine from being speared by a second arrow by knocking O'Neil unconscious!"

Fillingham leaned away to look Julie in the face. "With that swing, you may have a secondary career in pugilism, my love, or at the very least, tennis."

"Can we start with driving lessons?" Sarah asked.

Julie pulled a face. "I got us down to the pond, didn't I?"

"You took out an entire staircase," Sarah said.

"It's the result that counts," Julie said.

"How did you know where to find us?" Fillingham asked.

"We drove into High Park to look for Wayne when he hadn't been found anywhere else," Sarah answered. "We saw your car parked near Colborne Lodge. After we stepped out of our vehicle, we heard a child scream."

"Why didn't you find us on foot?" Fillingham asked Julie.

She shook her head. "No time. Plus, we're not armed. I knew about the staircase, so I took the shortcut down."

"Did you hear the tow truck driver when he saw the patrol car?" Sarah said.

"He had a few choice words," Fillingham responded.

They laughed.

"When you save the day, sometimes there's collateral damage," Julie said dismissively.

"WB1 is headed for the scrapyard," Sarah said sadly. "I'll miss her."

"Que sera, sera," Julie sang.

"Christine," Sarah said, leaning forward in her chair, "Where did you get the ax? I was shocked when I saw it in your hand when you charged off the ice."

Christine said, "I grabbed it from the lodge."

"I can't believe you hit O'Neil with it," Sarah said.

"It wasn't a bull's eye," Fillingham said.

"You're criticizing my aim?" Christine said.

Fillingham answered, "I'm just saying you've thrown better."

She felt a rush of emotion for her partner, who had risked his life for her and her brother. "Every time I play you at the station, I throw better."

"Christine!" a child's voice called. Wayne ran into the room and threw himself at his older sister, hugging her hard.

Christine winced as he pressed against her bandaged thigh. The anesthetic must be wearing off, but she held him tight, one hand cupping his head, the other arm squeezing him to her. She inhaled the sweaty boy smell of his hair. Her brother was here, in the flesh, safe.

Phyllis followed Wayne into the room.

"Let's give them a few minutes," Sarah said. As the officers filed out, Christine heard Julie ask Fillingham, "Am I allowed tea, or is that verboten, too?"

"Hey, Mom," Christine said. "Wayne check out okay?"

Her brother had been driven to the hospital from Grenadier Pond in a police car, accompanied by Sarah and Julie. After Christine was loaded into an ambulance, Fillingham hopped in and sat on a box of medical supplies beside the attendant. O'Neil was placed in a second ambulance, and a truculent Roy was taken into care by a social worker.

Phyllis said, "The marks on Wayne's skin are swollen," she pointed at Christine's face, "like yours. But the doctor says it's just bruising. He'll be fine."

Wayne hopped off the bed, scanning Christine's body. "Where's the arrow?"

"They took it out," Christine said.

"Did you keep it?" he asked.

Christine coughed a laugh. "I didn't ask for it."

Phyllis scanned the room's medical equipment. "This is the second time you've been in a hospital since being on the Island."

"A few stitches, Mom, that's all," Christine said, trying to interrupt the familiar lecture regarding the danger of her policing job compared to Records. "And we found Wayne."

Her mom smiled, thin lines webbing her eyes. "Yes, you did." Phyllis placed a hand on Wayne's shoulder. "You've seen Christine. Now she needs to rest. We have to pick Donna up from the Derringers as well. A patrol car is waiting to take us home."

Christine nodded. "I'll be back for breakfast. Don't eat all the Cheerios," she addressed Wayne.

Steering Wayne by the shoulder, Phyllis walked him in front of her and out of the room. She said, "I'll meet you at the elevators, Wayne," then stepped back into the room.

"Did you forget something, Mom?" Christine asked.

"Hans Jansen is not your father," she said.

Christine twitched into alertness.

Phyllis stared at Christine with her deep brown eyes. "That picture, the one in the frame. I saw it in the newspaper one day and got a friend who worked in the ads department to get me a copy. It's a photo of a Norwegian pilot, Hans Jansen, as you found out. But he's no one. I never knew him. I just picked out the photo and told you he was your father, Thomas Lane."

Christine waited.

Phyllis broke eye contact, scanning the room. Taking a deep breath, she regarded Christine again. "I don't know a Thomas Lane, either. I met your dad at a dance. He was a guy who had extra time on his hands and a rich fiancée he was marrying in two weeks. He moved on and never looked back." She paused. "I wish it was different, but it's not." After a few seconds, Phyllis turned on her heel and left.

Alone in her hospital room, Christine stared at the institutional gray wall across from her. Her dad wasn't a Norwegian pilot. Or Canadian Air Force Captain Thomas Lane. She didn't even know if her father had been in the military. He had been engaged when he met Phyllis, which meant Christine was a bastard abandoned by her father.

After a while, she closed her eyes, blocking out the olive faces of the monitors, the shelves of boxed gauze and the equipment carts. She had her family: Phyllis, Wayne and Donna. And her Women's Bureau friends who had risked their lives for her and Wayne tonight. And, of course, Fillingham, who had her back.

She didn't need a father.

A knock fluttered her eyes open. It was Dr. Jim, whose calm demeanor and dry humor were renowned amongst his police patients.

"Sorry to disturb you," he said. "I heard you were clamoring to get home. I'll do a final examination and then the nurse can start on your discharge papers."

Christine said, "I feel good. Very little pain."

"May I?" he asked. Lifting the sheet at her nod, he surveyed her bandaged thigh and then felt the area around the wound with his fingers. He asked her to bend her leg and rotate her ankle. A dull pain started when she moved her leg; the anesthetic must be wearing off.

"Looks good," he said. "No impact on mobility or range of motion. I'll give you some painkillers for home. Monitor the area around the wound. If it becomes streaky red, feels warm to the touch or you feel nauseous or run a temperature, come right back in." He waited for her to nod before saying, "Let's look at the pellet welts."

Leaning in, he examined the marks on her face, neck and hands. She had others on her torso and legs, but her clothing had cushioned the pellets' impact, and these welts were less swollen. "Can't say I've seen this combination of arrow and pellet injuries before."

"It's a first for me."

"You were far enough away that the bullets didn't penetrate the skin. Apply ice when you get home to reduce the swelling, and they should heal nicely."

A male voice said, "Dr. Jim?"

They turned toward the doorway. Deputy Chief Darlow stepped into the room, his six feet three inches almost brushing the top of the door frame.

Oh, no! Not him again.

"Deputy Chief," Dr. Jim acknowledged.

"Sir," Christine said, sitting up. Why was Darlow assigned to visiting injured officers? This was the second time he had seen her in the police ward—it made her seem injury-prone. Furthermore, he had told her explicitly to back off the Jacob Nowak case—to leave O'Neil and the Nature School alone.

"In the thick of things again, PW Lane?" The deputy crossed his arms in his dark wool coat. He was wearing a suit underneath, not his uniform, so he mustn't be making a statement to the papers.

"I'm fine, sir, just a few stitches," she answered. "Ask Dr. Jim." She looked at the doctor with imploring eyes.

"I see you two know each other," Dr. Jim said as he scribbled on a clipboard. With a flourish of signature, he said, "You're good to go, PW."

"You left a mess in High Park," Deputy Darlow said to her. "We needed a crane to lift the patrol car out."

The state of the WB1 patrol car was hardly her fault, but no point getting Julie in trouble. Christine was lucky that her friends had come to the rescue. Their entrance had given Fillingham time to get Wayne safely off the ice.

"John," Dr. Jim said, addressing the deputy, "she was saving her brother and fellow police officers from attack."

Deputy Darlow raised his hands in surrender. "Even the medical establishment sings your praises."

Dr. Jim said, "Not to mention she solved the mystery of a child's drowning."

The deputy frowned at Dr. Jim. "I believe I see you enough at the curling rink."

Smiling, Dr. Jim said, "We're playing Sunday night, by the way. Seven o'clock."

Deputy Darlow turned to Christine. "I can't decide if you are insubordinate or a hero."

She remained quiet.

He continued. "Despite explicit orders, PW Lane, you continued with the Jacob Nowak and Ginny Rogers investigations. Both cases were outside your jurisdiction. In the police force, we need bravery and investigative skills, but orders must be followed and hierarchy respected. Otherwise, the organization devolves into chaos."

Should she apologize? Explain why she continued her respective investigations?

"I'll bid you goodbye, PW," Dr. Jim interrupted. "A nurse will be in shortly to discharge you." He turned to the deputy. "Are you heading out, John, or is there more chewing out to be done?"

The deputy stood there, looking far from pleased as he regarded his friend and then Christine. "I'll walk out with you," the deputy said to Dr. Jim and headed toward the door.

Over his shoulder, Dr. Jim said, "I'll reserve a bed for you, PW Lane, for next time."

"I won't be back!" she exclaimed, hoping Deputy Darlow heard her declaration.

Ten days later, Christine and Fillingham shivered in the bow of the

Onigara, coat collars lifted as they headed out for their overnight shift on the Island. Her leg was healing—only a slight limp if she stood too long. Dr. Jim had encouraged her to walk and signed her ready for duty several days earlier than expected.

While they waited to disembark, Fillingham slid his hands into his pockets. "This place is like the seventh circle of hell in the winter."

Pressing her hat down over her ears, she said, "I thought you liked winter. Isn't the Island our little Artic playground? And don't you ski?"

"At a ski chalet, where a fireplace and a hot toddy await me after my run. Quite different from patrolling a windswept island or sitting in that drafty shack of a police station."

The police car idled twenty feet from the dock, exhaust puffing white smoke; Sergeant Bard and Pilkington waited for the pair to hop inside to receive report.

Fillingham and Christine climbed into the back seat of the car. Sergeant Bard turned to Christine from the driver's seat. "Got a problem for you, Lane."

She pulled her memo book from her purse to record the details. It was probably a domestic call—a drunk husband roughing up his wife. Not a great way to start a shift.

"Yes, Sergeant." Her pen was ready in her gloved hand, her teeth clenched to stop them from chattering.

"How do I put this, Pilkington?" Sergeant Bard turned to the officer in the passenger seat.

Pilkington's face flushed red, and he looked away.

Bard gave a dramatic sigh and placed his arm over the top of the seat so he could face her more fully. "A group of naked men are singing and dancing around a bonfire on Ward's Island Beach."

Ah! She suppressed a smile. Just like the complaint from September regarding the three naked men tanning on a rooftop. Could they be the same Islanders? The red-bearded Karl had reminded her of Hawk with his honey skin and broad chest. He'd been a good sport, too. Pushing Karl off the roof to shock her fellow officers had been a satisfying prank.

"It's a pagan male ritual," Pilkington mumbled. "Something to do with the full moon."

Christine said, "Naked men on a beach. No problem, sir."

"Your specialty!" Fillingham added dryly.

Sergeant Bard faced forward. "Off we go, then. My warm bed awaits."

The two off-duty officers exited the front seat and hurried toward the ferry.

Climbing out of the back seat, Christine said to Fillingham, "We should pick up pails from the station garage so we can dump sand on the fire to extinguish it."

"You can take the call," Fillingham said as he got out of the car.

"You'll miss all the fun," she said.

Standing beside the car, he said, "I've seen you throw a man off a roof and take down another with an ax. I think you can handle a group of naked, chanting males."

Christine paused at the driver's door. "Shall I take the wheel?" Without waiting for an answer, she opened the door and settled into the driver's seat.

FREE SHORT STORY!

Use the QR code below to receive a free short story featuring Christine Lane and her friends when you sign up for my monthly newsletter at DianneScottAuthor.com/Newsletter.

LEAVE A REVIEW

If you enjoyed MISSING, I invite you to leave a review at your favorite bookseller site. Reviews guide readers to my books and help me reach a new audience, so they are much appreciated.

If you enjoyed MISSING, which is Book 2 in the Christine Lane mystery series, you'll want to check out Book 1 FINAL LOOK.

In an island full of intrigue, the best kept secret is a killer's identity.

Policewoman Christine Lane felt the humiliation like a slap. Transferred to this sleepy island station, she could almost hear her career screeching to a halt.

During a violent protest on the island, a resident is found dead and Christine is hurt. Her boss threatens to sack her for incompetence and she vows to mantain a low profile.

When the homicide leads dry up, Christine is shocked when investigators move on to their next case. So she secretly gathers information on suspects, digging up local dirt. When Christine is ambushed, she knows she is closing in on the perpetrator. Can she flush out the murderer before she is shut down for good?

Use on the QR code below to buy Final Look or go to diannescottauthor.com/books to order it from your favourite bookseller.

Acknowledgments

I have many people to acknowledge for their part in the creation of *Missing*. My conversations with past and current residents of Toronto Island provided insights into the political, cultural and social milieu of Toronto Island in the 1960s. These Islanders opened my eyes to the landscape's beautiful geography, fascinating history and unique community. I am happy to say these conversations continue. I have researched extensively the subject of women in policing and have been impressed by female officers' courage, strength and resilience. I have been most deeply affected by my interviews with female officers who worked on the Toronto Police Force, and I thank them for their honest reflections regarding the quirks, rewards and challenges of their profession.

I thank my writers' group for their feedback on *Missing*. Thanks to Leanne Lieberman, Roz Spafford and Ania Szado for their encouraging and constructive comments.

Finally, thanks to my sister, Ann Marie Scott and my mother, Rose Marie Scott, who have always supported my creative work. And of course, thank you to my husband Michael Shin and my children Claire and Matthew who support, encourage and inspire me daily.

About the Author

Dianne Scott lives in Toronto, Canada, a short ferry ride away from Toronto Island which is the setting of her mystery novels. She is the award-winning author of the Christine Lane mystery series, including *Final Look* and its sequel *Missing*. News about the third book in the series will be out soon.

When Dianne is not writing, she is walking Toronto's neighborhoods, reaching unsuccesfully for her toes in yoga and testing her Sudoku speed (slow!) She also teaches literacy skills and hangs out with her young adult children playing board games and table tennis.

Dianne loves connecting with readers and book clubs. You can contact her via social media, email at info@diannescottauthor.com or scan the QR code below.

www.ingramcontent.com/pod-product-compliance
Lightning Source LLC
Chambersburg PA
CBHW051146190726

48290CB00006B/2012